D1470291

An **Arab**, a *Jew*, and a Truck

by

Moustafa M. Soliman

All rights reserved. No part of this book shall be reproduced or transmitted in any form or by any means, electronic, mechanical, magnetic, photographic including photocopying, recording or by any information storage and retrieval system, without prior written permission of the publisher. No patent liability is assumed with respect to the use of the information contained herein. Although every precaution has been taken in the preparation of this book, the publisher and author assume no responsibility for errors or omissions. Neither is any liability assumed for damages resulting from the use of the information contained herein.

Copyright © 2012 by Moustafa M. Soliman

ISBN 978-0-7414-7460-5 Paperback
ISBN 978-0-7414-7461-2 Hardcover
ISBN 978-0-7414-7462-9 eBook
Library of Congress Control Number: 2012935595

Printed in the United States of America

This is a work of fiction. Names, characters, places, and incidents either are the product of the author's imagination or are used fictitiously. Any resemblance to actual events or locales or persons, living or dead, is entirely coincidental.

Published August 2012

INFINITY PUBLISHING
1094 New DeHaven Street, Suite 100
West Conshohocken, PA 19428-2713
Toll-free (877) BUY BOOK
Local Phone (610) 941-9999
Fax (610) 941-9959
Info@buybooksontheweb.com
www.buybooksontheweb.com

For my grandson
Chase Alexander Soliman

TABLE OF CONTENTS

INTRODUCTION

When I started writing this novel in 1977, I chose the characters of my story to represent a topic that was in the front page of every major newspaper and on all TV news channels. The hot topic was the historic visit of President Anwar El-Sadat of Egypt to Israel, and the start of peace negotiations between the two countries.

I thought at the time that the new Peace accord would just be the beginning. Egypt and the Middle East would return to that of my boyhood experiences. I vividly remember an Egyptian society where Jewish businesses flourished and many Jewish families were members of the country's high society. I can still hear the laughter coming from our living room where my parents played weekly card games with Jewish and Christian friends. They discussed kids, schools, business and the latest community gossip. There was no talk of who was a Muslim, a Jew or a Coptic Christian. We were all Egyptians.

A graduate student at the University of California, Berkeley, in the early 1960's, I remember fierce debates between Arab and Jewish scholars. Each side stubbornly stuck to his or her rigid position and claimed ownership to that piece of land that comprises the state of Israel, the West Bank and Gaza. At that time, the option of two independent states, Israel and Palestine, living side by side, was rarely discussed. The Palestinians wanted it the way it was before the 1947 partition of the country. The Israelis and their supporters argued that Israel should always remain a Jewish state.

Those debates often disturbed me because they left me feeling that there was an endemic hatred between Arabs and Jews. Talking heads, think tanks, politicians and the media spread this concept while ignoring the fact that Arab societies historically included Muslims, Christians and Jews. The act of 9/11 by a handful of fanatics somehow became proof that 1.3 billion Muslims not only had hatred for Jews, but for the entire Western world.

I live in the West. I married a Christian woman. We raised a son who grew up to respect all religions and we have a grandson who embodies the three Abrahamic faiths.

It is my deepest belief that hostilities between Muslims and Jews are a product of recent history and not deeply rooted in ethnicity or religion. As a matter of fact there are many similarities between Jews and Muslims in both their old traditions and the practice of their religions.

My wife and son felt that it was imperative for me to finish this novel I had started thirty-five years ago and had to abandon because of my work responsibilities and family demands. There can be no peace in the world if we only talk about our differences.

What Jews and Muslims have in common is the basis of my story. It takes place in the Bronx rather than somewhere in the Middle East. The reason for that is my belief that the American society with its diverse factions of moderate Christians, Jews and Muslims to right wing Evangelists, Orthodox Jews and fanatic Muslims have and will play a crucial role toward establishing peace in the Middle East.

The main theme of the story is an unusual and unexpected partnership between a devout Palestinian Muslim and an American Orthodox Jew who share an apartment in the Bronx. The two main characters, Ali and David, while devout are not fanatical believers, and they learn to live together, share a kosher kitchen, and recognize the similarities rather than differences between them. These two roommates end up forming a unique moving business called "An Arab, a Jew, and a Truck" that opens the door to a number of engaging, educational, and entertaining encounters highlighting some of the ironies and conflicts that parallel the progress of the Arab-Israeli peace process.

The story line leaves readers wondering whether the children of Abraham, the patriarch of the three monolithic religions, might begin a process of reconciliation, and end centuries of war and hostilities between Christians, Jews and Muslims. They may all soon realize that God never intended to have his children kill each other in His name or for His sake.

I'm most grateful to my closest friend, partner and wife, Lynn Skynear, whose unwavering support, enthusiasm and humor helped me finish this novel. Thanks to my creative and resourceful son Omar Soliman and my talented nephew Tarik Soliman (himself a Hollywood writer/director) for their valuable suggestions. My special gratitude goes to Len and Libby Traubman, dedicated supporters of peace in the Middle East, and the award-winning author Gloria Miklowitz, for their encouragement after reading the first draft of this novel. Thanks to Andrew Bosley for his clever design of the book cover, Audrey Hoffer for her input on Jewish traditions, and Melissa Burley and Michael Walker for editing the manuscript.

Finally, my special thanks to all the peacemakers throughout the world. May you succeed.

CHAPTER 1

Meeting

Today, David Goldstein hated his life. If he had followed his heart and ambition rather than his father's, he wouldn't be glaring at a phone that refused to ring. If his father had financially supported his business idea of Kosher Deli on Wheels, he'd now be hiring a lawyer instead of studying to be one. With visions of Park Ave dancing in his head, the fantasy life of David Goldstein was interrupted by the sound he'd been waiting for, "Hello," he answered his interrogator on the other end of the line "Yes, it is a two bedroom. It's got lots of light. How big? Big enough for two people. One bathroom, yeah, yeah, we share it. It's got a tub and...hello, hello?"

What do people want for $500? The fourth floor walk-up in a worn-out bland 1960s building was on one of the noisiest streets in the Bronx. Exhaust emissions mixed with cooking from around the globe filtered into the entire apartment building. Today the pronounced smell of duck fat and pungent Asian spices rose from Mr. Chang's carryout across the street, overtaking every other worldly smell in his compact hot apartment.

Compact, he said to himself, *but clean. Clean and near a subway. That should count for something.*

It's been three weeks since his roommate moved out without notice. The call came in the middle of the night and by morning one half of the rent rushed back to Chicago to take care of a father on life support.

1

David felt guilty about seeing his roommate and friend as a rent check, but he couldn't help it. David needed a different kind of life support and he needed it now. His own father's health was in decline. He unselfishly gave his meager savings to pay for tuition and books. David couldn't turn to him for rent money.

The day after his roommate's emergency exit, he placed a four by ten-inch card on the synagogue bulletin board advertising a room for rent while emphasizing a kosher kitchen and the proximity to both the synagogue and Marty's Deli. On the school bulletin board, he promoted the subway, the vibrant Bronx life, and of course the cheap rent.

Free ads, including the craigslist, produced zilch. This time he bought a two lines ad in the *New York Times:*

Share clean 2 bdrm 1 bath nr subway, shops, restaurants avail. immed. $500 plus util. 555-289-1345

David placed a lot of hope on that ad. He dreaded facing Dorothy, his gentile landlady who invested in this 1960s eyesore with the insurance money left by her dead husband ten years ago. David saw Dorothy as a kind person who was good looking for her undetermined age. She liked and respected him, and treated him as a friend. But Dorothy was a businesswoman and she expected to receive the rent on the first day of the month. David didn't want to damage their friendship or lose his status as a model tenant.

Suddenly, Mr. Model Tenant's thoughts were interrupted by a soft taping. *Damn, Dorothy must already be playing rent hardball.* David was always punctual with his rent. Personal delivery was his style. Every month he placed the check in an envelope and knocked on her door. If she were home, she'd ask him in for a hot or cold drink depending on the weather. Like a schoolboy, he looked forward to those brief encounters. It wasn't difficult to erase a few facial lines and imagine the younger, flawless, All-American Dorothy. Her flirting skills hadn't diminished with time. She still had a way of holding a gaze a little longer than

David was comfortable with. It excited and embarrassed him at the same time.

Now his embarrassment was about money. *Let me get it over with and face the debt collector.*

Adjusting his thick eyeglasses and straightening his yarmulke on his thick chestnut-colored hair, he opened the door with a broad, welcoming smile on his face.

Startled by a foreign-looking man in his mid-twenties, David could only say, "You're not Dorothy!"

That was the only thing the equally startled young man was sure of. He was not Dorothy and he probably had the wrong apartment.

David eyed this stranger who was smoothing a thick, dark mustache with one hand and holding the *New York Times* classified ads with the other.

Suspicious, David's head was spinning. *I didn't put the address in the ad. I only had enough money for two lines.* Suddenly he heard his mother's voice, "Never open the door to a stranger...have an unlisted phone number...just because you're a man, it doesn't mean you won't be stalked." Returning to his senses he remembered... *Oh yea, I gave a few callers the address. I must have given the apartment number and the floor without thinking.*

David studied the man standing before him in a short-sleeved white shirt that emphasized powerful bronze-colored arms and a strong chest. His eyes rested on the carved Semite features. A revelation. *God has answered my prayers and sent me a Jew...a Sephardic one.*

The visitor, watching the perplexed look on David's face, said in a thick foreign accent as he extended his hand, "Good afternoon, my name is Ali Nasrallah and I'm here to see your room for rent."

No longer a revelation, the excitement and smile faded from David's face. He looked at Ali in disbelief realizing that the man standing in front of him wasn't a Jew. Not even a Sephardic Jew would have a name like Ali.

David spoke without cracking a smile, giving no hint of his confusion, "Hi, I'm David Goldstein." He shook Ali's hand quickly then turned around and said, "Please come in."

He strode toward the back of the apartment where the second bedroom was and with his voice rising to hide his uneasiness, he said, "This is it."

Ali followed David. *My God. I've responded to an ad to share an apartment with a Jew, and probably an Orthodox one.* The ad for the apartment had been exactly what he was looking for. On his way to David's place, he noticed the Jewish deli two doors down and the kosher meat store on the corner of the street. But he hoped it just meant it was one of those ethnically diverse neighborhoods found in the Bronx. He'd been excited about the low rent and the proximity to his engineering school. It would mean he could sleep an extra hour in the morning. He thought of his father, a Palestinian farmer living in the West Bank who was struggling to support him. His father's dream had always been for his oldest son Ali to go to college in America and become a civil engineer like his wealthy uncle Ali, whom he was named after.

Ali assumed it was an exercise in futility, but decided it would be rude to leave right away. The room was small, but clean and sparsely furnished with a single bed pushed against the wall, a small old wooden desk and a dresser with a mirror. One window overlooking the busy street below brought plenty of sunlight, the smell of the eating-places around the building, and also a lot of street noise. In spite of the smell and noise, Ali liked the room. He was impressed by its size and cleanliness. He thought it was cheerful and the rent was reasonable. Unfortunately for him, it came with the wrong roommate.

David continued the tour barely making an eye contact, "There is only one bathroom in this place. The kitchen is there." He didn't invite Ali to step into the kitchen but Ali walked anyway. Cooking was one of his favorite hobbies. He liked the ample counter space and the new-looking gas stove.

4

As he turned around to follow David, he saw a sign above the stove in English and Hebrew: This is a kosher kitchen.

Ali stared at the sign for a couple of seconds. *Oh my God. He is one of those.* David turned around, their eyes met uneasily and Ali smiled just to break the tension. David finally smiled back, "Are you working or are you a student?" David asked.

Is he seriously considering this? "I'm an engineering student at Bronx College and how about you Daveed?" Ali quickly apologized, "Am I pronouncing your name correctly? This is the way we say it back home."

David's smile got a little wider, he was amused by Ali's accent, "We pronounce it David in this country."

"Sorry, sorry, David, right?"

"Yes, yes, you're doing just fine. I'm in my first year in law school at New York University."

"Scholarship?" Ali asked and wondered if he'd gone too far again. But he knew the tuition at NYU was high.

"No, my parents send me money for the tuition. They're retired and live in Florida. They live on a fixed income and they are scraping every penny to pay this tuition. I also work as a busboy in a Chinese restaurant to pay for my other expenses."

Ali laughed, "My first job in the United States was washing dishes in a Chinese restaurant. The owner offered me some sweet and sour fish to eat and I vomited all over the kitchen! Arabs are not used to eating sweet and sour foods. Especially fish!"

David relaxed as they laughed together. Ali liked people with a good sense of humor. Then he chided himself. *What am I thinking? This could never work. What would my Palestinian friends say?* He thought first of Yasser, with whom he was staying. They grew up together in the same small town in the West Bank. The Israelis had made their lives miserable on a daily basis. Yasser's family used to own large acres of farmland that were confiscated by the Israelis to build one of the dozens of Jewish settlements in the West Bank. People in their town had to spend hours going through

5

Israeli checkpoints and get humiliated by Israeli soldiers on what Ali and Yasser believed to be their own land. And some of those Jewish settlers came from New York and many of them were Orthodox Jews like David.

But maybe David was different. Ali kept thinking about his living situation with Yasser. In David's apartment, he'd have his own room and would pay less rent than he was paying Yasser. He had no comfortable place to study. He also had to take the subway to school, costing him more money and wasting a lot of his time.

Encouraged by David's laughter Ali went on, "You must be sick of Chinese food if you work there."

"I never eat it!" The laughter was gone as fast as it had come.

Ali knew he'd made some kind of mistake, "Why?"

"Didn't you see the sign? I only eat kosher food."

Ali stopped laughing. "I beg your pardon," Ali said, feeling himself blush. "But I don't actually know what that consists of. I'm sorry if I offended you."

Ali tried to switch the subject, "Do you have someone in mind for the room?"

David exhaled. "Well, I've promised a friend from my synagogue to have the first choice. He is still thinking about it. Why don't you call me in a few days?"

Okay, it's over and it probably wouldn't have worked anyway. That's good. Ali could read his face. *There was no one else interested in the room.* He thought about the few encounters he had with people like David who accused him of being one of those Hamas members or Arab terrorists who killed innocent Jews and wanted to drive Israel into the sea. He was even accused once of sympathizing with the 9/11 terrorists. He also recognized that David's dilemma was similar to his. They both had preconceived feelings of hatred and mistrust toward each other although they had never met. But suddenly they found themselves in a situation where their mutual interests intersected. David needed a roommate for his apartment that didn't appeal to too many people, and Ali was having a hard time finding a place that met his requirements of low rent and proximity to school. There was something in this arrangement for both of them.

In spite of the attractive features of the apartment, Ali was relieved. He extended his hand to David, smiled amicably, and said, "Okay, thank you for showing me your beautiful apartment and nice meeting you, David."

"Nice meeting you Ali ---Baba," David grinned.

They both laughed.

With the newspaper rolled up under his arm, Ali moved slowly down the steps. In a bizarre way the building felt right. *How could a place in the Bronx remind me of the West Bank? Perhaps the smell of age is universal.* Ali inhaled the familiar odor of cracked plaster, waxed worn wood and tobacco smoke combined with years of cooking. Long after he walked out of the apartment the strong scent from the corridors and the stairway lingered in his head. *Strange, David seemed familiar. But why wouldn't he seem familiar? I grew up surrounded by thousands of Davids.* In the West Bank, Ali avoided eye contact with all Jews. The only time he spoke to a Jew was going through a checkpoint. *Today, like a sacrificial lamb, I voluntarily entered the lion's lair. Why did it have to be so clean and perfectly located? But--- David was not an unlikable lion. He was polite and seemed to have a sense of humor.*

Oblivious to the street racket and the sounds of humanity, Ali moved toward the subway. *It's almost too bad.* Ali thought. *In another world I could have been friends with that man.*

CHAPTER 2

Getting Acquainted

Ali felt hopeless. Classes would begin in a few days. There seemed to be no way out of Yasser's cramped, dark apartment. Every place he saw was too small, too far, or too expensive. As he was about to give up his search, his spirits were lifted by a crazy idea. *David. Maybe he is as desperate as I am.* He remembered David's expression when he asked him whether he had someone in mind for the room. He could see in his eyes that there was no friend from the synagogue thinking about renting the room. *My room.* He thought again. *I must be insane. How can I think of this as my room? Is it possible to share a small space with an Orthodox Jew who keeps a kosher kitchen and maintain peace and harmony? I can only imagine what would happen if we got into a heated political or religious argument. He'd probably throw me out in the middle of final exams.*

Time had run out. Ali's practical self came to grips with reality. Living conditions with Yasser took their toll on him. He could no longer concentrate, or study for exams.

The struggle was over. With a great deal of trepidation he pulled out the crumpled ad and made the call, "Hi Daveed, this is Ali Baba."

Buoyed by David's laughter at the other end of the phone, he continued, "I have consulted with the forty thieves and they said that it's okay for me to share the apartment with you."

"I hope they're not planning to move in with you," David responded with a chuckle.

David hadn't had a single call for his room since he met Ali. Neither his advertisement in the *NY Times* or his note on the bulletin board at the synagogue brought any serious inquiries. He was getting discouraged and rent was due. But he was apprehensive about sharing his apartment with an Arab. What if he was one of those militants he'd read about? Or what if he invited his Arab and Palestinian friends to the apartment and they started hanging posters of Hamas and Hezbollah on the walls? He'd never met an Arab before and never understood why he held such hatred toward them as a people. David, however, understood the law and the fact that the apartment lease was in his name. If he had any problems with a new roommate, he could easily and legally kick him out of the apartment.

Feeling desperate, and at the same time slightly amused by Ali's sense of humor, David invited Ali for a cup of tea to talk things over with him.

Ali and David sat across from one another in the living room sipping tea and chatting. The main room was modestly furnished with a large sofa, two armchairs, a wood coffee table and a small metal side table between the two chairs. In the corner of the room was a dinette set with six chairs. A painting of the City of Jerusalem showing the Temple Mount and the Old City hung on one of the walls. Next to it was a picture of the Western Wall in the Old City. The wall across from the sofa was adorned with a large picture of a menorah.

David continued to be amused by Ali's strong accent, often pronouncing the "p" as "b" and saying "beoble" instead of "people." He teased Ali a couple of times about that and Ali responded by telling him an Arab joke that after President Mubarak of Egypt visited President Bush in the U.S., he ordered all the doors of the public bathrooms in Cairo to have "Mubarak" written on them. When he was asked about the reason behind his decision, he told his staff that all the bathroom doors in America had "Bush" written on them.

David decided to confront the elephant in the room. He looked at Ali and asked in an earnest voice, "You know I'm Jewish, right?"

Ali wondered how he could ask such a question with the big kosher kitchen sign and all the Jewish decorations on the walls. But he was prepared for such a question and responded, "Of course, David, I have several Jewish friends at the school."

That was a lie. The truth was that he always avoided Jewish male students after an encounter he had in the college cafeteria when he sat, by accident, at a table across from a Jewish student. The two of them got into a heated argument about Israel and the Palestinians. Each of them cited historical facts about who was the true owner of that land. The argument almost ended into a fistfight when a few students came and separated them.

"Unfortunately, I can't say the same thing," replied David, "You're the first Arab I've ever met." David continued in the same earnest voice, "I maintain a kosher kitchen, do you know what that means?"

"I know of kosher kitchens, but I don't know what that entails. Would you explain that to me?" responded Ali.

David explained that he kept two sets of dishes and silverware, one for meats and the other for dairy products. He also emphasized that he washed and stored those two sets separately.

Ali reassured David, "Don't worry, I've got my own dishes and silverware, and I can keep them away from yours. I can even hide them under my bed, if you wish."

Ali continued in a serious tone, "I also have to tell you that I'm a Muslim and I'm a religious one. I pray five times a day. My father taught me how to pray when I was seven years old. He used to take me to the town's mosque every evening after dinner. You know, David, my father believes that there are two things that matter in life, religion and education, and he is spending his life's savings on educating my three brothers, two sisters and me. The whole family has to cut corners so that my father can send me to engineering school in America."

"Your parents sound like Rachel and Sam Goldstein," interrupted David.

Ali looked perplexed, "Rachel and who?"

"Sorry, my folks," David clarified. "Religion was the centerpiece of our lives and education was our daily food. Seldom an evening meal went by without discussing the importance of a real profession. My father always wanted me to become a lawyer."

"He must be proud of you now. Do you have brothers and sisters, David?"

"Yes, I have one older sister. She is the real pride of my parents. Besides having uncommon beauty, she has the kind of drive that would leave most men in the dust. She was always an excellent student, skipped grades, maintained a 3.9 average, and was recruited by one of the most prestigious investment firms in the country. She now owns her own loft apartment in the Tribeca district."

"I'm sure you also will be making a ton of money when you finish law school."

"Hate to burst your bubble, but being a lawyer is my father's dream and my nightmare. It would kill the old man if I left school. The only thing that rivals Catholic guilt is Jewish guilt." David gazed at a frame on the table showing an old picture of his parents on their twenty-fifth wedding anniversary, and continued, "Sam and Rachel seldom complained about the pleasures they denied themselves for their children. My mother, Rachel, never had a fashionable day in her life and Sam didn't even know what fashion was. I don't call my dad an old man for nothing. I'm the late in life prodigy."

"What's a prodigy"?

"I'm my father's wunderkind."

Ali was lost and David didn't care. "My dad is a living memorial."

David thought about his father's stories of his own childhood. The only sweet memory Sam had of life in

Warsaw, Poland was when he'd escape the heart of the ghetto and find his way to the university. Unlike his older twelve-year old brother, Sam was not forced to wear the Star of David on his sleeve. Invisible and full of envy, he peered through the gates and pretended that he was wearing brand new clothes, carrying an armfull of books while racing from one class to the next.

"My father's parents could barely put food on the table. College was the impossible dream for him, but not for me."

Ali was touched by David's story because it reminded him of his own father.

"Sounds like our fathers are interchangeable. My father also isn't an educated man. He grew up in Palestine and had to leave school at a young age to help his own father cultivate the land they owned. This was their only source of income. He always felt that he'd missed out on life for not finishing his education. He looked with envy at those men in suits sitting in offices with phones in their hands and wished he could switch places with them."

He paused for a few seconds, and then continued in a sober tone, "I feel, David, that we have at least one thing in common in our rather dissimilar backgrounds. Both of us seem to be fulfilling our fathers' dreams. We're getting a good education, and we're strict observers of our own religions."

David drifted slightly as he listened. *I'll give him an A for sincerity, but how do I find out if he is a religious zealot? Let me review my copy of How to Screen Your Future Roommate for Dummies. Question one: Are you one of those fanatical militias, survivalists, or militant Muslims who have scared the shit out of us? Question two: Do you go to a church, a temple, a mosque, or a clearing in the woods that breeds terrorists? Let me give it a try.*

"Ali, let me get right to the point. Do you go to a mosque?"

"Of course, every Friday at noon. Every good Muslim does. Don't you go to the synagogue on Saturday?"

"Well, yeah of course I do, but that's a little different. There are so many stories about what goes on in some of the mosques."

"Guess you're the expert, what goes on?"

"Listen Ali, I don't want to seem like I'm politically incorrect, but I read that some of the terrorists responsible for 9/11 frequented one of those mosques." *God I feel like an idiot. I even hate the concept of political correctness. He probably doesn't know what the hell that means.*

"Let me get right to the point, David. I don't know anyone who wasn't horrified by what happened on 9/11. Those criminals didn't only hijack planes and kill thousands of people, they also hijacked a billion people's religion. You think I like having to prove I'm not a terrorist every day of my life?"

"Sorry, I'm only asking because I want to clear the air. If this housemate thing is going to work, we've got to be honest with each other."

He's dangling the housemate carrot. I'll take that as a bit of encouragement and clear the air even more. "Let me tell you about my religion and suicide. We view suicide as one of the gravest sins. In fact a verse in the Qur'an says, 'And do not kill yourself, surely God is most Merciful to you.'"

"I can one up you on that. Suicide is forbidden in Judaism. If you are a Jew and commit suicide, say goodbye to your loved ones, because you will be buried in a separate part of the Jewish cemetery and you won't receive mourning rights. We Jews may not shun you in life, but we sure will if you die the wrong way."

The drill wasn't over. David needed more assurances, "Ali you claim your religion forbids suicide. Let us assume 9/11 was a criminal act carried out by political extremists. How do you explain Palestinian suicide bombers who kill thousands of people inside Israel?"

This guy doesn't give up. Am I being indicted or interviewed? "David, I can't explain how anyone takes another person's life, but what I can tell is that some Palestinians feel victimized, oppressed, and desperate under the Israeli occupation."

David noticed that Ali was getting tense and his rent check was slipping away. He decided to change the subject since he couldn't change the roommate.

"I understand that Muslims don't drink alcohol or eat pork." *What am I saying? We're talking about suicide bombers and now I'm asking about booze and swine. Pretty soon I'll want to know his favorite color.*

Relieved by David's change of tone Ali thought, *Thank God the inquisition is over.*

"I've never tasted either one. Some of my friends tease me and try to get me to drink a glass of beer. So far they haven't succeeded. How about you?"

"Pork has never touched these lips. I only drink wine occasionally on some Jewish holidays. If I had a choice, I'd abstain. I think I'm allergic to the damn stuff." David paused, and then continued in a sarcastic voice, "Nothing turns a woman on more than a man ordering a Coke."

Ali laughed, "I know what you mean. I'd rather tell my date I have an old man's ulcer than admit that I don't drink."

You mean a good Muslim like you goes out with women? Don't tell me you date Christian women?"

Amused by the question, Ali stroked his mustache and said in a deep mocking voice, "I'm afraid so David. In fact, I would go out with any woman regardless of race or creed." As if sharing a secret, Ali added, "An old wise man once told me that God would forgive anything except if a man refuses to go to bed with a woman when she asks."

"I think I agree with that man. But wait a minute, you mean that God would never forgive us if we ate pork, but would look the other way if we slept with any woman?"

"You will have to ask the old man."

Ali's mood quickly changed. Initially enraged and then discouraged by his potential roommate's questions and insinuations, he was now relieved. He understood the mathematical equation: 9/11 plus suicide bombers equal Muslims. He couldn't blame David for being another victim

14

of the six o'clock news. *Thank God it's out in the open.* It was like sixty years of animosity were sucked out of the air. *Now we can get down to business of living together. Americans are always talking about family values. In a weird way, David and I share that.* Smiling to himself, Ali thought. *The most important thing is that he laughs at my lame jokes.*

At first David had done his best to disguise the palpable distrust he had of all Arabs and Muslims, but he knew he had gone too far and was genuinely sorry he had hurt Ali. *I like the guy. At least he occasionally sins. He's not the perfect Muslim and nobody will accuse me of being the perfect Jew. How does that song go? If you can't be with the one you love, love the one you're with----It might not be love, but it sure is convenient.*

"Do you want more tea?" David asked in an attempt to set the stage for the most important decision of the meeting.

"No thanks, I have to get going so I can look at a few apartments west of here," replied Ali with a slight grin.

For God's sake, I feel like I'm setting the stage for a marriage proposal. Feeling slightly ridiculous, David went on, "I thought you were going to move in with me. Anyway, you shouldn't consider any place west of here, because you'd be getting further away from Mecca."

"I've never thought the Bronx is the closest place to Mecca, but I may ask you one of those days to stand next to me and face east."

"I may do that, but I will be standing at a slight angle from you. In the direction of Jerusalem," David said teasingly. Then with a serious expression on his face, he addressed Ali in a friendly tone, "I'd like to have you as my roommate. So if you agree, you may go and bring your things and suitcases."

"Suitcases? Who told you I have suitcases?" clowned Ali.

"I don't care whether you have any clothes. I only care about your set of dishes and silverware." David shot back.

15

"Ok. I will be back in a few hours," Ali said, rushing out of the door. "Please clean a shelf in the kitchen for my underwear. I mean my silverware."

CHAPTER 3

Living Together

Ali was up at six o'clock in the morning on his first day in the apartment. He jumped out of bed and walked to the bathroom in his blue striped pajamas to wash himself in preparation for his prayers. Ali adhered to one of the basic tenets of Islam. He prayed five times a day--in the early morning, at noon, in the afternoon, at sunset and in the evening. Ali washed his face, arms, hair and feet, as required, before each prayer. He wore his head cap to cover his hair, a tradition followed by many Muslims when they pray to demonstrate their respect for God.

As he walked out of the bathroom David was heading there, also in blue striped pajamas, almost identical to Ali's, and had his yarmulke on. The yarmulke looked very much like Ali's head cover except it didn't cover the entire hair, but rather fit in the middle of the hair. Jews wear the head cover as a sign of respect when they pray and to remind them of God who is the Higher Authority above them.

They both looked at each other in disbelief. *There must be a fire sale on striped pajamas,* thought David. Ali pointed at David's yarmulke, "David, I wasn't serious last night when I told you that you may stand next to me and pray."

David smiled, "Listen, you keep wearing that thing on your head and you may be the first Ali Baba to join my synagogue."

Ali walked to his room, spread out his prayer rug on the floor, and faced east toward Mecca. He stood solemnly on

17

the carpet and whispered his prayers. As he knelt down he could see David standing in the hallway, arms folded, watching the unusual ceremony with curiosity. Ali continued his prayers undeterred. He knelt down for the second time signaling the end of the morning prayers. He then sat on the prayer rug with his legs crossed, pulled out his copy of the Qur'an and read some verses with his voice rising slightly above whispering and his upper body gently rocking forwards and backwards. David was still watching and surprised by the way Ali was moving his head and upper body in a way similar to the way he recited his own prayers.

David finally pulled himself away and went to his room to perform his own morning prayers. An Orthodox Jew, David prayed three times a day-- in the morning, in the afternoon, and in the evening, and faced Jerusalem when he prayed. The similarities to their rituals were uncanny.

Ali and David, each in his room, were immersed in their religious rituals that were different, but intended for the same God, the God of Abraham who is considered the father of the three religions: Judaism, Christianity, and Islam. Followers of the three religions, Jews, Christians and Muslims, are referred to as the People of the Book who worship the same God worshipped by Abraham.

Ali got dressed and stayed in his room waiting for David to finish his breakfast and leave the kitchen. He didn't want to start any problems on his first day by stepping in the kitchen and doing something terribly wrong. When Ali heard David leaving the kitchen, he got up and walked slowly and quietly in that direction. As he got closer to the kitchen door he heard David calling him. He froze for a few seconds before turning around wondering whether he should have walked in a certain way to get into the kitchen, or whether he should have kept his head cover on. But he was relieved to hear David asking him whether he would like to have a cup of tea with him.

"Yes, I'd like that," Ali replied.

David poured Ali a cup of tea as they sat in the living room and said apologetically, "I'm sorry, Ali, for staring at you while you were praying. I've read a little about your religion, but I've never seen it practiced before. Tell me, why do you face that way when you pray?"

Ali answered in a serious voice, "Because Muslims have to face the Kaaba, the black cubical building in Mecca, Saudi Arabia. The Kaaba is the most sacred site in Islam.

David had never been curious about the Kaaba until now, "Who built that sacred place?"

"According to our religion, Adam built the original building at the site that was destroyed by the great flood. The current Kaaba was built by Abraham and his son Ismail (Ishmael) on the same site. All Muslims must face the Kaaba during their prayers no matter where they are."

"But considering the earth is round, you could face the Kaaba or Mecca in one of two ways. I mean in one of two opposite directions," asked David probingly.

"Yes, David, that is why we always face east in our prayers," replied Ali with a slight amount of exasperation.

"I guess it makes sense. I'd like you sometime to tell me more about your religion," David said diplomatically. He knew well the answer to his question because Orthodox Jews also face east toward Jerusalem when they pray.

"That's a deal. You explain Judaism to me and I will tell you more about Islam. But you have to promise never to try to convert me to Judaism, and I promise the same."

"You know, we Jews never try to convert anybody to Judaism because we believe that we are God's chosen people. You've got to be born from a Jewish mother to be a true Jew."

"Listen, David, you may be God's chosen people, but we Muslims are his favorite ones. Look how much oil he gave us."

When they stopped laughing, David changed the subject, "I think I should give you a guided tour of the kitchen. I told you that I keep a kosher kitchen, and you probably don't really know what that means."

Ali agreed and showed enthusiasm for the idea. He followed David into the kitchen. David explained to Ali that the fundamental thing behind a kosher kitchen was the separation between milk and meat.

"We Jews believe that life of the flesh is in the blood. Because of this we're forbidden to eat the blood. When we kill an animal or fowl we must remove the blood from the animal or fowl before eating the meat. But we are also forbidden from combining the life-giving element of an animal, its milk, with the death element, its flesh." David scrutinized Ali's face to make sure he was concentrating on the kosher kitchen rules. "This separation must be observed in preparing, cooking, and eating the two elements."

"Unbelievable, we Muslims do the same. We also must remove the blood from the animal when killing it. We call the meat halal. We are not supposed to eat the meat of an animal or fowl that is killed in any other way."

A smile came across David's face as he listened to one of the people he thought were his archenemies tell him that he ate what sounded like kosher food.

Ali, heartened by David's smile, continued to explain that Muslims could mix meat with dairy products and didn't have to separate them. It then became clear to both of them that halal and kosher food started diverging after the animal or fowl was killed.

David started his guided tour of the kitchen by pointing out the two sets of dishes and silverware he used separately, one for meat and fowl and the other for dairy products. He showed Ali how he stored them in separate cabinets.

Ali stored his dishes and silverware in a cabinet on the other end of the kitchen. But he kept looking at the only double sink in the kitchen wondering how they would both use it without starting some serious religious conflicts. He felt that some ground rules would have to be established and agreed upon before he could venture to use the kitchen.

David noticed the perplexed look on Ali's face and interrupted his thoughts by explaining that he had two sets of sink liners and dish drainers for meat and milk dishes.

"I would appreciate it very much if you never use my things in the kitchen," David talked in a firm voice. "You can wash your dishes, pots and pans in the sink, but please don't use my sink liners. These liners will ensure that my utensils don't come in contact with the sink."

Both Ali and David knew at that instant that coexistence in the kitchen could make or break this apartment sharing arrangement. David made a great concession by allowing someone who didn't know anything about kosher food, not to mention an Arab, to share his kitchen. He knew that he had to watch every step Ali took in the kitchen to make sure that the kosher rules were never violated.

Likewise, Ali, who loved to cook and eat Middle Eastern food, had to compromise a great deal on the use of the kitchen. He thought that the only way he could make this arrangement work was for him to limit his use of the kitchen.

A certain amount of tension was building up as they discussed when and how each of them would use the kitchen. Each one of them thought he was making a greater compromise. Ali couldn't anymore invite his friends to spend Fridays (the Muslim Sabbath) preparing and eating a meal of lamb and rice as they used to do back home. He felt somewhat cheated, paying half the rent but not allowed to use the kitchen freely.

David also started feeling the burden of the concession he'd made. How on earth could he convince his Jewish orthodox friends, when they were invited to his apartment, that he still maintained a kosher kitchen? No one from his synagogue, even his friend Ben Katz, would step a foot in his place if they found out that there was an Arab living with him and sharing his kitchen.

As Ali and David were leaving the kitchen, Ali stopped and looked at the sign saying that the kitchen was kosher and asked, "Can I also put a sign at my end of the kitchen?"

David looked at Ali to see if he was serious, and asked suspiciously, "What would your sign say?"

But Ali was not smiling, "It would say, this kitchen is fifty percent kosher and fifty percent Arabic."

David wanted to laugh but he had to control himself for fear of Ali taking this as a sign of relaxation of his rigid kitchen rules.

"No," David said firmly. "But you can place a sign on your cabinet saying that it was an Arab corner in a kosher kitchen."

David chuckled, but Ali was not amused, and dashed out of the kitchen and went straight to his room.

He grabbed his school notebook and decided to get the hell out of the apartment before starting another argument with David. He kept whispering a few Arabic curse words: "Yahudi ibn kalb," meaning a Jewish son of a dog. Such an expression would be considered mildly offensive in Arabic, a language rich with swear words that range from calling the mother or the sister a whore to naming their vaginas. The more he thought about the kitchen situation, the louder his Arabic swearing got, calling David "son of a donkey," and declaring that he would screw David's mother.

He was on his way out when he passed by David's room. The door was partly open. He looked discreetly inside and saw David standing inside facing east and whispering his prayers. His upper body was moving gently back and forth the same way Ali's was when he was reading the Qur'an and sitting on his prayer rug. He had seen Orthodox Jews before standing and praying at the Western Wall in Jerusalem, moving their bodies back and forth the same way Muslims do. *That must be for the same reason. We should pray not only with our heart, mind, and soul, but with our whole body as well.* He froze for a few moments. *How can this guy face God when he is denying me equal rights in my own kitchen? He is praying to the same God I pray to and who teaches us to be fair. Guess he missed that lesson.*

Ali left the apartment and descended the stairs talking to himself and reiterating his kitchen rights. The ceiling lights were slightly dim. As he was about to make the last turn near the bottom of the stairs, he heard the clack of heels and the scent of Jasmine filled the air around him. The smell had a calming effect on him. For a few seconds he drifted away thinking about those Jasmine trees back home with their dark green leaves and small white flowers. Then he noticed a female coming up the stairs. He couldn't see her face very well, but did notice her shoulder-length platinum hair and her well-proportioned figure. Ali immediately hushed his voice. His anger gave way to this instinctive signal that had served to alert him when the prospect of sex was on the horizon. He slowed down to a stop. Just as she came in full view, he wanted to appear comfortable and casual.

"Good Morning." Next, he blurted out, "Do you live here?" It almost sounded accusatory. *My God, I sound like I'm asking to see her papers.*

Attempting not to burst out into laughter, she answered with a smile, "Do I live here? I own the place." There were days she wished she never saddled herself with this property. She dreamed of traveling. Carnival in Brazil, bull fights in Mexico, and Tango in Argentina. She understood that her full figure, translucent skin and light hair would be irresistible to Latin men. At this moment she was drawn to this exquisitely machismo specimen slightly blocking her passage on the stairway. *I don't have to leave home after all. South of the border just arrived.* "I have not seen you here before. Are you visiting someone?"

Ali, embarrassed, hastened to say, "My name is Ali Nasrallah and I've moved into the apartment on the top floor with David Goldstein."

"Ali who?" she asked mockingly.

"Ali Nasrallah."

"In that case welcome to our building. I'm Dorothy and I live in apartment number one on the first floor," Dorothy said extending her hand to Ali. "Where are you from Ali?"

"I come from Palestine," Ali replied, shaking Dorothy's hand.

"You're a Palestinian and you're living with David Goldstein? I don't believe it. You mean peace has finally come between the Arabs and the Jews? For heavens sake, this sounds great."

"No Dorothy. I only moved in after David had promised to join the PLO."

"Why don't we see how that living together thing goes first." Dorothy said with a grin.

Ali acted as if he were interested in the conversation, but both his mind and eyes were wandering. Once his vision adjusted to the dim, overhead lighting, he noticed that she wasn't as young as he thought. *She must be at least twenty years older than me, old enough to be my mother. Well, maybe not my mother.*

The next thought that crept into his head was football. *Am I crazy? Did this roommate thing push me over the edge? I'm face to face with one of the most alluring creatures I've met in a long time and I'm thinking of mother? Football?*

"Of course football," he murmured under his breath.

Like most of his friends he transitioned from loving the game of soccer to enjoying American football. His friends would taunt him every time he'd say that he equally admired the prowess of the football players as he did the cheerleaders, "Save it for the Imam, Ali. Don't give us that BS." But deep down he believed that football cheerleaders exemplified the haute cuisine of the American melting pot.

Suddenly, as if plucked out of his mind, there stood an American cheerleader. *Well maybe a retired one.*

She still had beautiful powder blue eyes, but deep creases began to replace the girlish dimples. The extra twenty pounds didn't deter Ali. The most desirable women where he grew up had soft rounded curves and warm heavy breasts. *This woman would reign in my village.*

A few seconds went by and neither of them uttered a single word until Dorothy interrupted the silence.

"I have to get back up to my apartment. Nice meeting you Ali, I will be seeing you around."

"Nice meeting you too, Dorothy."

Dorothy walked past Ali up the stairs to her floor, his head turned around in the true Arab way to watch the rhythmic sway of her hips. He loved the way the cloth clung to every curve of her body revealing just enough to wet a hungry man's appetite. She could feel Ali's eyes piercing her back and instinctively gave her hips an extra swing. As Dorothy turned around the corner of the stairs, she turned her head slightly to look at Ali who was still standing in the same place. Ali snapped out of it and continued walking down the few remaining steps toward the front door of the building. His anger toward David gave way to lust for Dorothy. *He can keep his kosher sign up as long as I have the lady who owns the whole building.*

CHAPTER 4

The Militant Friend

Ali sat in the school cafeteria eating his usual turkey sandwich and reviewing his class notes. He couldn't concentrate well on all the complicated mathematical equations he copied during the morning lecture. His thoughts wandered between his agitation with David over the use of the kitchen and Dorothy, the sexy landlady. Ali had not been successful with American women since his arrival in the United States. Back home he was considered a good-looking man. Girls in his hometown admired his masculinity and loved his mustache. While living in the New York area he dated three girls from the school but was never able to develop a lasting relationship with any of them. After one or two dates, he always got the same response when he asked them out again. He heard all the familiar excuses ranging from how busy they were with homework to having other commitments that week, the week after and the one after that. He was smart enough to recognize that being a foreigner and new in the country was the reason behind such rejections. He wasn't on top of the latest TV shows, the current music hits, or the latest fads. He didn't drink or smoke pot. He wasn't one of the mainstream young men that attracted young women. He tried to make up for his shortcomings by being funny, or by mimicking one of the college administrators or one of the professors the girls knew. He managed to make them laugh, but laughter didn't take him far enough. Furthermore, the only subject he could dwell on was politics and the Arab-Israeli problems. He always found a way to bring up that subject, and then he became emotional and spoke on it at great length. The women found his conversations to be boring and consequently were turned off and didn't want to see him again.

He started thinking of Dorothy and the fact she was older and more mature. He felt that she had given him meaningful looks and he saw raw sex in her eyes. But his recent lack of success with women made him lose his self-confidence, and he wasn't sure whether Dorothy's looks were a real invitation or a figment of his imagination conjured by long sexual deprivation.

His thoughts were interrupted by a loud voice from behind him saying, "Salam Allukem."

He turned around and saw his friend Yasser. He gave him the usual Arabic hug and kiss on both cheeks that made other students sitting around the cafeteria gaze at them as if they were from a different planet.

Yasser was born in the same small town in the West Bank where Ali came from. But, unlike Ali's family who lived in the same place for generations, Yasser's family originally lived near Haifa that is now part of Israel. The family owned few acres and a house there for generations before they resettled in the West Bank after the establishment of the state of Israel. A few years later, however, the Israelis confiscated their land in the West Bank to build a new Jewish settlement and Yasser's family had to move again; this time to Ali's small town. Yasser never saw his family's house near Haifa but he heard many stories from his parents and grandparents about that house, and how the family had to abandon their business and their roots and flee just before the Arab-Israeli war of 1948. He never clearly understood why his family had to leave, whether they were driven out or left on their own. The answer to this question was irrelevant to Yasser. He only cared about one thing; he wanted his family to go back to that old family house which, unbeknownst to him, didn't even exist anymore. He was obsessed with this dream, a vision he could not shake. The

27

further confiscation of their land in the West Bank compounded his hatred for the Israelis and anybody who showed any support for them.

Yasser pulled a chair and sat next to Ali. He was fuming. He found it hard to believe that his childhood friend Ali was sharing an apartment with an Orthodox Jew. He lectured Ali that he couldn't and shouldn't trust David. Ali listened to his reasons and nodded his head as though he agreed with him. He mentioned to Yasser the details of the skirmish he just had with David over the kitchen, and shared with him that he probably had made the wrong decision in moving into David's apartment.

But Ali was more rational and moderate than his friend Yasser. He discussed his conflict with David calmly and displayed a great deal of restraint that annoyed Yasser.

"Listen carefully, Ali," Yasser said with a serious look on his face and raising his hand as if he were lecturing a group of Arab students in a rally, "you either kick this guy out of the apartment or move out. You can't coexist with these people."

"Why not?" Ali asked in a cracking voice, "I thought we could live together in peace, and respect each other's religion and traditions. I believe David and I could share this kitchen as well as the rest of the apartment and live together as friends."

Yasser jumped off his chair and yelled, "This is very naïve, Ali. You sound like those peace advocates back home. They all forget one important thing. The Israelis will never want to coexist with us. They want to take over our land the same way they took our country, Palestine. They want to be the masters exploiting us Arabs and making us their slaves. You know about Apartheid. That is what the Israelis want in our country: a Jewish Apartheid."

Yasser continued, bringing his voice down to a whisper, "My friend, your experience is a lesson to all Arabs who talk about peaceful coexistence with the Israelis. You pay half the rent but you don't have half the rights. You're a second class tenant."

Ali tried to interrupt Yasser and explain to him that the dispute with David over the kitchen was not that serious, and that he only was worried that things could get worse between them over time.

Yasser, however, didn't give Ali a chance to talk. He continued pointing his finger into Ali's face, eyes burning, signaling to Ali to listen and not to interrupt, "We have to develop a good strategy to defeat this damn Israeli!"

"But he isn't an Israeli! He is American," interrupted Ali, now equally passionate.

"It doesn't matter. They are all the same. We should get some of our Arab friends involved."

Ali jumped up, openly annoyed by Yasser's oratory, "Yasser, I've my career to worry about. My father and my family are suffering to pay for my education. I want to live in peace. I don't want to fight anybody."

Ali walked toward the door of the cafeteria followed by Yasser who jumped in front of him blocking the door and mumbling, "Ali, don't be a traitor. Think of your people who're killed every day by the Israelis. Let us unite and fight them back."

Ali pushed him gently out of his way and continued walking.

Yasser's irrational ranting wore him out and made him sad. He shared some of Yasser's bitterness and animosity toward the Israelis for the hardships they were causing his people in the West Bank and in Gaza. He thought of the hours he and his father had spent going through one Israeli checkpoint after another to reach a destination that was only thirty minutes away from their town but took them four hours. He felt like a prisoner in his own country. He used to watch new settlements being built for Israeli families that had running water, electricity, new roads, and all the modern conveniences while their small town continued to decay.

In spite of his bitterness, Ali was rational and didn't believe in armed struggle, but rather in dialogue and compromise. He felt as he walked home that if he couldn't share an apartment with David and overcome the problems brought up by their cultural and religious differences, how could the Palestinians hope to have their own country adjacent to Israel? How would his people be able to have economic and cultural ties with the Israelis if he couldn't, as a Palestinian living in the Bronx, coexist with someone like David?

When he got closer to his apartment building, he calmed down, and managed to convince himself to work harder on making his living arrangement with David successful. Moreover, he had another incentive to make that arrangement work-- it was Dorothy. As he thought of his encounter with her, a broad smile came across his face and his steps got faster. He was hoping to run into her again as he climbed the stairs. He stood for a minute in front of her door, hoping that she would accidentally open the door and see him. That would give him a second chance to test the water with her and find out if she were really interested in him.

He became suddenly embarrassed by his schoolboy antics and continued up the stairs to his apartment.

David was sitting reading in the living room when Ali walked into the apartment whistling an Arabic song. When he saw David he blurted out a loud friendly hello and started chatting with him about any subject that came to his mind. He wanted to make up for his dashing out of the apartment in the morning and to demonstrate that there were no hard feelings between them, "You know, David, I'm always shocked to see so many homeless people in the streets of a country that is considered to be the richest place in the world."

When he got no response, he continued, "I've got to tell you about the funny incident that happened to me on my way home. I saw a homeless man sitting on the corner holding a cup. Without thinking or looking carefully at the man, I took a quarter and dropped it in his cup. The man screamed at me because I'd dropped the quarter in his coffee. The man wasn't even homeless. He was just sitting down resting and drinking his coffee."

David put his book aside and laughed.

Ali then switched the subject and asked David in an animated voice, "Guess who I met today?"

"Who?" David inquired without showing any emotion.

"This lady, Dorothy; I understand she owns this whole building," Ali answered so eagerly that it made David uneasy. "What a knockout. When I laid my eyes on her, it was sex at first sight. You should have seen the way she glided up those stairs." Undeterred by David's scornful stare, Ali couldn't stop. "Our women back home have a rhythm to their sway, but this Dorothy can lead the entire orchestra."

His lust-filled voice went on to describe the details of how they had met on the stairs and the inviting looks she gave him. David stared at Ali without cracking a smile and grew impatient as Ali continued his account of every curve, valley, and point of interest as if Dorothy's body were a roadmap.

Agitated, David interrupted him, "You're definitely mistaken. Dorothy is a nice older lady. You may have misunderstood her friendliness as a sexual overture. She is friendly with everyone in the neighborhood."

Ali ignored his explanation and kept clowning, "David I know she has a few miles on her, but following the old wise man's advice, I would never be able to say no to her."

David was getting more and more irritated with Ali's talk, "I want you to know that Dorothy has lived in this neighborhood for years and she has been a great friend of the neighborhood Jewish community. She and her late husband, Mr. Kaplan, are very popular among all the residents and the merchants in this area. They always invited the neighbors to their home during the Jewish holidays."

"Is she Jewish?" Ali became concerned.

"No, her husband was. Dorothy is Christian and is active in her church. I don't know whether you understand that there is a strong bond between Christians and Jews in this country."

"I know, I know," Ali replied. He sensed that David was jealous and irritated at the thought of an Arab, who was new in the country, running away with Dorothy the All-

American Christian woman who had been a great friend of the neighborhood Jewish community for years.

David was hoping that Ali was mistaken, and that Dorothy was not taken by his naturally tanned skin, his bulging muscles, or his dark curly hair and thick mustache. He hoped that Dorothy was smarter than that. He had known her for two years and had a crush on her. He, too, thought she was attractive and voluptuous and he would have loved to have an affair with her. But he never expressed his feelings to her, first because she was not Jewish and he dated only Jewish girls, and second, because she was a lot older than he.

It suddenly dawned on Ali that there might be something else that was causing David to be tense. *Maybe there is something going on between David and Dorothy.*

"David, are you involved with Dorothy?"

"Absolutely not," David replied emphatically. "I just don't want you to build false hopes and embarrass yourself."

David tried to cover up his initial reaction to Ali's comments. He became worried that his jealousy might have been obvious. Ali, noticing David's uneasiness, tried to comfort him, "I guess you're right. Maybe I shouldn't have listened to that wise old man."

He then excused himself and went to his room and David to his because it was time for each of them to perform their afternoon prayers.

CHAPTER 5

Dinner Party

The doorbell rang. Alone in the apartment, David's head was pounding from the day's assignment, Chapter 3, The Libel Plaintiff's Burden of Proof. Libel Per Se, Libel Per Quod. *Libel per who in the hell is bugging me at this time of day?*

He threw the door opened and was ready to slam it on the wrong face. Instead it was an unexpected one.

Typically he'd be elated to see Dorothy. But not this time. She seldom came up to the top floor. His heart sank and he had a foreboding premonition that included Dorothy and his new roommate.

Uninvited, she took a few steps inside and casually scanned the room perhaps hoping Ali would emerge, announcing to David that she was having a dinner party that evening and hoped David and his new roommate could come. She told him she'd met Ali the other day and congratulated him on choosing such a nice person to share his apartment with.

Yeah, thought David. *Mr. Nice guy whose mentor is a wise old man. The widow Dorothy is old enough to take care of herself.*

She explained that the dinner was intended to introduce Ali to another tenant in the building. "By the way, I invited Satish, I think your roommate ought to meet him," Dorothy said playfully.

David was stunned by the speed of Dorothy's dinner invitation. She met Ali only two days before. He remembered that he had lived in the building for weeks before he was invited to Dorothy's apartment, and it was only for an afternoon tea.

Here we have the burden of proof. Your honor, such a swift invite proves that my client Ali was not hallucinating.

This was not the first time he and Satish had been invited to dinner by Dorothy. There were birthdays and Thanksgiving, but he was certain that this dinner was primarily for Ali and Dorothy's benefit, and that he and Satish were merely the sideshow.

Now he had two reasons to grab the aspirin bottle off the counter. *My first dose will hopefully dull the pain caused by the law chapter on defamation. My second dose will prepare me for dinner foreplay between Dorothy and Ali.*

David was hoping he was wrong. *The last damn thing I want to hear is Ali giving me graphic play-by-play of his affair with my friend and landlady.*

David stayed in his room to avoid seeing Ali when he came back from school. He wanted to choose the moment to tell him about Dorothy's dinner and make it appear that the invitation was intended for himself as much as for Ali. He waited until he ran into him in the corridor.

"By the way, Dorothy invited us to dinner tonight. She also invited our neighbor Satish."

Ali's face lit up. He tried to hide his excitement but couldn't hide the smug look on his face.

"Who is Satish?"

"Satish is a good friend of Dorothy and mine."

Ali ignored David's explanation and said, "Great. I look forward to tasting her food. If she cooks as well as she walks, we are on for a great meal."

"Don't hold your breath. She probably will order the food from one of the kosher restaurants around here."

"Kosher kitchen. Kosher dinners. Is there any freedom of choice in this building?" Ali mumbled as he walked into his room.

At seven o'clock Ali and David went down to Dorothy's apartment. David brought her a bottle of wine and Ali opted for flowers. Dorothy opened the door with a loud hello and an exaggerated thank you. She had a glass of white wine in her hand and it seemed that it wasn't the first one. The form-fitting creamy white sleeveless top she had on left little to Ali and David's imagination. Since 9/11 she was never without her small-jeweled flag pin that always had a place above her left breast.

Lucky pin, mused Ali.

A slit in her long soft cinnamon skirt showed a firm tight thigh that definitely belonged to a Dallas Cowboy cheerleader and not to a woman of her age. She wasn't even one of those obsessive women you'd see on a stair master to nowhere in some hyped-up trendy New York gym.

God must have loved making this woman, David thought. *This well-formed body is a birthright. Who can blame her for showing it off? Who could blame Ali for desiring it?*

Ali and David struggled to keep their eyes politely above Dorothy's neckline. The struggle was over when she introduced Ali to Satish who was born in Mumbai, India, and had lived in Dorothy's building since his arrival in the United States.

David teased Satish by saying hello in a made-up Bollywood accent, and Satish welcomed Ali as if he were the evening host.

Satish was a proper, serious man in his late twenties. He wore thick glasses and his dark long hair occasionally fell over his ears. He was only 5'4" tall and so thin that his ribs could be seen underneath his white short-sleeved shirt. His baggy grey pants were long enough to partially hide his sandals and his long toenails. He was studying for his doctorate in business administration at Columbia University. But he had a special interest in international relations, a field he'd studied during his undergraduate years.

Satish sat erect at the edge of the sofa next to Dorothy facing Ali and David who sat in the two arm chairs across from them. There was an expression of amusement on his face as he watched Ali and David sitting next to each other. The fact that an Arab and a Jew were roommates obviously intrigued him. He also knew that David was a conservative Jew who held strong views about the Arab-Israeli problem that he assumed wouldn't agree with Ali's.

Dorothy asked Ali whether he wanted a glass of wine. She knew that both David and Satish preferred soft drinks. Ali politely explained that he didn't drink alcohol. In response, Dorothy murmured, "For heaven's sake, you guys are a wholesome bunch. Do any of you have any vices?"

Ali immediately exchanged meaningful looks with her suggesting that he'd one vice she'd be interested in, and David hastened to say, "Of course Dorothy, we just don't tell the landlady."

Dorothy passed around the ice tea she'd prepared and got up to set the table for dinner. David was quick to volunteer to help her while Satish sat chatting with Ali and asking him the usual questions like where he was from and where he was going to school.

Ali felt comfortable talking to foreigners, particularly those who came from developing countries. With Dorothy and David out of the room, Ali and Satish discussed the hardships in their own countries and in the developing world.

"How would the average American know what it's like to go through food shortages, or to have no running water and no electricity?" Ali said in a hard voice. "I'm always amused by those boutique-like grocery stores that sell so called organic foods to the well-heeled at outrageous prices. Many shoppers spend hours reading every ingredient on a package to make sure there aren't too many bad carbs or too few good ones."

"Don't forget the obsession with thin," added Satish. "This is the ultimate luxury when there isn't enough food, organic or even polluted, to feed the world. You know, Ali, I have a theory. When a nation starts to fight fat, anorexia and bulimia, it means that it has finally graduated from the third world to the first."

Ali and Satish talked as if they had known each other for a long time. In spite of the clandestine critical chat, both men expressed their respect and admiration of the United States. They agreed that it was the land of opportunity, or as Satish fondly called it, "The land of plenty."

Dorothy and David finished setting the table and dishing the food specially prepared by Cantor Kosher Restaurant around the corner. In a lilting voice, Dorothy announced that dinner was ready. With a wine glass in one hand and the other hand reaching for Ali's hand she led her guests to the table. Her thumb gently rubbed Ali's hand and he, in turn, pressed on hers. She turned her head and gave him an encouraging smile.

David sat at one end of the rectangular dining table in front of the plate and silverware he had brought with him. Satish sat at the other end and, by design, Dorothy sat across from Ali.

The meal had something for every one. It was a kosher meal but had plenty of rice and vegetables that suited Satish who was a vegetarian. Dorothy, however, had no clue of Ali's diet. Unbeknownst to her the food was also good for him because it had no pork and the kosher meat would pass for halal meat.

Dorothy got giddier after a few glasses of wine. She teased everyone as she passed the food around, stopping at Ali for few extra moments to examine his powerful arms one more time. Ali's eyes were focused on her and he wasn't paying attention to anyone else at the table. They exchanged meaningful smiles every time their eyes met. David sat uncomfortably watching this exchange of looks and smiles between the two. Satish, on the other hand, continued to eat his food, totally oblivious to the fuss around him.

Dorothy asked whether everyone liked the food, and Ali immediately raised his glass of iced tea and said, "Dorothy, I was expecting a typical American meal of roast beef and mashed potatoes, but this went beyond my expectations."

"Honey, you will have to thank the Cantors for this meal. I only set the table and even on that I got help from David."

The light conversation around the table, the laughing and the giggling were interrupted when Satish, like a true provocateur, turned to Ali and asked in a serious voice, "Ali, your people in the Middle East must hate Americans for what they're doing in Iraq."

Ali's laughter faded quickly, he put down his fork and answered Satish, looking at Dorothy and David, "We don't hate Americans, we resent American policy in the Middle East. Look at what happened to Iraq; millions have fled the country and are refugees in Syria, Jordan, and other Arab countries. Imagine, hundreds of thousands of people were killed or maimed." Ali could not hide the emotion in his voice, "Now sectarian fighting and destruction are taking place everywhere in the country."

"Don't forget the thousands of young American men and women who lost their lives or were severely injured, and the hundreds of billions of dollars spent on this war," interjected Satish. "Saddam Hussein was a terrible leader, but his people would have gotten rid of him at some point and the country would have changed like others did. Think about this. Not too long ago Russia and China had leaders who were worse than Saddam Hussein. But look at them today. They did it on their own."

David shook his head, "I don't know how we will get out of this mess."

Dorothy raised her hand as a student who wanted to express an opinion in a classroom, "I think I'd rather fight those terrorists over there than here in our backyard. We will never forget what they did on 9/11."

"But there were no terrorists there," Ali, Satish, and David shouted at the same time, and David continued. "The terrorists showed up there only after the United States had invaded the country."

The three of them were in agreement that the Iraq war was a huge mistake. Ali felt that Dorothy was not well informed on that subject, and she was just repeating an argument she might have heard on one of the conservative news channels.

Satish loved political debates and was not satisfied to see an agreement between Ali and David on the Iraq war. He quickly switched the subject and asked Ali, "I'm interested hearing your views on the Arab-Israeli issue. What do you think of the U.S. position in this conflict?"

That was Ali's favorite subject. He answered in a deliberate voice, determined not to get emotional as he usually did when he discussed this issue, "I believe America's one-sided policy and bias for Israel is making extremism flourish among some Arabs."

Satish nodded in response to Ali's reply, but David raised his voice to say, "Our policy isn't one-sided. And even if it is, Israel is our most reliable ally in the Middle East."

Dorothy smiled and raised her glass, "I'll drink to that."

David continued without acknowledging Dorothy's remark, but encouraged by her support, "Israel is our best defense against terrorism in that region. Besides, more than one hundred million Arabs surround Israel. If it wasn't for our support, they would destroy her."

Ali ignored David and looked at Dorothy with disappointment because she didn't come to his support. He addressed her in an injured tone, "I don't want to destroy Israel. I want to live in peace with dignity on my land, Palestine. And I'm not advocating that America abandon Israel but just be a fair referee. Just think about history; the Arabs have always been your friends. They stood with you against Nazi Germany, and we are great consumers of your products. The oil-producing Arab countries have been partnering with US companies for decades. This is my question, why can't your policy makers understand that it's not in America's interest to antagonize the Arab world?"

Dorothy looked at David for support, hesitated for a few seconds and replied without looking directly at Ali, "But look at what the Israelis have accomplished. They formed a democratic society, developed modern industry and agriculture, and built schools and hospitals. They made a piece of America over there. I think the Arabs can learn a lot from the Israelis and work on developing their countries and educating their people rather than fighting them."

Satish interrupted Dorothy and talked as if he was lecturing her, "This is irrelevant, Dorothy. You can't take my house against my will and every time I ask you to give it back you tell me about the excellent job you've done fixing it. It's still my house."

Dorothy was persistent, "You know, Satish, Americans feel a deep commitment to Israel because it's a reliable ally, its culture is similar to ours and Judaism is more familiar to Americans than Islam which is the dominant religion among the Arabs."

David found himself jumping in, "We all loved and cheered Sadat of Egypt when he traveled to Jerusalem and started his famous peace initiative. He emerged as an American and Western hero and we all hoped that was the first step of peace in the region." *Wow, I'm forgetting what side of the table I'm on.*

Ali became emotional in spite of his intent not to do so. He raised his voice while addressing Dorothy and Satish and ignoring David, "He forgot to tell you that the Camp David Accords signed by Sadat and Menachem Begin of Israel called for a process guaranteeing the full autonomy of the West Bank and Gaza within five years. That was in 1978, and now we are in 2008, and we still have no real autonomy."

Satish nodded approval of Ali's argument, but David objected, "It was your militants and suicide bombers who destroyed the prospects of peace."

Dorothy became concerned that the political arguments would ruin her carefully planned dinner, "Listen, Ali. The fact that we have a special relationship with Israel doesn't mean that we are oblivious to the Palestinian plight. On the contrary, my church congregation fully supports peace and the establishment of an independent Palestinian state."

Ali listened to Dorothy and looked around the table feeling that he was in the middle of one of those meetings of the United Nations General Assembly he'd frequently watched on television back home. Dorothy was stating the American position he'd often heard. Satish's arguments were consistent with those of many developing countries who sympathized with the Palestinians and identified with their cause. As for David, he was like many Jewish Americans. He had a strong connection with Israel. As an Orthodox Jew he strongly believed of the Jews' right to the ancient land of Israel even if the Palestinians had lived there for centuries. He blindly supported any position taken by Israel's leaders.

The mood around the table grew tense. Ali and David were not looking at each other, and Ali ceased his flirtation with Dorothy who suddenly stopped her giggling. Satish, realizing that he'd started this hot and divisive debate, attempted to diffuse the tension by asking Dorothy about her plans for the apartment that was about to become vacant in the building. Dorothy seized the opportunity to change the subject and asked all of them to move to the living room to have dessert and a cup of tea and to learn about her plans for that apartment.

The three men moved to the living room as Dorothy went into the kitchen. Ali felt betrayed by Dorothy because he expected her to side with him. Instead, she showed little sympathy for his people. He also felt some contempt toward David. He'd hoped that David was moderate in his views about the Arabs and the Arab-Israeli conflict. It hadn't occurred to him that he wasn't moderate himself about the same situation.

Dorothy soon came to the room with a tray of kosher cookies and tea. She was cheerful and determined to turn the page on the tense situation at the dining table. As she poured the tea for everybody she declared that she'd decided to rent the soon-to-be vacant apartment furnished. She thought that if she decorated it nicely, she'd be able to attract a young professional and demand a high rent. She asked their opinion in an attempt to get them all talking again. She knew that

Satish, being a graduate student in business administration, would be the most knowledgeable among them. Satish quickly approved of the idea and explained the financial merits of renting a furnished apartment. He explained to Dorothy that she'd not only receive higher rent, but she also would be able to depreciate all the furnishings over a few years and that would give her an additional tax advantage. Ali and David listened quietly. Neither of them was good in the field of finance.

But Dorothy, attempting to get them involved, asked whether they could help her in moving the furniture into the new apartment as well as painting and decorating the place. They were both quick to show their readiness to help her. Ali went further and told her, while flexing his muscles, that he had worked for a few weeks in a moving company in Queens. He jokingly asked Dorothy to feel his arm and she gladly placed her hand around his bicep and gave a sigh of admiration.

David watched the charade and said with a smile, "I will certainly help Ali move your furniture. I may not have the same muscles, but I know how to maneuver all the turns in the staircase, and I'm an expert in getting large pieces of furniture through narrow doors."

Dorothy became visibly excited and said in a loud voice as she clapped her hands, "It's a deal."

Dorothy managed, at last, to make everyone smile again. When it was time to leave, she kissed each one of them on the cheek as they walked out of the door. Ali was the last one and he placed his arm around her waist and pressed his body gently against hers. He could feel her breasts pressing against his chest. She placed her hand on his bare arm, looked at him straight in the eyes, and said in a tender voice, "Thank you for your offer to help. I'll see you soon."

CHAPTER 6

The Affair

Two days later, after finishing his evening prayers, Ali decided to go for a walk. He passed by David's room, and again saw him standing, exactly like he had been, facing east and totally consumed in his prayers. He shook his head and continued on his way out. *How in the world did this Muslim-Jewish feud really begin? Look at him facing east and praying to the same God I've just finished praying to five minutes earlier. It's like he picked up where I left off.* Always the engineering student, Ali thought. *This mathematical equation just doesn't add up. We both are Semites and we're descendents of Abraham. Even Moses, one of the important prophets in Judaism, is considered a prophet by us and is repeatedly mentioned in the Qur'an.* He then smiled. *We are even circumcised according to Abrahamic law.* He kept questioning his feelings for David that oscillated between contempt for his disregard of the Palestinians' rights and admiration for his commitment to the same God Ali prayed to.

Ali walked the streets of his busy neighborhood. He could hear the roaring sounds of the window air-conditioning units above him. The water drops from those units gave him a slight relief from the late summer heat. He went by the corner deli that was a destination for many people seeking the best pastrami and corned beef sandwiches, and the Cantor restaurant, famous for its gourmet kosher food. In the middle of the hustling and bustling neighborhood, there was a small movie theater that showed only X-rated movies. Ali glanced at the nude pictures in the window and his thoughts immediately turned to Dorothy. He thought about her kiss on the cheek after the dinner in her apartment and her breasts pressing against his chest as he pulled her against his body. She thanked him for his offer to help moving the furniture in the soon-to-be vacant apartment. But he was certain that her "thank you" was an invitation for him to come and see her.

It was 10 pm and he wondered whether it was too late to knock on her door. What kind of an excuse could he give for his visit? He didn't want to show any sign of hesitation when she opened the door. He believed that most women admired masculine men. In his mind that meant courage and confidence. But what if she were sleeping, or what if she would snub him? That would completely close the door on any hope for a relationship. He knew it was a gamble, but fire burned inside his belly and only Dorothy could put out the flame.

When he got close to the apartment building he looked up and saw a light in her living room. He was certain she was there, probably watching TV. But was she alone? He obviously didn't know and actually didn't care. He was willing and ready to take his chances.

He stood in front of Dorothy's door for a few minutes listening to hear whether she had any guests while gathering enough courage to make the move. Not hearing any voices he pressed the doorbell half way, taking his finger off quickly as if that was a discreet way of bell ringing.

She opened the door, looked at him and smiled. She didn't show any sign of surprise. He attempted to hide his sense of relief and demonstrate the confidence he'd been trying to build all the way up to her door, "Good evening Dorothy, did I wake you?"

"Heavens no, please come in," she said.

Dorothy wore a gold threaded light blue kimono-styled robe that ended just above the knee and jade green slippers.

What lies beneath that modest cover? Thought Ali. He imagined a laced crimson low cut bra and matching bikini panties. He was certain that Dorothy would never settle for practical white cotton underwear.

She grabbed Ali's hand to lead him in and closed the door, "Come and sit down; do you want something to drink?" That was the last thing Ali was thinking about. He kept holding her hand, walking toward the sofa and looking at her admiringly. He suddenly turned his body to face her, pulled her hand and placed it around his neck and wrapped his arm around her waist. There was no resistance on her part, and she put the other arm around his neck. Ali pulled her body against his with his hands going down on her hips. His lips searched for hers and the two met in a long passionate kiss. His hands stroked her thighs and her back until they reached her breasts that he had been yearning to touch.

Ali put one arm around her back and the other around her legs and lifted her in his arms and walked toward the bedroom. She leaned her head against his shoulder and he placed his cheek on hers. He lowered her gently on the bed and started taking off his clothes as she lay down looking at his thick broad shoulders. Unfastening the silken belt, Dorothy's kimono slid open revealing everything that he had imagined. She stretched her arm and gently pulled him toward her. Her sighs turned into muffled screams as Ali's youthful energy radiated throughout her body. Her screams got louder and louder and her arms held him tighter hoping that time would freeze and those few orgasmic seconds would last for hours or days.

She lay down next to him caressing his muscled arms, gently pulling on his chest hair and playfully biting his earlobe. Neither of them spoke; they didn't wish to ruin the moment.

As the night wore on, Ali displayed his youth and stamina and Dorothy was eager to please him. They were both full of intoxicating desire and felt that they had found in each other a sexual treasure.

At six o'clock in the morning, Ali jumped out of bed and announced that he should go back to his apartment to prepare for school. Dorothy, with a broad smile on her face, feeling that she had just finished the Boston Marathon, got out of bed, walked him to the door and gave him a long kiss, "Please come by after school. I will prepare dinner for you."

"Thank you, I will see you around eight."

Ali opened his apartment door hoping not to face David and to have to explain to him where he had been that early in the morning. As he walked into the living room, David was coming out of the bathroom with a towel over his head. He looked up and saw Ali's face covered with lipstick, his wrinkled shirt and messy hair, "Where were you? Were you in a fight?"

"No, No, I spent the night at my friend Yasser's place."

Ali had to lie. Lying was against his nature and his religious upbringing, but he wasn't sure how David would react to his affair with Dorothy.

"What did you guys do? Did you go together on a suicide mission?" David asked without cracking a smile or expecting an answer. He suspected Ali was with a woman, perhaps Dorothy, and this annoyed him a great deal.

David's feelings toward Dorothy were convoluted. He liked her and was sexually attracted to her but never dared to express his feelings to her. He had that strong belief that when it came to premarital sex he'd be forgiven only if he slept with a Jewish woman. Furthermore, he never wanted to risk jeopardizing his friendship with her because he felt that she was one of his links to the gentile community of this country. Suddenly he felt threatened because he had to share this friendship and affection with Ali.

He was concerned that an affair between Ali and Dorothy, driven by sexual attraction, could detract from his special relationship with her. The mere thought of her siding with Ali against him and Israel in a future discussion infuriated him and made him feel both jealous and insecure.

After a quick shower Ali stood facing Allah for his morning prayers and asked for his forgiveness for the sin he'd committed. He knew deep in his heart, though, that he was about to commit the same sin that night, the following night, and possibly many other nights.

CHAPTER 7

Sex and Politics

Dr. Butterworth should have been a tyrant rather than a professor of structural engineering. At the beginning of each semester, in a deep rumbling voice, he'd give a warning, "I want one hundred-percent of you. Not ninety-nine...I want it all...I'm greedy. Don't look sideways, stare off into space or utter a syllable to your neighbor. Write down every word I say...including my sneezes."

Some students swore he was telepathic; most agreed he was less than human. Break the Butterworth edict and the miscreant would suffer the dreaded long reptilian stare before being humiliated and devoured in front of his peers. The reptile could spot a wandering mind a mile away. Once he captured the prey's attention he'd invite him or her to stand before the class and regurgitate the morning lecture.

"Mr. Smith, explain to the class the precise difference between tensile stress and shear stress." If the student failed, Butterworth would go in for the kill. "Quit! You are undeserving to be in my class." Pointing to the door in anger he would command the student to leave.

Banishment was not permanent, but it did require an appropriate amount of groveling, pleading, a couple of visits to his office, and a strong promise to work a lot harder.

Ali took copious notes in class so he would be prepared for such a dreaded moment. He was always ready, but not today. His mind was not focused on mathematical equations or engineering principles. He was focused on the night before. Like a starving man who stumbled on a source of food, he could not wait until his next meal. The Dorothy countdown began as erotic images played in his head. *Bending moments...Dorothy, tension...Dorothy, ...compression....Dorothy.*

Suddenly an unwelcome intruder entered his thoughts. Butterworth, the mind reader, stood in front of him shaking his head in controlled anger. "Mr. Nasrallah, I invite you to stand before this class and explain the engineering principles and how to calculate bending moments."

Ali tried to quickly get Dorothy out of his head and think bending moments instead. But his brain wasn't responsive. He stood up, looked down at his notes, and hesitated. His eyes stared at the stone face in front of him pleading for mercy. Butterworth knew Ali to be a good student and the usually unsympathetic professor took pity on him and asked him to sit down and pay more attention.

Ali decided to skip the rest of his classes that day after the Butterworth embarrassment and go to his favorite Arabic grocery store in Queens to buy a box of baklava for Dorothy. He knew she loved that Middle Eastern desert. He passed by the cafeteria on his way out of the school. He saw Kamel, an Egyptian student, sitting in a corner laughing and chatting with Judy Gardner, a girl from one of Ali's classes. They were holding hands and it was obvious that they were more than close friends. Ali knew Judy, and had tried a few times to go out with her. But she kept making excuses until he finally realized that she wasn't interested.

He looked at them and shook his head. *Why Kamel and not me? He isn't even good looking. He is short, chubby, and doesn't have my sense of humor.* But deep inside, Ali knew the answer. Kamel was part of a group of Arab students who came from well-to-do families. Many of them went to English or American schools in their countries. They had money, wore designer clothes, and spent their weekends dancing in N.Y.'s trendy nightclubs. They were different from Ali's group who came from modest families, had to work to support themselves through school, weren't on top of the latest music or men's fashions, and generally adhered to their culture and traditions.

I don't care if she likes Kamel because he drinks and goes to clubs, I want a woman who likes me the way I am. Like Dorothy. The thought of Dorothy renewed his confidence and brought a smile to his face.

At eight o'clock he was at Dorothy's door. The moment he entered she put her arms on his shoulders, kissed him on the lips, and whispered in his ear how much she'd missed him.

Ali felt like a new man; he was confident and knew what to expect. The night before he stood in the same place hesitant and unsure of how Dorothy would react to his visit. This time he felt that the script of the evening had already been written by Dorothy herself leading to the end they were both looking forward to.

He looked around the living room noticing that it looked different from the night before. The lights were dimmed, there were candles in every corner of the room, and Frank Sinatra was singing, "When I was seventeen, it was a very good year." Dorothy was visibly happy and excited. They both sat on the sofa holding hands; she was sipping white wine and he held a Coke in his other hand. They made small talk. She asked him about his school and stroked his ego by telling him how impressed she was by his engineering background.

Ali resisted opening his favorite subject about Middle Eastern politics and the Israeli-Palestinian dilemma. Besides engineering, this was the topic he was most informed on. But it was only his second night with her and he didn't wish to detract from the main course of the evening.

Dorothy took his hand and led him to the dining table. She'd prepared a delicious meal of ribeye steak, baked potatoes, and mixed green salad. They hurried through the meal, skipped dessert and rushed into bed to have uninterrupted sex until the wee hours of the morning.

David watched with relative envy Ali disappearing every night after his evening prayers, and showing up early in the morning for his shower and morning prayers.

As days went by David grew more apprehensive of the new relationship between Ali and Dorothy. He knew deep down that there was no logical reason behind his feeling. But he still feared the unintended consequences of a strong bond developing between a Palestinian Arab and a Christian American woman like Dorothy. David's head was swarming with thoughts of millions of Arab men like Ali coming to the United States and having affairs or marrying mainstream American women. As this ridiculous scenario continued to unfold in his head, David ramped it up by imagining a new America that no longer supported Israel. *Future scholars would be asking when did America cease to support Israel? Ah yes, it all started early in the twenty-first century when Ali met Dorothy.* Unable to shake this ridiculous vision, David could not disguise the disdain he had for Ali.

His bitterness showed when he ran into Ali one morning after they both had finished their morning prayers, "How could you face God and pray one moment and in the next you're downstairs sleeping with a Christian woman to whom you aren't married? I thought you were a good Muslim."

David's sudden opening of the subject he had been trying to avoid surprised Ali. "David, in our religion there are simple vows a man and a woman have to say to be married before God. Admittedly, governments in Muslim countries or in America don't recognize such marriages. But who cares about that? Do you know that a Muslim can marry a Christian or a Jewish woman? There is nothing in Islam that forbids such a marriage."

David was stunned to hear that and hastened to ask, "Are you telling me that you and Dorothy are now married?"

Ali laughed, "No, no, for heaven's sake. I just asked her to repeat some vows, and she did to make me happy. She didn't care."

"I'm sure she cares. She is a good Christian."

"I'm also a good Muslim and you're a good Jew. But what if a man and a woman are attracted to each other? Remember what the old wise man said? I thought you agreed with him."

Seething, David said under his breath, "Doesn't this old wise man's crap have an expiration date?"

Ali wasn't listening and kept examining his face for clues. He was sure that David wouldn't care if he were having an affair with another Christian woman. But he felt that David was against his relationship with Dorothy and couldn't figure out the reasons behind that, or perhaps he did. *Is he secretly in love with her? Or is it because she was married to a Jew? Or is it because she is a good friend of all the Jews in the neighborhood?*

David finally uttered in a hushed voice, "I just wish you wouldn't have an affair with our landlady. I don't like mixing sex with business." Then he got up and went to his room.

Ali wasn't convinced by David's argument and as David walked away his voice followed, "Remember, David, I don't have a lease agreement with Dorothy and you are not having an affair with her. Therefore, neither of us is mixing sex with business."

As days went by, Ali became more and more confident of Dorothy's feelings for him. He believed that she liked him, both emotionally and physically. But he remembered the conversation they had during the first dinner with David and Satish and how she was adamant in her support for Israel. He thought that her late husband, who was Jewish, and her many Jewish friends, had influenced her. He was anxious to explore whether their hot and steamy relationship and her feelings for him had any impact on her views on the subject. He was hoping that she'd softened her position and become more sympathetic to the Arab side.

While lying in bed holding her in one arm and fondling her hair with the other hand, he gently approached the subject of the miserable conditions his people were living under in the West Bank and in Gaza, and their desire to have their own independent country Palestine. But he was shocked to find her unshaken in her support for Israel. He couldn't comprehend how she was lying in the arms of a Palestinian Arab and not supporting his views on a subject that was of paramount importance to him. He noticed, however, that she started to show more compassion for the Palestinian situation than she'd displayed at their first dinner. She kept insisting that there was no reason why the Israelis and the Palestinians couldn't live next to each other in peace and harmony.

She noticed that Ali was annoyed and felt betrayed because she wasn't siding with him. She tried to comfort him and said, while rubbing his arm, "Look at you and David. You both manage to coexist and respect each other's religious and political views, and share an apartment with one kitchen and one bathroom. Why can't the people over there do the same?"

Ali had no response. He knew the problems in his region were far more complicated than the simple way presented by Dorothy. But deep inside he felt she was right. *Why couldn't the Israelis and we live next to each other in peace? If David and I, who are religious and come from completely different cultural backgrounds can do it, the others over there should be able to do the same.*

CHAPTER 8

The Uninvited Arab Guest

David went to visit his parents in Miami. He wanted to spend some spiritual time with them. Unexpectedly, Ali received a phone call from his cousin Aisha and learned from her that she'd been accepted as a graduate student at Columbia University. She competed and won a scholarship for a Ph.D. degree in the field of international relations. She asked Ali where she'd stay while searching for a suitable place to live near the university. In the true Arab way of hospitality that sometimes seems to be overbearing, he insisted that she stay with him in the apartment. He never thought about first asking David's opinion or approval. Aisha reluctantly accepted his offer, not knowing that the apartment had only one bathroom and that Ali's roommate was an Orthodox Jew who maintained a kosher kitchen.

Ali grew up with Aisha in the same town in the West Bank. She, like Ali, was in her early twenties. He always thought she was a beautiful girl. She had large brown eyes with long eyelashes, and long silky black hair. She was religious and dressed herself in the traditional modest way of Muslim women. She covered her hair with a scarf wrapped around her head (hijab) and wore long dresses down to her ankle. Ali always told his family that his cousin's beauty and sex appeal shined in spite of her hijab and the long dress that hid her youthful and full figure.

Aisha came from a large family, three brothers and two sisters. Ali knew her parents to be religious but mostly open-minded and moderate in their political and religious views. They never demanded that she wore the hijab. As a matter of fact, her sisters did not cover their hair or wear long dresses, although they were equally religious. Ali was always impressed by the fact that the family had several Israeli friends who lived inside Israel. Her oldest brother, Hassan, had worked for an Israeli building contractor, Amon, before the 2000 Intifada and before Israel sealed the borders with the West Bank. The relationship between Amon and Hassan started as a business arrangement that was mutually beneficial. Hassan was a skilled carpenter and was reasonably priced compared to his counterparts inside Israel. Amon was a general contractor and had excellent business contacts. The business relationship grew into a close friendship, not only between Hassan and Amon, but also between their families. They celebrated family birthdays and some holidays together.

Aisha used to tell Ali stories about her trips with her brother during her school holidays. She stayed all day with the Amon's family inside Israel while her brother was busy working with Amon. She developed a close friendship with Amon's daughter, Alia, who was her age. They both were in tears when the tense political situation following the Intifada made it difficult to see each other. They continued, however, to talk to each other on the phone and to exchange e-mails and text messages on a daily basis.

Ali knew what Aisha's friends used to call her, "the peace maker." Whenever some of her friends got into a fight with each other, or had an argument, Aisha was quick to intervene and made sure that the warm and congenial friendship was maintained.

In her political views, she also was a peace advocate. She argued with her friends about the need for compromise with the Israelis and the need to stop violence and focus on economic development. She steadfastly held those views independent of her close friendship with Alia. On many occasions during the height of the Intifada, her friends scorned her and accused her of being a traitor because she wasn't supporting the armed struggle of her Palestinian people. But she constantly reminded them of how great leaders like Mahatma Gandhi of India and Nelson Mandela of South Africa were able to achieve their goals and free their people through passive resistance. Gandhi helped India's struggle for independence from Britain through a campaign based on nonviolence and civil disobedience. His doctrine of nonviolent action had a profound influence on Martin Luther King Jr., the leader of the civil rights movement in the U.S., and Mandela, the most prominent figure of the Black opposition to Apartheid in South Africa.

Ali considered Aisha's views and moderation to be the antithesis of his friend Yasser. Although they both grew up in Ali's small town in the West Bank and only a few blocks apart, their views were on the opposite ends of the political spectrum. Aisha and Yasser were both religious and closely followed the tenets of Islam but they diverged in their interpretation of these tenets. While Aisha believed in dialogue, compromise, and passive resistance, Yasser was convinced that the only path to re-establish the Palestinian homeland was through armed resistance. He always dreamt that one day he'd go back and live in his grandparents' house near Haifa, which he'd never seen except in pictures carried by his parents.

Aisha was popular in her hometown, and many eligible men, including some of Ali's friends, were interested in marrying her. But she wasn't interested in starting a family or raising children in the prevailing environment of hostility and economic hopelessness in the West Bank. She watched one peace initiative after another fall by the wayside on basis of intransigence and shortsightedness by both the Israelis and the Palestinians.

Ali enjoyed his political discussions with her because she was intelligent and well informed. She could never comprehend why the Israelis had to have settlements in the West Bank and not in Israel, and why the Palestinians insisted on the "right of return." Why did they want to go back and live in Israel as second-class citizens when they could live as masters of their own destiny in a Palestine made of the West Bank and Gaza? And why Jerusalem, the holy city cherished by all the People of the Book: Jews, Christians and Muslims, couldn't be administered by all the interested parties. She felt that all those world experts in international law could certainly develop a workable system to administer Jerusalem that was fair and equitable to every one.

Those questions and paradoxes were constantly on her mind. Through her frustration she chose a career that, in her mind, might put her in a position to help resolve the political dilemma that was destroying her hopes of living and having a family in her homeland. Consequently, she decided to study international relations and was fortunate to receive a full scholarship from a distinguished school such as Columbia University.

Aisha arrived at Ali and David's apartment while David was still in Miami with his parents. She immediately realized that she was encroaching on David's rights in the apartment. Ali arranged for her to sleep on the sofa in the living room and stack her suitcases against the wall. She was uncomfortable about the fact that Ali hadn't asked David's permission to invite her to stay with them. She felt like she was one of those settlers in the West Bank whom she despised and considered to be one of the sources of tension and animosity between the Israelis and the Palestinians. She immediately started to look for an apartment to rent. But the search was more tedious and time consuming than she'd expected. She became convinced that it might take her a few weeks before she could find a suitable place, and that made her more anxious and ashamed of the situation she was in.

In a matter of days it became clear to Ali the difficult situation he had created by inviting Aisha to stay with them. He wasn't able to see Dorothy as frequently as he wanted. He managed to slip away a couple of times for a few hours to see her. He didn't want Aisha to know about his affair because he wasn't sure how she would react to such a relationship. As for Aisha, every day that went by without success in her search, she became more exasperated and more homesick.

Ali started to worry about her and decided to organize a nice dinner for her to make her feel at home. He invited his friend Yasser whom she hadn't seen for two years and his other Palestinian friend Ahmed, and cooked a Middle Eastern meal for them.

Although Ali knew that Aisha wasn't fond of Yasser and his extreme political views, he thought the gathering would take her mind off the frustrating process of the apartment search. He was sure that she would enjoy meeting and talking to Ahmed who came from the West Bank and was acquainted with some of Aisha's friends.

After dinner, the four of them sat in the living room sipping mint tea, chatting about the families back home, and listening to some Arabic music, including some of the old songs of Um Kulsum, the famous Egyptian singer.

As the four of them sang and repeated her lyrics, the doorbell rang and Aisha opened the door. The man there saw Aisha in her long dress and the scarf around her head and immediately looked up again at the apartment number. It was obvious that he thought he had made a mistake and rang the wrong doorbell.

"Is this David Goldstein's apartment?" he asked with a grin, expecting to be told that it wasn't.

Ali jumped up and went to the door, "Yes, this is his place. I'm Ali Nasrallah, David's roommate. He is in Miami visiting his parents. Please come in."

Aisha repeated Ali's invitation, "Please come in and have some tea with us."

The man at the door couldn't hide his shock at the scene in front of him. He hesitated then stepped cautiously in, looking around the room, "My name is Ben Katz and I'm a good friend of David. I'm sorry to disturb your dinner; David never told me that he had a roommate."

Ali quickly explained that he had been living there for a short time, and introduced Aisha, Yasser and Ahmed to him.

Aisha watched Yasser shake hands with Ben, and she almost burst into laughter. The two had long beards and head covers, Yasser in his traditional Muslim head cap and Ben in his yarmulke. They both looked a little alike. They had dark skin, because Ben was a Sephardic Jew, and they were the same height and had similar body shapes. She recognized right away that Ben was an Orthodox Jew, and was amused to see him shaking hands with Yasser whom she considered to be an orthodox Muslim and a militant Palestinian.

But what Aisha didn't know was that Ben was as extreme as Yasser in his political views. His mother's family was one of the first settlers in the occupied West Bank. They built one of the largest of the seventeen settlements that made a block called Gush Etzion. He and his family believed that they had a divine right to settle in the land where, according to their belief, David and Abraham once walked. They were against any international effort to dismantle or limit the expansion of the settlements in the West Bank.

Yasser reviled those settlers who had sliced the land that once belonged to the Palestinians, took scarce resources like water, constructed settlers-only roads, and built checkpoints that made his and his family's lives miserable.

Aisha looked at Ben and Yasser and could see that they were noticeably uncomfortable with each other in spite of their physical similarity. That apparent animosity didn't surprise her.

Ben looked around the room and saw her suitcases against the wall with a pillow and blanket on top of them. He discreetly turned his head toward the kitchen and saw dishes and silverware piled in the sink. He became suspicious and concerned about David's safety. He never trusted Arabs, and he'd not seen David at the synagogue for over a week. Moreover, David never mentioned that he had an Arab roommate.

He excused himself and left in a hurry. He rushed home and immediately called David in Miami. Upon hearing David's voice he shouted in the phone, "David, I'm very happy to hear your voice and find you're safe."

"What do you mean, Ben?" David asked probingly.

"You better hurry back or call the police. Your place has been taken over by a bunch of Arabs who claim they're your roommates. They have suitcases and blankets all over the place, and above all, they have violated your kosher kitchen. I'm telling you, David, your place looks like a Palestinian refugee camp."

David was embarrassed because he'd never mentioned to his good friend that he had an Arab roommate. He hadn't found the right opportunity or had the courage to tell him. Suddenly he found himself in a corner and tried to bring the news to Ben in a joking way, "I forgot to tell you I have a Palestinian roommate. His name is Ali and he wants to join our synagogue."

Ben wasn't amused, "Wake up, my friend, Ali has brought his forty brothers and sisters with him, and one of them has a veil on her head and the other has a long beard and wears one of those skullcaps the fanatic Muslims wear. I'm telling you this guy looks like a real terrorist."

Ben had his yarmulke on his head and was holding the phone in one hand and stroking his own long beard with the other.

CHAPTER 9

The Arab Settler

David became concerned after Ben's call and was on the first flight back to New York. Deep in his heart he knew that Ben was opinionated and mistrusted all Arabs. But what if he was right and Ali and his friends had taken over his apartment? He considered calling Dorothy and asking her to check the place, but decided against that idea. He was determined to resolve this matter by himself and to confront those people, regardless of their ethnic background, who were illegally residing in his place and using his kitchen and his furniture.

He arrived at the apartment late in the evening, opened the door quietly to surprise the intruders inside, and walked into the living room. The lights were dim, and Aisha was standing in the corner of the room praying. He looked around and saw a bed sheet and a pillow on the sofa, and a couple of suitcases leaning against the wall. He walked past her heading to Ali's room, and she continued praying unperturbed by his presence. He looked inside and saw Ali also kneeling down in his prayers. David walked back to the kitchen to wait for him to finish. In the meantime he looked around the kitchen, examining every corner to find out whether Ali and his gang had violated his kosher kitchen. He was partially relieved to find the kitchen clean and his dishes, silverware and sink strainers exactly in the same place he'd left them.

He looked through the kitchen door and saw Aisha sitting on her rug, and turning her head to the right and to the left whispering her greetings to the angels as Muslims do at the end of their prayers. She got up, folded her rug and walked straight to David greeting him with a big smile as if she'd known him for years, "Shalom David, my name is Aisha and I'm Ali's cousin. Please forgive me for imposing on you, I had no idea before I arrived that Ali had a roommate."

Then she started speaking to David in Hebrew, telling him that she was familiar with kosher kitchens and kosher cooking.

David froze in his place in the kitchen and couldn't understand even half of what she'd said. He couldn't hide the surprised look on his face. He was looking at a woman in a long dress, her head wrapped in a hijab, and obviously a devout Muslim, who spoke Hebrew fluently.

Who could this woman be? Was Ben correct in his assessment of the situation? Was she one of those female suicide bombers he'd seen on television? Was Ali, his roommate, on some mission here in America and his school attendance just a front?

He finally responded to her in a hushed voice, "Hello. Where did you learn Hebrew?"

As he finished the question, Ali joined them in the kitchen and explained to David that Aisha had been awarded a scholarship by Columbia and that she was searching for an apartment. He apologized for not checking with him before inviting her to stay in their place.

David was slightly relieved, but remained apprehensive. "Is she the only one staying here? Are there other Palestinian students from Columbia staying here?"

Ali and Aisha laughed and responded teasingly, "Our cousins are on their way with their tents."

David wasn't amused, and continued questioning Ali, "How long is she planning to stay here?"

Aisha was quick to assure David that it was only a matter of days, and that she had narrowed her search to a handful of apartments near the campus.

David felt slightly embarrassed by his overt inhospitality and attempted to cover up his deep concerns about her presence by saying ingratiatingly, "You're welcome to stay until you find a place. I'm just concerned that our place may not be comfortable for you, considering we have only one bathroom. I also maintain a kosher kitchen, and I don't know if you know what that means."

Aisha repeated again what she said earlier in Hebrew and assured David that she was quite familiar with kosher kitchens. She mentioned to him her friend Alia in Israel, and the times the two of them had spent together in Israel and in Aisha's town in the West Bank, and how she used to help Alia and her mother prepare kosher meals.

David was somewhat puzzled and at the same time impressed by this Arab woman who was obviously a conservative Muslim, but spoke Hebrew, had a close Israeli friend and knew everything about Judaism and kosher food. He wondered about her feelings toward Israel and her views about the Arab-Israeli problem. He knew Ali's views; he heard them at Dorothy's dinner and never broached the subject with him again.

After several days, David felt that Aisha's presence in the apartment was a nuisance in spite of her gentle personality. She was neat and tidy, and was constantly cleaning the place, including the kitchen and the bathroom. But the apartment started to feel smaller and overcrowded. In the morning each one of them had to race to the bathroom to prepare for their morning prayers. David prayed in his room, Ali in his, and Aisha in a corner in the living room. After their prayers they congregated in the kitchen to prepare their breakfast and ate together at the small dinette table in the living room.

Every day David noticed one more of Aisha's belongings appearing in the living room. One day it was a copy of the Qur'an placed on the small table between the two armchairs. Another day it was a picture of her and her father in the Old City of Jerusalem standing in front of the Al-Aqsa Mosque the third holiest place for Muslims. Under the picture a caption read: My Beloved Jerusalem.

David liked her and found her to be intelligent, broad-minded and entertaining, but he felt that she was taking over his living room with her stuff. He thought that she was infringing on his freedom of movement in his own apartment. Furthermore, he wasn't sure when she would ever move out. Although he wasn't dating anybody at the time, he kept wondering how he'd be able to invite a girl to his apartment with Aisha and her suitcases filling his main entertainment space.

It occurred to him that he'd use Aisha as an excuse to call Hadassah, the girl he'd recently met at a dance organized by his synagogue. He was interested in her. She was a bright, attractive girl who graduated from NYU and majored in international relations. Although she was a Conservative Jew, she didn't live by all the rules of Conservative Judaism like David. She also was a rebel when it came to Israel. She didn't agree with Israel's policies and all the settlements being built in the West Bank. On her first meeting with David she lectured him on the need for Israel to compromise and to allow a Palestinian state in the West Bank and Gaza.

Hadassah, like David, was in her mid-twenties. She had blonde hair and a slender figure that was the product of regular exercising. He liked her looks and her intellect, but was slightly taken back by her lack of Jewish nationalism and support of Zionism. They left the dance together and went for coffee to continue their conversation. He found her to be knowledgeable on a variety of subjects. She traveled all over the world, including Israel, Jordan, and Egypt. David never traveled outside the United States. She told him about the wonderful time she had in Cairo and the Muslim friends she'd made during her visits. David sensed that she thought of him to be too conservative for her, and he wanted to prove to her otherwise. He decided to call her and invite her to lunch or dinner with Aisha, and tell her about his new

Palestinian roommate and his female cousin who was staying in their place. That would show her how liberal and broadminded he was. He thought that if his plan worked, Aisha's unexpected visit and the inconveniences he had endured would have paid off.

David gathered his courage and called Hadassah, and in a cheerful voice said, "Hi Hadassah, this is David Goldstein. I enjoyed our coffee together after the dance and I'd like to see you again."

There was a brief silence on the other end. David didn't want to give her a chance to make an excuse for not being able to see him again, so he continued without waiting for her response.

"I'd like you to meet this interesting Palestinian girl who is visiting my roommate, Ali, and staying for a few days in our apartment. She will be going to graduate school at Columbia to study international relations; your field, isn't it?"

"What? You have a roommate named Ali? I don't believe it, I'm astounded. And who is this girl? I'd very much like to meet her," She exclaimed in disbelief.

"It worked," David murmured. "Now I can be cool."

His initial anxiety faded and was replaced by self-confidence. He asked her in a deliberate voice, "How about dinner one night this week? We can go to one of those kosher restaurants around here."

David wanted her to meet Aisha alone and not with Ali. The last thing he wished for was to have her engaged in a trilateral discussion with Ali and Aisha, and he'd be left out. Alone with the two girls he could better manipulate the situation and make a very good impression on Hadassah.

"Sure, I'm free this week. Which evening?" she asked enthusiastically.

"How about Wednesday evening? Let me check with Aisha and call you back."

"Perfect. I'll wait for your call."

David was excited by his clever ploy, and became convinced that Aisha might provide the catalyst for him to build a close relationship with Hadassah.

Aisha was equally eager to meet her, particularly when she learned that Hadassah had spent some time in the Middle East and had made many friends over there. Furthermore, they both majored in the field of international relations and they would have a lot to talk about.

On Wednesday evening, the three of them met at Lieberman, a well-known kosher restaurant not far from David's apartment. The restaurant was located on a busy corner, wedged between a Chinese carryout and a fish market. Inside the restaurant the eating area was large, open, and modestly decorated. The walls showed photos of celebrities and politicians being greeted by the owners of the restaurant.

Hadassah was dressed in her secular street clothes, David had his yarmulke on, and Aisha wore a long dress and the traditional scarf around her head. They looked rather odd together, particularly in a place frequented by many Orthodox Jews. There were several Hassidic families eating there that evening. The men were dressed in their usual black suits and black hats and the women had long dresses and wrapped their hair in scarves. Although the women's dresses weren't very different from Aisha's, the headscarves were. Aisha's scarf covered her hair and was wrapped around her face while the Hassidic women covered only their hair; and that made a world of difference.

As soon as David, Hadassah, and Aisha sat down at a table, many heads turned around to look at them and Yiddish whispers could be heard from across the room. Both Hadassah and Aisha understood some Yiddish and overheard whispers about what such a nice Jewish man like David was doing with a Gentile and an Arab woman. They assumed Hadassah was a Gentile because of her blonde hair, her lack of distinct Semitic features, and the way she was dressed.

Hadassah looked at Aisha with concern.

"I hope you don't mind being here." Then turned to David, "I'd have chosen another restaurant."

David was quick to defend himself, "This is the best kosher restaurant in the Bronx. Do you see the photos of the famous people who ate here? Wait until you taste their food."

Aisha assured both Hadassah and David that she didn't mind the stares and that she enjoyed being with the two of them and meeting Hadassah.

"I've become immune to the stares. Honestly, the first couple of weeks were tough. I'd get on the subway, or enter a store, and I felt that all eyes were stuck on me. Finally I told myself, it's not my business what people think of me; it's what I think of myself." Then she continued in a disappointed tone, "Imagine, the landlord of one apartment I was trying to rent wouldn't even look at me when I met him. He told me that the apartment had been rented while looking the other way."

Hadassah shook her head in disbelief, and said sympathetically, "I admire your courage. You should stick to your beliefs and pay no attention to those ignorant people."

Aisha smiled, "Thank you, Hadassah, I appreciate that. You know the problem is that many people have been brainwashed by the media and the distorted images they see on their televisions. Particularly after 9/11. They associate my scarf with radicalism. I'm far from radical. What amazes me is that people readily accept an Indian woman wearing her Sari and having a scarf around her head, or a Catholic woman with a scarf, but they frown on mine."

Hadassah nodded, showing her agreement with Aisha's argument, and told Aisha about her female Arab friends in the Middle East, "What I found to be interesting when I was invited to an Egyptian home in Cairo was that female members of the same family acted differently when it came to dress and religion. One of them was dressed in a long dress and wore hijab, like you, while her other sisters wore western clothes and apparently weren't very religious. The point is there are differences among Muslims in the degree they adhere to their religion just like Jews and Christians. We have Hassidic, Orthodox, Conservative, and Reformist Jews. We are all Jews, but we may differ in the ways we practice our religion and the way we dress."

"We are the same in my family," Aisha responded, "I wear the hijab, and I pray five times a day, but my younger sister doesn't cover her hair and isn't religious."

Noticing that the waitress was intentionally ignoring his party, David waved to her to bring the menus. The old grumpy waitress dropped the menus on the table and walked away whispering as she passed the table behind them, "I hope she isn't hiding something under that long dress."

David heard the comment, but Aisha and Hadassah didn't. They were oblivious to the rude waitress and to the people around them who were discreetly turning their heads to sneak a look at them.

Hadassah quickly glanced at the menu, put it down, and continued talking to Aisha, "I understand from talking to many people during my Middle Eastern trip that there was a resurgence of Islam in most Muslim countries. For instance, an Egyptian friend took me to Cairo University to prove his point. He pointed out that years ago female college students were always dressed in the latest French and Italian fashions, but now most of them wore long dresses and wore the hijab."

"You're right, there's a wave of religious conservatism sweeping across the Muslim world. But I don't think it's limited to Islam. The same thing is happening in Christianity and Judaism. You see how strong the Christian Evangelists have become in this country. The same thing is happening in Israel where the religious political parties are gaining more and more power."

David wanted to insert himself in this discussion, and to display his moderate views to Hadassah, stating, "I don't fully understand the reasons behind these trends."

Aisha turned to David, "I believe that in many Muslim countries, people are taking refuge in the religion hoping that it will rid them of the corruption they see among their rulers. They believe that if every Muslim adheres to the tenets of

Islam many of their social problems will be solved, and they will gain respect among friends and foes."

Hadassah added to Aisha's thesis, "I think, based on my observations while visiting Israel, the rise of power of the religious political parties is a reaction to the wave of liberalism sweeping the country. The religious leaders play on the fear and the insecurity of the average Israelis. They managed to convince them that the liberals would make major concessions to the Palestinians that would come to haunt them in the future. But, I don't understand how the right-wing Christian Evangelists have become such a powerful movement in a country like ours."

David grabbed the opportunity and answered Hadassah.

"Religions are also feeling the threat of modernization and scientific developments. Christian Evangelists are no exception. Scientists are encroaching on one of the basic beliefs in our religions when they start cloning human beings, and ultimately making babies in a laboratory. Evangelists are also alarmed by the spread of free sex among young people, and the continuing increase in teenage pregnancies and abortions which they deplore."

Both Hadassah and Aisha agreed that such developments could pose a serious dilemma to Judaism, Christianity and Islam.

The discussion was interrupted when the waitress reluctantly returned to take their orders. Hadassah ordered the matzo ball soup and a plate of falafel. Aisha ordered the house specialty of poached new potato with crème fraiche, smoked salmon, and black olives. David asked for the matzo ball soup and mixed grill.

The waitress looked at Aisha and said in a subdued sarcastic tone, "Honey, if you didn't have that thing around your head, I'd have thought you are one of us."

"But I'm one of you," Aisha replied calmly. "We all are the children of Abraham."

The waitress picked up the menus and walked away quickly when she noticed that Hadassah was about to explode. She was infuriated by the waitress' overt rudeness.

David took the opportunity to hold her hand trying to calm her down. He kept rubbing her hand as he looked at it admiringly. He remembered it was her beautiful feminine hands and long manicured nails that attracted his attention at the dance.

Aisha, in an attempt to diffuse Hadassah's anger, asked playfully, "Tell me, Hadassah, how did you learn to like falafel?"

Hadassah smiled as she reminisced about her trip to the Middle East.

"I started eating it in Israel, and when I told the Egyptians that falafel was an Israeli dish, all hell broke loose. I remember one of them saying, 'They may take our land, and the homes of millions of our Palestinian brethren, but they can't take our falafel.'"

They all laughed and Hadassah calmed down by the time the food was served. None of them acknowledged the waitress when she placed the dishes in front of them, and they continued chatting. David was flattered when Hadassah praised the matzo ball soup.

"This is the best matzo ball soup I ever had; Aisha you've got to try it," Hadassah said while pushing her bowl of soup in front of Aisha.

"Excellent, almost as good as my recipe," Aisha said playfully after tasting it.

"What, you know how to make matzo ball soup?" David exclaimed in disbelief.

Hadassah didn't want the conversation to turn to a lighter subject, "I truly believe that there is a lot in common between Arabs and Jews, and there are many similarities between the Islamic and Jewish religions."

Aisha immediately picked up the subject and continued, "Many people don't know that Arabs and Jews coexisted and lived in peace together for centuries. During the glorious period of the Arab history from the eighth century to the fifteenth century AD, Jews played an important role in the Arab societies whether in the government or in the business, arts, and science communities. When the Jews were expelled from Spain during the Spanish Inquisition in the fifteenth century, the Arab countries opened their doors and welcomed them."

As David listened to this amicable but intelligent dialogue between Aisha and Hadassah, his fondness of Hadassah and respect for Aisha grew stronger. He was happy to see them getting along and comfortable with each other because he was confident that he'd benefit from such a friendship. He looked at them and interjected, "Listening to both of you, I feel that these current animosities between Arabs and Jews must be recent."

"Absolutely," Aisha and Hadassah responded in a single voice. Then Hadassah asked Aisha, "Don't you think that the so-called hatred between them is politically motivated? I really believe that once a just solution is achieved between the Israelis and the Palestinians, this animosity will gradually disappear."

"In my opinion, the extremists on both sides have hijacked this historically friendly relationship. They don't believe in compromise and in win-win solutions. They believe in winner takes all, and that breeds more hatred and more violence. I'm sure each of us knows of a person who fits this criterion. I for one know a man from my town in the West Bank who now lives here in New York that fits this extremist description. His name is Yasser. He isn't a violent person or a terrorist, but he is rigid in his religious and political beliefs. He doesn't believe in compromise."

"Oh my God, I know of a similar person who fits that description," David interrupted. He started telling them about the phone call he received in Miami after Ben had visited his apartment and saw Aisha and other Arabs there. "He thought I had been kidnapped by Hamas," David joked.

Hadassah became excited, "I've got a great idea, David. Why don't we invite these two characters to dinner at your place? I think it would be interesting and we may succeed in making them reassess their unbending positions."

David loved the idea since it provided an excuse for Hadassah to come to his apartment. He knew that the first visit to a man's apartment, particularly by a serious person like Hadassah, was the hardest. After that visit, it would be easier for him to invite her to come to his place when no one was there.

"Who is going to do the cooking?" David asked.

"We will," Hadassah and Aisha answered enthusiastically.

Excited by the dinner idea they all got up and left the restaurant not paying attention to the whispers and curious looks emanating from the tables around them. David walked Hadassah to her apartment and Aisha rushed home eager to tell Ali about her meeting with Hadassah and their plan to invite Yasser and Ben to dinner. But Ali wasn't home. She waited for him until David came back. It was getting late and she asked David if he knew where Ali was. David had a good idea where he was, but hesitated to tell her. She kept questioning him until he finally told her about the ongoing affair between Ali and Dorothy.

For days Ali couldn't see Dorothy. He was stuck with Aisha either showing her the way around the city while she was apartment hunting, or staying with her at home in the evening. In true Arab tradition he didn't want to leave her alone with another man like David, even though he trusted him. During those days, and except for a couple of times he was able to sneak out for a short period of time, he had no chance to see Dorothy. As soon as Aisha left with David to meet Hadassah, he ran down to Dorothy's place. He was happy that David hadn't asked him to join them for dinner. He planned to return to the apartment before they got back. But Dorothy wouldn't let him leave and was acting like a hungry tiger that had not been fed for weeks.

Ali rushed back at dawn hoping that Aisha was still asleep. As he walked into the apartment, she was finishing her early morning prayers. She looked at him in disgust, examining his messed-up hair and the lipstick all over his face. He looked the other way and walked straight to his room.

After taking a shower, Ali stood for his prayers in his room with the door closed. Aisha's disgusted look awakened his tormented conscience. At the end of his prayers he spent a long time fervently asking God for forgiveness. He had done that in the past, yet he would set off again in spite of himself to see Dorothy and then return to beg for forgiveness once more.

After he finished his prayers, he collected his courage to face his idealistic and religious cousin who was about to grill him. As he expected, Aisha didn't lose much time confronting him, "Doesn't that relationship trouble you since you are a believer?"

Lowering his eyes in embarrassment, Ali answered in a near whisper, "Aisha, some things can't be helped. I'm a man living in a foreign land, and I'm not ready to get married. I hope you understand that and accept it."

Aisha was an idealist, but certainly not an ideologue. She never intended to impose her ideals on her cousin. Her own brother drank alcohol, played poker with his friends, and chased several women from the neighboring towns. She never once tried to interfere with his life or his practice of the religion. Aisha was the kind of a Muslim who, though strong in her convictions and adherence to the tenets of Islam, believed in a true secular society where every individual would live according to his or her beliefs. She always quoted a verse from the Qur'an that read, "You have your own religion and I have mine."

But what bothered her about Ali was his hypocrisy. He spent the night having sex with a woman whom he wasn't married to, and then he rushed home to take a shower and stand before God for his prayers as if water had wiped out all his sins.

The short and tense exchange with Ali distracted Aisha from what she'd been waiting to tell him about her meeting with Hadassah. She continued, brushing aside what Ali had said.

"My dear cousin, this is your life and your own relationship with God. Who am I to interfere?"

She started telling him about her evening and their decision to organize a dinner and invite Yasser and David's friend Ben. "We all thought it'd be interesting to have a religious right wing Muslim and his Jewish counterpart sit at the same dinner table and share a meal."

"I thought David was a right wing Orthodox Jew. Do you want to invite another one?"

Aisha interrupted him, "I disagree with you I've found David to be quite moderate in his religious and political views and open-minded, almost as much as Hadassah."

Ali shook his head, completely baffled by her impression of David's views. His own impression during Dorothy's dinner was quite different. He asked sheepishly, "Is Hadassah pretty?"

"Yes, she is very beautiful, intelligent, and what you men call sexy."

"Now I understand." He smiled like a person who'd just solved a difficult puzzle. He knew that David, like himself, would sometimes say or do anything to appeal to a woman he is interested in. He concluded that David was playing the liberal game only for Hadassah's sake. But he went along with the idea of the dinner to please Aisha.

"Ok, I will call Yasser, but I can't guarantee that he'll accept. You know well how he is when it comes to socializing with Jews. I may need your help to persuade him to come."

73

CHAPTER 10

The First Supper

Ali picked up the phone and called Yasser while Aisha stood next to him.

"Yasser, good morning, how are you?"

"Good, thank you, how is Aisha? Has she found a place yet?"

"No, she is still looking. Listen, Aisha wants to cook dinner for us on Tuesday. Can you join us?"

"Of course, I wouldn't miss a meal prepared by Aisha. God bless her hands. I remember the delicious food I had at her house back home."

Ali quickly added, "She also invited David and his girlfriend."

Noticing a pause on Yasser's end, he hastened to explain, "Aisha met the girlfriend and was impressed by her and her sympathy to our cause. Apparently she'd traveled throughout the Middle East and has many Arab friends."

Yasser continued his pause for a few seconds, then replied in a hesitant voice, "Well, I respect Aisha's opinion. What time do you want me to come?"

"How about seven o'clock?"

"Good I'll see you then."

Aisha was flabbergasted when Ali hung up the phone without mentioning Ben. Ali noticed the angry look on her face, and before she opened her mouth, he explained, "Believe me; it is better not to mention to him beforehand the presence of some right wing Orthodox Jew. He'd never come to the dinner. I know Yasser better than you."

Aisha reluctantly accepted Ali's explanation and called Hadassah to tell her that the dinner was on, and that they were waiting for David to invite Ben. They were both excited about the prospect of having an engaging dialogue among Yasser, Ben, David and Ali.

David met Ben at the synagogue. They usually attended the Monday weekly lecture. As they walked out of the lecture hall, David told Ben about the beautiful, intelligent woman named Hadassah he'd recently met.

"Ben, you have to meet this girl. I think I may already be in love."

Ben gave him a look devoid of emotion and asked, "I hope she isn't one of the crowd I saw in your apartment."

"No, no. She is a nice Jewish girl. She is also religious and very worldly. By the way, she will be preparing a delicious dinner on Tuesday and she wanted me to invite you."

"I'd love to meet her," Ben responded quickly, relieved that she was Jewish.

"I also invited my roommate Ali and his female cousin. Believe me, this girl is amazing. She speaks Hebrew fluently and has close Israeli friends. She even knows how to cook kosher food," David added, intentionally omitting Yasser, the right wing Arab who was also supposed to be at the dinner.

Ben looked at David suspiciously. He never had the experience to share a kosher meal with two Arabs, but he was curious to meet the religious Jewish woman David was so enamored by. He met most of the women David dated, but he never heard such excitement in his voice about a woman before.

"Ok I'll be there."

David immediately called Hadassah to tell her that the coast was clear and that Ben had accepted the dinner invitation. She, in turn, informed him that Yasser would be there and that she and Aisha were planning the dinner menu.

Hadassah and Aisha treated the planning of the meal as a serious academic exercise. Hadassah took out her Middle Eastern cookbooks, reviewed several kosher recipes, and prepared a list of options. Aisha, on the other hand, never relied on cookbooks. Her cooking experience came from helping her mother and grandmother in the kitchen. The main dish of the dinner became the principle topic of their phone conversations.

"I propose that we have one kosher meat dish and one halal meat, preferably lamb. What do you think, Aisha?"

"Good idea."

"I honestly don't know what makes meat halal. I'm sure you know, right?"

"Of course. Slaughtering animals in Islam is a ritual process, just the same as in Judaism. The killing must be performed with a quick stroke across the throat that results in the complete draining of the blood."

"That is the same with kosher meat. But one thing I know is that for the meat to be kosher a pious man or a rabbi must carry out the slaughtering of the animal. Is it the same for halal meat? Do you have a sheik or a religious man kill the animal?"

"No, any Muslim can do the slaughtering but must recite a few words from the Qu'ran before and during the killing of the animal. I used to run away and hide every year when my father slaughtered a sheep during our religious holiday called Eid Al-Adha when Muslims commemorate the willingness of Abraham to sacrifice his son Ishmail before God sent him a sheep to sacrifice instead."

They finally decided on the menu and farmed out the responsibilities. Aisha was to prepare a halal lamb dish, Middle Eastern rice and one of her famous falafel dishes. Hadassah planned a kosher beef dish and one of the delicious salads she had learned during her visits to Israel.

The stage was set for the first supper among, what Aisha and Hadassah referred to in their private conversations as, the antagonists. What they knew for sure was that Yasser and Ben were religious zealots with uncompromising political views. On the other hand, both had an inaccurate impression of David's views and what he stood for. Ali was an unknown entity to Hadassah, but Aisha had known him all her life. She knew Ali to be religious and usually dogmatic when it came to the Arab-Israeli question. But he could be persuaded with logic and reason to change his preset views on certain subjects.

The fact was that, compared to Yasser and Ben, Ali and David were moderates. They both adhered to the tenets of their religions, but when it came to women they found a way to circumvent those tenets. On the political front, David consistently sided and defended the decisions made by the Israeli government, and was not eager for Israel to make any major concessions to the Palestinians. Likewise, Ali was adamant in his defense of the Palestinians' rights. He considered Israel to be a colonial power that had taken over their land and caused the Palestinians to live in misery. But considering that they had agreed to share an apartment showed that they were willing and capable of compromising. Ali and David, however, were still far to the right of Hadassah and Aisha who, though religious, were true liberals in their political thinking.

On Tuesday, at seven o'clock, the bell rang, and Ben was the first to arrive. Hadassah, Aisha, Ali, and David were already there. David introduced him to everyone, and a few minutes later Yasser arrived and Ali made the introductions. Hadassah, the only one who often drank wine with dinner, decided to refrain from drinking on that evening, out of respect for the Muslim guests. Yasser sat across from Ben with his arms crossed in a defensive position. They both had their head caps on, and occasionally stroked their long bushy beards. Yasser held his prayer beads in his right hand and moved the beads through his fingers indicating that he was reciting some Muslim prayers even though he was having a conversation with Ali. To an inexperienced American, Ben and Yasser could have been close relatives. They could have been standing praying in front of the Western Wall in Old Jerusalem, or standing next to each other facing Mecca in the

Al-Aqsa Mosque right next to the Wall. But, in reality, there was a mountain separating them both religiously and politically.

Hadassah and Aisha looked stunning that evening. Hadassah had a blue knit dress with a short skirt that showed her beautiful legs. The blue color of the dress accentuated her blonde hair that hung on her shoulders. Every time she crossed her legs, David's eyes followed their movements, attempting to see more than she'd intended to show. Aisha wore a long dress that was tighter than her usual dresses, thus showing her small waist, thick thighs and sensuous hips. That evening she wore her hijab around her hair but didn't wrap it around her neck as usual, showing more of her beautiful face. The hijab ceased to detract from her round black eyes, her long eyelashes and thick lips.

Ben was chatting with David and Hadassah, but his eyes kept drifting toward Aisha who was engaged in a conversation with Ali and Yasser. Ben traveled to Israel a number of times and spent time with his relatives in their settlement in the West Bank. But he never mixed with the Palestinians or spent any time talking to them. This dinner was his first experience sitting face to face with them and chatting with a Palestinian woman whom he found to be attractive.

Eager to provoke a dialogue between Ben and Yasser, Hadassah asked everyone to come to the dining table. Each one of them blessed the food in his/her way, and she and Aisha explained the various dishes, including the kosher and halal meats. As the serving plates were passed around, Hadassah looked at Yasser and asked, "Yasser, I understand you're from Aisha's town in the West Bank."

"Yes, I'm from Palestine."

Taking note of the tone and meaning of his response, she continued, "What do you think are the prospects of peace? The whole world wants to resolve this problem and to have the Palestinians and the Israelis live side by side in peace and harmony."

"The Israelis want it all; they want peace and the land. They want us to live in cantons like prisoners surrounded by their settlements."

Ben, so far quiet and ignoring the Arab male guests, jumped in, "Israel is surrounded by enemies who advocate its destruction. There can never be peace as long as terrorist organizations like Hamas continue to exist."

Ali protested, "Terrorist organizations to some are freedom fighters to others. The Jews called the Stern and Irgun gangs of the 1940s freedom fighters. But in today's jargon they would also be referred to as terrorists. And when Israel was established, some of the leaders of the so called terrorist organizations became statesmen like, for example, Menachem Begin who became Prime Minister and signed the peace agreement with President Sadat."

Ben was undeterred, quoting an Israeli politician, "If the Arabs put down their weapons today, there would be no violence. But if the Jews put down their weapons today, there would be no Israel."

Ali interrupted him, "This is not supported by facts. If the Arabs put down their weapons today, there may not be Jordan, Lebanon, Syria, Iraq, or even Egypt. They would all be part of the great land of Israel. You know very well that some of the right-wing religious Jews, the same ones building settlements in the West bank, believe that the land of Israel extends from the Nile of Egypt to the Euphrates in Iraq."

The atmosphere around the table grew more tense and Hadassah and Aisha knew that they had to interfere to direct the arguments into more constructive channels. Aisha spoke in a calm and comforting voice, "We all know there's a lot of blame to share. Hamas, the right wing Israelis, and even some of the Arab countries like Syria and others are all part of the problem. But, it's up to people like us sitting around this table to find a solution that is fair and satisfies all sides. I mean a win-win solution. If we can't do that sitting here, eating delicious kosher and halal food, how can we expect our people over there to reconcile and arrive at a solution?"

Hadassah nodded in approval, "I feel that we, around this table, represent all the warring factions over there. I'm glad that none of us is carrying an AK-47 or an explosive belt around his waist. But, philosophically, I feel that almost all the views of those factions are represented here."

She then added apologetically, "I know there are three Palestinians sitting around the table and no Israelis. But I'm told that several members of Ben's family are Israeli citizens and are among the strongest supporters of the settlements in the West Bank. Am I right, Ben?"

Ben leaned forward and answered Hadassah stoically, "You're right. So, what do you expect us to do? Surrender or let Hamas move into the settlements we had built with our hands and sweat."

Aisha waived at Hadassah asking her permission to respond to Ben. She looked at him with a broad smile on her face, and said in a soft persuasive voice, "Ben, nobody is asking you to surrender. All that we're trying to accomplish here is to reach some consensus on the sticky issues that have been obstacles to peace for so long. For example, why do the right wing Israelis want to continue building settlements in the West Bank on Palestinian land? They are the people who wish to maintain Israel as a Jewish state. But if you continue building Jewish settlements among Arab towns and villages, you'll ultimately transform the West Bank into a secular region that you were against in the first place. It doesn't make sense."

Ben was flattered by Aisha's smile and the way she addressed him, but he was unmoved, "The Palestinian Arabs can move into any of the Arab countries around us. These countries have more land than they can use."

At that point, all the guests around the table, including David, raised their voices objecting to Ben's remark. Ben immediately realized that he'd made a tactical error, and started retreating, "Well, they also can stay and we'll stay where we are."

Then he turned to Aisha and addressed her in a friendly tone as if he'd known her for some time, "Aisha, if we leave the West Bank, I may not be able to see you, or maybe even take you out to dinner."

Yasser put down his fork and stared at Ben for making, what he considered, an inappropriate move on Aisha. She, however, was flattered, "If and when you leave, Ben, I promise to come and visit you in Israel. I have many friends there."

"You promise?"

"Yes, I do."

Hadassah and Aisha were well informed of all the issues surrounding the Palestinian-Israeli peace negotiations that they had addressed in numerous papers during their studies. They both enjoyed playing the roles of John Mitchell, Dennis Ross, and other American peace negotiators around the table.

"The practical solution to this issue is for Israel to maintain only a few symbolic settlements that are contiguous along the borders of Israel," Hadassah attempted to focus the discussion on the thorny issue of settlements.

Yasser immediately protested, "How about the properties in Israel that were taken from us in 1948? We need to go back and claim these properties. My family owned several houses in Haifa. We've every right under international law to take ownership of those properties."

Aisha raised her hand taking the responsibility to address Yasser's complaint, "While I sympathize with you, Yasser, going back and seizing those properties isn't realistic. I believe that the issue of the right of return can be resolved through financial compensation and probably the symbolic resettlement of a number of moderate Palestinian families in Israel."

"That sounds like a reasonable and workable compromise, Aisha," Hadassah talked like she was the moderator at the table. "How about Jerusalem? I understand that this is one of the biggest stumbling blocks in all previous peace negotiations. Each side is adamant to have control of the City and to have it as their capital."

"I think Jerusalem can be administered in such a way to allow each side to claim it as their capital and to have all the religious sites managed by a commission of Jews, Christians, and Muslims. After all, this is a holy place for all three religions," Aisha responded.

Ali and David stayed quiet during this exchange, but both showed signs of intrigue at the clever and diplomatic way Aisha and Hadassah handled such complicated and sensitive issues. Yasser and Ben, on the other hand, didn't seem persuaded by the rationale and solutions offered by the two politically liberal women. But they chose not to prolong the argument and spoil the delicious dinner they were all enjoying. Furthermore, Ben was showing interest in Aisha and didn't want to place a wedge between them.

"These are delicious falafel. God bless your hands, Aisha." Yasser said.

Ben seconded, "I agree, they're excellent. How did you learn to master such a traditional Israeli dish?"

Yasser raised his hands and shouted in protest, "First they take our land and now they claim ownership of our recipes."

They all laughed because they noted that Yasser had sat passively during the division of Jerusalem but couldn't take the loss of the falafel battle to the Israelis.

Ben continued to needle Yasser and said, looking at Aisha, "I want you to know that the ingredients of falafel are documented in the Bible as food of the Hebrews."

"My friend, falafel became popular in Israel by the Jews who lived in Palestine and by the Arab Jews who immigrated to Israel. I doubt very much that Polish or Russian Jews had known of falafel before they came to Israel," Aisha interceded. "Why don't we equally share the ownership of the falafel and use this as a recipe and metaphor for compromise on the bigger issues."

The falafel discussion introduced an air of easiness among all the guests, including Yasser and Ben. For the first time in the evening they addressed each other by their first names. As the dessert and mint tea circulated around the table, Aisha led a discussion about some of the similarities between Arab and Jewish traditions and the historic bonds between them. They all agreed on one thing that the hostilities between Arabs and Jews could be measured only in decades but the cultural and economic bonds between the two peoples lasted for centuries.

As they all departed for the evening Hadassah and Aisha felt that the dinner was a success and that they had partially achieved their goal of climbing the first of several hills on the road to peace.

CHAPTER 11

Seeds of Collaboration

Over the two days that followed the dinner there was an air of friendliness in the apartment. Aisha was frequently on the phone with Hadassah, sometimes chatting about their families and personal matters, and at other times having a serious discussion on some domestic or international issue. David also was on the phone with Hadassah expressing his fondness for her and how much he was looking forward to seeing her on the following Sunday. Ali and David, who hadn't spent much time talking to each other before the dinner, found themselves chatting at every opportunity. More surprisingly was the conversation David had with Ben who expressed affection for Aisha. He even hinted to David that he would like to see her again.

The dinner gathering certainly planted the seeds of friendship among the four. Even Yasser and Ben, although they maintained their defensive postures throughout the dinner, nodded in agreement few times. They never showed overt hostility and were civil toward each other. The secret was the presence of Aisha and Hadassah. Listening to them and watching how quickly they became close friends made the four men see the light at the end of the long dark tunnel of hostility in the Middle East. Two girls who came from completely different cultural and religious backgrounds managed to become close friends in a matter of days. And none of the men could accuse them of being just some liberals who didn't understand or appreciate the subtleties of the region, the cultures, or the religions. They were intelligent, educated, well traveled, and almost as religious as any of the four men. But they managed to demonstrate to the uncompromising Yasser and Ben and to the less rigid Ali and David that there was more to gain from collaboration and friendship than dogma and hostility.

Aisha finally found a nice apartment near Columbia University and rushed home excited to share the news. Hadassah was the first person she called to tell the good news and they agreed to work together on decorating the place.

David was relieved that Aisha had found her own place. Although he liked her and found her friendship with Hadassah helpful to him, he was looking forward to some privacy. He was counting the days before he'd invite Hadassah to his place and be alone with her. He knew he could take advantage of the long evenings Ali was spending with Dorothy and he'd have the whole place to himself.

As for Ali, he also was happy to see her leave because she was watching all his moves. Every time he spent the night with Dorothy he had to face her in the early morning as he walked into the apartment and cope with her disappointed looks.

Shortly after Aisha moved out, Dorothy called on Ali and David to help her move furniture in the apartment she was planning to rent. She had discussed this move at the dinner she had for them and Satish, and they both agreed to help. She offered to pay all the expenses of renting a truck plus twenty-five dollars per hour for each of them. It was a generous offer they couldn't refuse.

The move wasn't as easy as Ali and David had imagined. The furniture included large pieces such as a full sofa, armchairs, a dining table, a queen bed and other items Dorothy had stored in a warehouse. Some of the furniture was antique and quite valuable. The little experience Ali had working for a moving company was of great help to them. He'd learned how to wrap each piece of furniture and the various home accessories, and how to fit all of them in the truck in such a careful way to avoid any damage during the drive from the warehouse to the apartment building. Once there, they had to maneuver the narrow staircase and its sharp turns up to the vacant apartment. They had a difficult time moving a large antique armoire through the narrow door of the apartment. They were both sweating profusely and swearing loudly in different tongues, surely startling anyone passing by. Ali was cursing in Arabic and David in Yiddish, as they turned the large wood monster sideways and upside down until it went through the door without a scratch.

People on the street stopped to watch them as they unloaded the truck in front of the building. They didn't look or act like professional movers, much to the amusement of others who chuckled as they awkwardly managed each piece through the door and up the stairs. Neither David with his thick eye glasses and yarmulke, nor Ali, wearing a short sleeve white shirt and dress pants, was the typical mover one would see unwrapping and moving large furniture pieces on the curbside. One passerby made a wise remark and recommended that they should hire professional movers for the job. They were quick to tell him that they were professional enough. Their response drew some laughter from a couple of people who stopped to watch them.

In spite of the negative remarks by a few bystanders, Ali and David sensed that they'd worked well together. Ali had the muscles and David had a good instinct on how to deal with winding stairs and how to move large pieces through narrow doors. In addition, they were both conscientious and treated each item they moved like it was one of a kind. These qualities were prerequisites for good movers. They felt that they complemented each other's strength and that they would make a good team.

Dorothy was pleased when she walked into the apartment and found the furniture arranged in exactly the way she'd wanted. She hugged both of them and said, "You guys make an excellent team. I'll recommend you to all my friends and the people in my church. May I?"

Ali and David looked at each other and replied at the same time, "Hell, yes."

Dorothy gave each of them a fifty-dollar tip. From the time they had picked up the truck until they returned it they spent eight hours on the job and each earned two hundred and fifty dollars; not bad for financially struggling students.

The first thing David said as soon as he got paid was that he'd take Hadassah to a nice dinner, and asked Ali, "What are you going to do with your money?"

"I'll use it for my rent," Ali replied. "My poor father is strapped for cash."

Dorothy was happy to see Ali and David work together as a team. She liked both of them, but for different reasons. She enjoyed David's intellect and Ali's sexual prowess. She found in their joint business venture a good and acceptable way to help them financially.

She got on the phone and called her friends, members of her church congregation and some of the stores she was doing business with. She told everyone about her good experience with the two-man moving team. She described them as clean-cut young students who were honest, conscientious, professional, and above all, less expensive than the commercial moving companies in the area.

Soon after, one of Dorothy's lady friends contacted them and asked for an estimate of the cost to move her furniture to another apartment in the same neighborhood. This presented a new challenge to them. She wasn't going to pay them by the hour as Dorothy had done. She expected an accurate estimate of the moving cost and they understood that once they gave their estimate they would have to complete the job within that budget.

After they had inspected the amount of furniture that had to be moved, they went back to the apartment to prepare their estimate. They realized that they had to factor in all expenses such as the number of boxes they would need, the cost of renting a truck, and the cost of gas and insurance. In addition, they had to estimate the number of hours it would take them to finish the job. They were well aware of the fact that if their estimate was too high she would look for other movers, and if it was too low they wouldn't be making enough money to justify their hard work. Dorothy's moving job, however, gave them confidence and provided them a benchmark from which they could make an accurate estimate.

Dorothy's friend was intrigued by the unusual business relationship between Ali and David and didn't even question their prepared bid. At the end of the move she was pleased with their performance and decided to give them a bonus. They ended up making a decent profit on their second job and no one made any wise remarks this time as they watched them load and unload the truck. They felt that they lost the awkwardness they had shown on their first move, and that they began to understand the moving business.

In the following weeks the calls for their services were sporadic, averaging one a week. Then the calls became more frequent. The money they earned stimulated their entrepreneurial spirit. They talked about how much they enjoyed the business more than going to school and sitting through one lecture after another. They felt the pleasure of being the masters of their own game. They didn't have to go and work for someone else at a meager hourly rate. They could schedule the jobs on their free days and they were earning far more money than they would from a part-time job.

On their way home after completing a moving job, Ali murmured as he was counting the money he'd earned that day, "I bet Dr. Butterworth doesn't make as much money in one day!"

"Dr. who?"

"Oh, he's my structural engineering professor. Every student dreads his class. He has an uncanny way of staring at you for several minutes without blinking if you don't answer his question correctly. My stomach churns every time he turns in my direction."

"I have a couple of those dreadful professors."

"This guy makes me hate going to school. I never have these feelings when I'm working on the truck with you."

David agreed with Ali, "I really enjoy being out all day talking to people, providing a service and getting immediate reward for my hard work. It feels good."

Within a few weeks they realized that owning a truck was essential for their business. In addition to the rental expense, a lot of time was wasted in making a reservation, picking-up and returning the truck. Furthermore, they felt they should have their own logo and phone number on the truck to attract the attention of potential customers as they drove through the city. They discussed the possibility of buying a truck, but they didn't have enough cash for the down payment or sufficient credit to obtain financing. Neither of them came from rich parents whom they could ask for a loan. The economy was bad and it was almost a hopeless case for them to approach any bank for a loan at that time. After considering all their options, they decided to continue renting their moving trucks until they could find some other way for financing their own.

One day Aisha was shopping at one of the Arab grocery stores in Queens when she overheard two Arab customers talking. One of them was saying, "I'm planning to move from my apartment next week, but I'm dreading the move."

"Why are you dreading the move?" the other one asked.

"First, my back is bothering me second, I hate packing and moving furniture, and third, I know how expensive the professional movers are."

"Listen, I heard about an Arab guy and his Jewish friend who move furniture at reasonable rates. They have a truck and someone told me that they are very good."

Aisha knew immediately whom they were talking about, and was quick to get into the conversation, "Excuse me, I overheard what you were talking about. I know these guys and they have a lot of experience and they are quite reasonable. I strongly recommend them."

She handed them Ali's phone number, "Tell them that Aisha has referred you and they will give you an extra ten-percent discount."

She acted as their salesperson for the first time and offered a discount without even asking them. It was a smart move on her part, and she knew they needed the business and wouldn't mind her promising a break on the price.

Aisha couldn't wait to tell them the story. She called them bragging that she'd brought them new business. She relayed to them the conversation exactly as she overheard it.

"The Arab guy and his Jewish friend---They have a truck," she kept repeating.

After they hung up the phone, David turned to Ali and started laughing, "We're the Arab and Jew movers, not just any movers."

"I think we should capitalize on that," Ali said without cracking a smile.

David, not convinced, replied, "Come on. Let's not mix business and religion."

"We aren't talking religion, David. You're a Jew, right?"

David shrugged his shoulders in agreement.

"Yes, of course I'm."

"OK, I'm an Arab, am I not?"

"You certainly are."

"So, what is wrong with being known as the Arab and the Jew movers? At a minimum, we may be able to get all the Arabs and the Jews in the city as customers."

"Let us cross this bridge later on," David interrupted impatiently, "The main question now is whether we should try to buy a truck, and where we can get the down payment and who would cosign for the loan."

David then looked at Ali and whispered in a sheepish voice, "How about asking Dorothy?"

Ali felt insulted by David's remark, "Are you crazy? I'm a proud Arab man. I can't ask a woman to support me."

"She wouldn't be supporting you. She'd be giving a business loan to both of us, not to you alone, and we will pay her back with interest. I bet you she'd be making more money off our interest than she is getting from her bank. Remember, the truck will secure her loan. She has nothing to lose."

Ali remained unconvinced, but David persisted, "I propose that we both meet with her and present our plans and ask for her opinion about the whole idea. I also think we should invite Satish to the meeting. I know Dorothy uses him as her accountant and trusts his business instincts and financial knowledge."

Ali became more comfortable with the idea. He wouldn't be alone with Dorothy asking her for money, but with David and Satish. If she turned them down, he'd have David to share the embarrassment with. He'd be totally devastated if she turned him down after asking her for such a loan while lying next to her in bed. He'd feel he was sexually inadequate, and would never be able to see her again. Or worst, that he was sleeping with her just to borrow money from her.

Ali asked David to make the call to Dorothy and tell her that they would like to discuss a business proposal with her.

When approached by David, Dorothy was enthusiastic about meeting with them and happy to hear that they had invited Satish.

Ali and David scrambled to prepare for the meeting. They identified at least two used trucks that were suitable for their business and in an affordable price range. They contacted several banks and selected one that was ready to make the loan for the purchase of the truck with a down payment of ten percent and the balance amortized over five years at an interest rate of seven percent, contingent on the review of their and the co-borrower's finances. They agreed to offer to pay back Dorothy's loan for the down payment within two years at the same interest rate of seven percent. They prepared a brief business plan showing their projected monthly expenses such as the truck payment, Dorothy's installment, gas and insurance expenses, telephone, parking, advertising and miscellaneous expenses. Based on their short experience in the moving business they were able to make realistic projections of the number of moving jobs they would be able to undertake every month. The numbers looked encouraging and they felt confident that Satish, who had a business background, would be supportive of their business plan.

They prepared a power point presentation showing a description of the business and their target customers, and projected monthly expenses, revenues and net income. The numbers were impressive. If they averaged three moving jobs a week, they would be able to pay off the loans in less than two years and still have a decent income to live on.

At the meeting, David took the responsibility of presenting their plan. He emphasized that their projections were supported by their analysis of the market and their experience over several weeks.

Dorothy was impressed by the methodical and analytical way David presented their plan and looked to Satish for advice. "What do you think? Do the numbers make sense to you?" she asked Satish.

Satish examined the numbers on the sheets in front of him for a few minutes, then looked up and said, "Yes, they make a lot of sense. I think David and Ali have a good business plan that can be profitable. But I'm wondering how they would be able to run this business and go to school at the same time."

Ali and David were prepared for that question, "We have been doing it for weeks and we arrange the jobs to fit our school schedules."

"Well, if you guys can manage schoolwork and simultaneously run a business, I wish you luck."

Dorothy agreed to provide them with the down payment and to co-sign the loan. Not only did she like and trust David, but she also was involved with Ali in a hot relationship that she wanted to last indefinitely. She asked, however, that they utilize Satish's business experience and have him involved in monitoring their books to insure that all loan payments and other bills were paid on time.

As the meeting was coming to a close and Ali and David stood up and were about to leave, Dorothy turned to them and asked, "What will be the name of your business?"

David hesitated and was reluctant to answer the question, but Ali couldn't help telling them about Aisha's story. He told them about her overhearing two men referring to them as the Arab and Jew movers. Dorothy's face lit up, "Your friendship may be the beginning of a successful business that could be the talk of the town."

Satish followed up, "You should consider a name that is an eye catcher. Business names can sometimes be the key to success. Use your name to your advantage."

David shook his head and continued to walk slowly toward the door, but Ali stopped and nodded in approval, "I agree with you, Satish, we will consider that."

CHAPTER 12

The Birth of a New Business

Dorothy's financial support gave Ali and David confidence in their new venture. All of a sudden their casual part-time business was about to be transformed into something more serious and official. They were going to have their own moving truck, displaying the name of their business, roaming the streets of New York. There would be no more anonymous rented trucks that nobody recognized. On one hand Ali and David enjoyed the anonymity of their partnership, but on the other hand they understood and appreciated the need for a more formal business with an identifiable name.

Initially Ali was excited by Aisha's encounter with the two Arabs in the grocery store who had referred to him and David as the Arab and the Jew. He thought then that incorporating the words "an Arab and a Jew" in the business name would be an eye-catcher and could result in more business. The importance of the name of the business was brought up again by Satish in front of Dorothy. But he soon realized that those two Arabs were strangers to him and became more concerned about what his conservative Palestinian friends would say if they saw such a name on the truck. Some of them might accuse him of being a traitor and collaborating with the enemy.

Likewise, David wanted to keep his business relationship with Ali discreet. He didn't wish to attract the attention of his Orthodox friends to his partnership with Ali. He was afraid that some of those people might find a business name referring to an Arab and a Jew, and displayed on a truck, offensive.

Both Ali and David were eager to see the business thrive as long as it didn't cause discord among their friends. The name of the business became the focal point of their discussions. David was influenced by the Jewish thought that a name wasn't merely an arbitrary designation, but it should convey the nature and essence of the thing named. He cautiously suggested, "How about a name like, West of Jerusalem Moving Company?"

Ali responded in a sarcastic tone, "You must be kidding! Are we serving the Jewish settlements west of Jerusalem, or are we moving them out of there and back into Israel?"

David wasn't amused by Ali's response, "Why don't you come up with something then?"

Ali thought for a while. He knew Arab names usually indicated the good character of a person or an entity, "How about Honest Bronx Movers? This should be an eye catcher."

"The only eye-catching thing in this name is that no one will ever believe there are honest movers in the Bronx."

David adjusted his skullcap, raised his hand and said, "Here is another one, Children of Abraham Moving Company, Aisha uses this phrase all the time. What do you think?"

Ali wasn't impressed, but recanted, "Children of Abraham! People will think we're working for a church, or some non-profit organization."

That dialogue went on for a few days without reaching an agreement on a name. Deep in his heart, notwithstanding the potential trouble he might have with his friends, Ali knew that highlighting the Arab and the Jew in the name of the business was a clever strategy. He finally came out and said it, "I think we should go back and consider the words, An Arab and a Jew, in the name."

To his surprise David didn't object this time but rather changed his focus, "Why do you keep referring to us as an Arab and a Jew; why not a Jew and an Arab? After all, Jews existed before the Arabs."

"This isn't true, David. The Prophet Abraham had his son Ishmael from whom the Arabs descended before he had Isaac the father of all Jews."

"Ali, let us not get into the history of our religions. We're trying to develop a business. This is exactly why I was resisting mixing business and religion."

"Forget about who came first, the Arabs or the Jews, but alphabetically the letter A comes before the J or the T in truck."

"Why are you mentioning the letter T or the word truck?"

"Because I think we should include it in the name."

"Are you proposing a name like 'An Arab, a Jew and a Truck'?"

"Exactly, this is a great name."

David hesitated for a minute eyes skyward, as if seeing the phrase in bright lights for the first time, then said, "I like it. Let's go with that."

They spent several hours afterwards designing the logo to be used on the soon to be purchased truck. Sometimes they were laughing at one idea and other times they engaged in a fierce debate. In the midst of their brainstorming session, Ali interrupted the debate to say in a sober tone, "You know, David, we Palestinians have a lot of experience in moving. We have been doing it for over sixty years."

David refused to let Ali get away with that statement, and said, "You may have been moving for sixty years, but we have centuries of experience."

The two of them looked at each other and jumped up, "That is it! That should be part of our logo--Moving is our specialty. We've been doing it for centuries."

Finally they agreed on their company logo:

AN ARAB, A JEW & A TRUCK

MOVING IS OUR SPECIALTY
WE'VE BEEN DOING IT FOR CENTURIES

They agreed that they needed some kind of a symbol in addition to the words and that symbol would have to be consistent with the name of their business. David was quick to propose the Star of David, claiming, "Since we've decided to use the word 'Jew' in our business name, I believe we should use the Star of David in our business symbol. As you know, this is the symbol of Jewish identity and Judaism. Please feel free to also include an Arabic symbol."

Ali felt trapped. After all, he was the one that insisted on including the words Arab and a Jew in the business name. But in his view the Star of David was part of the Flag of Israel and was associated with the Zionist movement, which he and some Arabs blamed for the Palestinian tragedy. He realized, however, that he had to go along with David's proposal and include some Arab or Muslim symbol to balance the business sign.

"Well David, you have a point. I propose to include the crescent moon, which is an internationally recognized symbol of the faith of Islam. Unfortunately, not all Muslims or all Arabs accept the crescent moon as their symbol like the Jews do with the Star of David or the Christians with the Cross."

Then the argument resumed about how to name their website and what kind of a phone number they should use. After considerable debate they concluded that their website and phone number should reflect the name of the business. Finally the full image of the logo and how it would appear on their truck evolved:

AN ARAB, A JEW & A TRUCK

MOVING IS OUR SPECIALTY
WE'VE BEEN DOING IT FOR CENTURIES

WWW.ANARABAJEWANDATRUCK.COM
Tel. 555-ARABJEW (272-2539)

The color of their truck was a relatively easy decision for them. They agreed on white, blue, and green. The white and blue reflected the Israeli flag and the green was the color of choice of several Muslim countries. Furthermore, they felt that the white and green colors displayed peace and tranquility.

They formed a Limited Liability Corporation (LLC) and named it the same as the Logo: An Arab, A Jew & A Truck, LLC. Each one of them owned 50-percent of the shares and they nominated Satish as the treasurer of the LLC. They thought besides being a good financial advisor for them, such a role for him would please Dorothy and make her more comfortable with her loan. For a nominal fee, Satish could also maintain their business books and take care of paying all their bills.

Within three weeks, Ali and David had purchased the truck, had it painted with their logo, designed white uniforms that had their logo printed on the back, and purchased cell phones with the new telephone number. They were ready to serve their new customers under the new business name.

The truck immediately attracted considerable attention as they drove through various neighborhoods. People in the street stopped and pointed at the truck, some laughingly, and others with their mouths open in shock. To help in advertising their new business, they sometimes left the truck parked at busy street intersections. They found that approach to be an inexpensive and effective way of publicity.

Their phones rang all the time. Some of the calls were from serious potential customers, and others were full of anti-Semitic, anti-Muslim, or just plain racist remarks. David answered the phone one time with his usual greeting, "Arab, a Jew and a truck, can I help you?"

"Am I speaking to the Jew or the Arab?" and not waiting for an answer, the caller continued, "You guys say you've been moving for centuries. I recommend you pack your truck and move yourselves out of this country. We don't need more Arabs or Jews here."

At the end of some days Ali and David were worn out by some of the abuse they received on the phone or from hecklers on the street. They started to wonder whether the choice of the business name was a good idea. They appreciated the positive business side of the name that had attracted the attention of many people and resulted in tripling their business volume in a matter of days, but the nasty comments and phone calls from those bigots depleted their enthusiasm for the business and weakened their spirit.

On good days, however, they wondered what they were doing at school when they could make so much money in one day of work. They talked about the jobs they would get at the end of their school years. If lucky, they would end up in an office somewhere in the city, or possibly they had to move to another state. They would certainly be working for a boss who would be telling them what to do, when they should arrive and when they could leave. They would be sitting at a desk all-day, arriving at eight or nine o'clock in the morning and leaving at five or six in the evening. They probably wouldn't be able to take a vacation for at least the first year. Even after that, they would have to schedule any vacation well in advance with a boss who might be a mean sadistic person. In the end, they would be receiving the same check at the end of a pay period, and every year they would wait with great anticipation for a raise based on their performance. Again the same boss would be in control of their livelihood and their income. This scenario wasn't appealing to either of them.

In spite of the cruel and nasty remarks they got from time to time over the phone, they enjoyed their business and each other as business partners. Most of their customers up to that point were good and generous. They were in complete control of their schedules. If they decided to take few days off and go on vacation, they could easily do that. They were the masters of their own destiny; they were their own bosses. No one was telling them when to come and at what time they could finish their work. On top of all these advantages they were making an excellent income after being in business for only a few weeks. They were quite confident that they would be able to substantially increase their profits as they expanded their client base.

The more Ali and David discussed the pros and cons of the business, the more they became convinced that their business offered a far better opportunity for them than a regular office job, even as an attorney or as a graduate engineer. Neither was thinking in the long term. They were making great money with little stress, which was all that mattered for the time being.

The biggest challenges confronting them up to that point were answering customer calls when they were both in class, and arranging their class schedules to allow them at least two free days to be able to work together.

One day the phone rang when they were both on the truck and David answered, "An Arab, a Jew and a truck, can I help you?"

"Shalom," a person on the other end answered in a voice that sounded like an African American male.

David thought that it was another crank phone call. But the caller continued to say a few words in Yiddish, and then switched to English, "My name is Achyan and I need your help in moving some stuff from our store in Brooklyn to the Jacob Javits building. We're preparing for the yearly Gift Show next week."

Although he didn't trust the caller and suspected some foul play, David scheduled the appointment. Then he turned to Ali with a bewildered look on his face and said, "This is strange; I don't think this job is for real. This caller is definitely an African American but he speaks Yiddish and his business is in an area in Brooklyn which is predominantly Jewish."

Ali wasn't as shocked as David.

"So what, Sammy Davis, Jr. was a Jewish African American. We used to like him in Palestine before he converted to Judaism and started supporting Israel."

Ignoring Ali's snide remark, David said in exasperation, "But I never heard Sammy Davis speaking Yiddish so fluently. Anyhow, we shall see when we get there."

On their scheduled appointment, Ali and David pulled the truck in front of a gift store. As they got out of the truck, an African American dressed as a Hassidic Jew came out of the store with his arms outstretched, "Shalom brothers, I'm very happy to meet you."

He had a black coat and a black wide-rimmed hat. He had a long bushy beard and side curls. Two young African American boys dressed the same way followed him, and he introduced them as his children, "Please meet my boys. This is Etan, he is nine years old, and this cute little one is Yosef, he is only seven."

David was surprised by the man's friendliness and his continuous use of the word "brothers" as he addressed them. David had met a few Hassidic Jews before and found them to be reserved and not usually friendly, particularly with strangers. This man was certainly different. Ali, however, had never met a Hassidic Jew before, and had no idea what to expect. But, he was still impressed by his warm reception.

David responded to the man, "Nice meeting you, Mr. Achyan. This is my partner, Ali. Let's see what you need to move."

"Please don't call me Mr., call me Brother Achyan."

Ali and David were visibly amused and said together as they followed him inside the store, "Ok, brother."

He introduced them to his wife, Ashira, who was sitting behind the cash register. She was an African American woman dressed like a typical Hassidic woman in a long black dress with sleeves past her elbows and a scarf around her head. She stood up and greeted them with a warm welcome.

"My husband and I have heard about you and are happy to see Jews and Arabs cooperating and forming a business together."

She continued in an earnest voice, "As African Americans we've been working hard on improving relations between Jews and Black Muslims in this area. I think your business name and your joint venture could be of great help to our efforts."

David thanked her and added, "You should expand your valuable efforts to include all African Americans and not only Black Muslims. I never understood why some African Americans have this feeling of hostility and resentment toward the American Jews. After all, we were at the forefront of the Civil Rights Movement. We always thought of American Jews as the whites most sympathetic to blacks. When three activists were murdered in Mississippi by Ku Klux Klan members during the summer of 1964, two of those killed were Jewish."

"Listen, Brother," Achyan responded, "You're absolutely correct. But the passage of the Civil Rights Act in the 1970s provoked tensions between us and the Black community."

"How come?"

"You see, Brother David, Black civil rights organizations started making demands for affirmative action and even quotas so that Blacks would be preferentially admitted to universities or hired in proportion to their percentage in the population. Jews generally opposed any quotas because of our small numbers, and that opposition caused a split between the Black and Jewish communities. You must have read about how Black Muslim leaders like the late Malcolm X used to blame Jewish store owners and landlords for the high prices charged to ghetto residents."

"But those Jewish store owners have now been replaced by Asians, and the Blacks still hate the Jews," David said in a sarcastic tone before he continued in earnest, "I'm sure you know that Louis Farrakhan, leader of the Black Muslims, is overtly anti-Semitic and anti-Israel, and has often referred to Zionism as a poisonous weed."

Ali didn't like being a bystander in that conversation.

"You can't accuse everyone who is against Israel as anti-Semitic. In my opinion, Blacks in this country in general, and Black Muslims in particular, sympathize with the Palestinians because they see people whose rights have been taken away and are treated like second-class human beings in their own country. They relate to the Palestinian tragedy."

David shook his head in disagreement.

"I think the Black Muslims' support of the Palestinians is based merely on religion."

Ali shouted back, "David, the Palestinians aren't all Muslims. A significant percentage of them are Christians. As a matter of fact, some of the most militant Palestinians are Christians. Did you know that?"

"This is fascinating Brother Ali, I never knew that before," Achyan responded to Ali's question, and continued, "I'd love to have both of you come with me and talk to our brothers in the Black Muslim community. You two could provide the bridge to peace we've been looking for."

Achyan and his family were an anomaly among the Hassidic Jews who owned stores on the same block. Not only were they converted Jews and Black, but they were sociable and politically active. They were good friends with Black Muslim families with whom they regularly shared meals, and festivities. Achyan was the kind of man who was always smiling, laughing, and cracking jokes, contrary to the typical Hassidic Jew who is reserved and rarely laughs in public.

Achyan, his wife, and their two kids followed Ali and David as they started loading the truck. Several Hassidic Jews, who were store owners on the same block, gathered near the truck looking at the sign and the words on the truck. A visible expression of disbelief could be seen on their faces.

Achyan called them as he approached the truck, "Shalom Brother Yaakov, hello Brother Moshe, come and meet Brother Ali and Brother David, the best movers in town."

Yaakov and Moshe approached Ali and David and shook hands with them, and Achyan continued to express his admiration of the example they were setting for business cooperation between Arab Muslims and Jews. His Hassidic friends, though not totally convinced, nodded in agreement.

When Ali and David were about to close the truck and leave for the Jacob Javits Center, Achyan held their hands and said, "I like you Brothers, and I'd like you to come and have dinner in our home and meet some of my friends. I will invite two of my Black Muslim friends and their families. You're welcome to bring your wives."

Ali and David looked at each other and said with a smile, "But we aren't married."

"Well, bring your girlfriends. You'll enjoy my wife's cooking. You'll have a soul kosher meal." Then he looked at Ali, "My Muslim friends eat kosher food. I hope you do too."

"Being in business with David, I've learned to like kosher food," Ali said with a grin.

CHAPTER 13

The Crossover Dinner

Achyan was sort of a maverick. He was an African American who adopted a strict form of Judaism and transformed himself into a Hassidic Jew. Nevertheless, he never forgot or abandoned his ethnic roots, and continued to build cultural and social bridges between the Jewish and African American communities, including Black Muslims whom many Jews accuse of being anti-Semitic.

Achyan confirmed his dinner invitation to Ali and David and informed them that two Black Muslim families, who were good friends of his family, would be at the dinner.

David was excited to invite Hadassah to the dinner. He knew that she'd love to be in the middle of political and religious extremes, and to practice her role as a moderator and peacemaker. These kinds of gatherings stimulated and excited her, and anything that excited Hadassah was good for him. Ali, however, had no girlfriend to invite. He couldn't invite Dorothy because he thought she wouldn't fit well and might feel uncomfortable in the middle of such a group. However, his cousin Aisha would have no problem talking to Black Muslims, Hassidic Jews, or anyone regardless of his or her cultural, religious, or political backgrounds. He also thought that Aisha and Hadassah would have fun bouncing off each other in any conversation with the host and his guests.

Ali, David, and the girls drove to Achyan's house in Hadassah's car. The Achyans lived in a mixed middle class

105

neighborhood in New Jersey. The modest brick rambler house looked like any other house on the block with a small lawn in the front and a double garage to the side. Achyan met them at the screen door. He led them into the spacious living room, which connected to a dining room. He introduced them to Muhammad, his wife Fatima, and their seven-year old daughter Latifa, and to the other Black Muslim couple named Abdul Raheem, his wife Zeinab, and their eight-year son Elijah. Achyan was, as usual, warm, smiling and joking with everyone. His wife Ashira, Aisha and the two Black Muslim women were dressed in long black dresses with long sleeves and black scarves covering their hair. Achyan wore his traditional Hassidic black suit and a black hat on his head and the two Black Muslim men also had black suits and their traditional black hats. The only different colors in the room were those of the sofas and the clothes worn by Ali, David, and Hadassah. If it weren't for those colors, the scene would have looked like an old black and white movie.

Achyan, looking at his guests, said, "When we sit at the dining table, I'll make sure to place those people dressed in colors between us dressed in black. Otherwise we won't know who is who."

Hadassah laughed and asked, "I understand why Hassidic Jews are dressed in black. It's in the Torah that you should do whatever the elders demand, and in the eighteenth century when Hassidism started, the elders were dressed in black. But, I don't understand why Black Muslims dress in black."

Aisha volunteered to answer her question, "Muslim women don't have to dress in black. As a matter of fact, many Muslim women wear dresses in different colors. But some women consider colors to be immodest and they stick to black as an expression of modesty."

The two Black Muslim ladies nodded in agreement, and Fatima added, "I think modesty is the main reason behind wearing black. You also see Catholic nuns and Catholic women in the villages of Italy, Spain, and Latin America dressed in black."

Fatima's husband, Muhammad, followed up, "It isn't only the color but also the shape of the dress that shows modesty. To be modest, the dress should cover the woman's arms and legs. And religious Muslim women, Hassidic women, and Catholic women, who live in small rural communities and haven't been influenced by the big city life, follow that principle."

Hadassah felt slightly uncomfortable since she was the only woman with bare legs and arms and her blonde hair wasn't covered but rather hanging down on her shoulders. She noticed that everyone was looking at her legs and she kept pulling down on the hem of her skirt, but it wouldn't go below her knees. She wasn't a person, however, who couldn't face a challenge, and offered, "I believe that modesty isn't in the clothes you wear, but in how you connect with God and with your fellow man."

At that point Achyan interrupted and asked all of them to come to the table, and he guided the children, Latifa, Elijah, Etan and Yosef to a small table in the kitchen. Ashira presented the delicious spread on the table, which she described as soul kosher cuisine consisting of southern-style barbecue chicken, West African vegetable stew, and salads.

Ali complemented Ashira on the food, but couldn't help asking, "I'm curious as to how you all became such good friends?"

Achyan smiled and pointed to his friends, "You know, Ali, both the Black Muslims and the Hassidic Jews are on the fringes of their religions. That is what attracted us to each other." Then he looked at Muhammad and Abdul Raheem and teased them, "But they're further out than we are. We limit ourselves to religion and don't get involved with politics."

Achyan started on a joke he'd probably told a few times before about a Muslim, a Christian, a Hassidic Jew, and a Black Muslim who died and on the Day of Judgment, God told them that he'd ask each of them to spell a word and whoever got it right would go to heaven. He turned to the Muslim and asked him to spell Muhammad and he obviously spelled it correctly. He turned to the Christian and asked him to spell Jesus and he did, and asked the Hassidic Jew to spell Moses and he also did correctly. He then turned to the Black Muslim, paused for a minute, and then asked him to spell Engelbert Humperdinck.

Achyan and his Black Muslim friends laughed, and it was obvious that they'd often teased each other before. Aisha and Hadassah, on the other hand, laughed in a reserved way because they didn't appreciate racial or religious jokes.

Aisha seized the moment to comment on Achyan's statement about Black Muslims, "I disagree with you, Achyan, I don't believe Black Muslims are on the fringes of the Muslim world. We don't have mosques for black people and mosques for white people. When we pray, we stand shoulder to shoulder regardless of skin color, ethnic background, or social status. I know you too don't discriminate between people in your synagogues. You may have temples for Hassidic Jews, and others for Orthodox or Reformist Jews, but those are based on religious beliefs and not on ethnic backgrounds."

Abdul Raheem, who was a thoughtful and rather reserved man, nodded in agreement, "Sister Aisha, you hit the nail on the head. I believe that one of the factors that drove some American Blacks from Christianity toward Islam was the fact that they felt discriminated against in their own religion. I grew up in the South as a Christian, and I never understood why I had to go to an all-Black church. All the pictures of Jesus I saw as a child depicted him as a white man. I never believed that Jesus, who was born and raised in the Holy land in the Middle East, could possibly look like the white people around me. I felt then that the white people had hijacked Jesus' image and deprived us from a sense of connection with him. This was one of the reasons that drove me to read about other religions until I found Islam."

Achyan had a similar story. He also couldn't comprehend belonging to a religion that allowed slavery and discrimination, even in the house of worship. He and his wife first converted to Judaism, and shortly after that Achyan befriended a few Hassidic Jews who convinced them to join their synagogue.

Ali took the initiative to respond to Abdul Raheem and Achyan's stories, "This discrimination in churches you're talking about may have existed in this country and maybe in the South, but it has nothing to do with the religion. Christians in our part of the world can attend the church of their choice regardless of the color of their skin. I'm sure that good Christians anywhere in the world would object to any form of discrimination in their churches."

Achyan then attempted to lighten the conversation that was turning serious and philosophical.

"Listen, my friends, Black Muslims may not be on the fringes of the Muslim world, and also the Hassidic Jews may not be on the fringes of the Jewish people, but I certainly feel I am. I don't know if you ever heard of the scam committed by two white guys on West Forty- Sixth Street, in the heart of the diamond district. They wore fake beards, black hats, and black coats and acted like two Hassidic Jews. They went into a diamond store and nobody bothered to check them out, and walked away with millions of dollars of diamonds. If I'd walked in dressed the way I am, a lot of bells and whistles would have gone off."

Hadassah enjoyed listening to the honest views and feelings of such a disparate group of people. She looked around the table and thought *How did this odd lot find each other?* Studying each face, she felt a special admiration for Achyan. She turned to him, "Achyan, I've got to admit you're a unique one. Are there any other American Hassidic Jews like you out there, or are you in a pretty exclusive club?"

"Isn't that exclusive," he said with a wry smile. "We let in a few members."

"Well, the point is, you picked the strictest sect of our religion. That's no way to increase your membership. But you're always trying to extend your hand and connect with people from other religions. You sure don't allow the rigid rules of your religion to limit you from having fun and sometimes laugh at your own situation."

"Thank you, sister Hadassah. This is a very nice compliment."

As soon as Achyan finished his sentence, his son Etan ran into the room crying, "Father, Elijah says that if he and I commit sins, we'd end up in the same hell."

"What hell is that?" Achyan asked with a wink.

"Elijah says hell in Islam is called Jahannam. Is that the same like Gehinnom to us?"

Elijah stood back looking to his father for support. Achyan smiled, hugged his son and explained, "I'll tell you Etan what Gehinnom stands for in Judaism. We're lucky that we've several good Muslims here who can explain to us what Jahannam stands for in Islam. Gehinnom is a place where people who die in sin may suffer temporarily. But certain serious sins may merit eternal punishment."

Aisha volunteered to explain the meaning of Jahannam in Islam.

"This is a good question Etan. I don't think there is much difference between the two. The two names are even similar. Jahannam is a place where sinners go after they die, same as in your religion. It's a place of torment and fire. It has several levels and, depending on the sins, a person may not necessarily spend eternity there. But I'm sure that you and Elijah are good boys and neither of you will go to Jahannam or Gehinnom."

David interrupted, "Can I get a word here? I agree with Achyan's explanation about Gehinnom. But I'd like to emphasize that the ideas of afterlife vary among different Jewish groups. As a matter of fact, the Torah talks more on the here and now, and more about living a good life than on what happens after death. Some scholars explain that such emphasis could be due to the fact that ancient Egyptians, at the time of the Torah, focused entirely on the afterlife."

Etan, feeling that the conversation was becoming too complicated for him to understand, left his father's arms and turned around to run back to the children's table behind Elijah. In doing so, his hand hit the glass of cranberry juice in front of Hadassah and the juice spilled all over her dress. Etan broke into tears again and Hadassah comforted him, "Don't worry Etan, this is an old dress and it can be cleaned." Etan's mother, however, jumped up and insisted that she would clean the dress herself. She asked Hadassah to come with her to one of the bedrooms. When Hadassah came out, she stopped in front of a wall mirror in the living room, looked at her clothes, and shook her head in disbelief. She was dressed in a black dress that had long sleeves and went down to her ankles. As she entered the dining room, the rest of the women sitting around the table took one look at her and chuckled, "Hello Sister, you look like you're one of us."

Achyan followed up, "Sister Hadassah, I told you it isn't an exclusive club."

Ali turned to Aisha, "You should place a black scarf around Hadassah's head and take her for a walk, and let her experience firsthand the stares you keep talking about."

Hadassah wasn't amused by all the sarcastic comments, "I don't have to experience those stares firsthand. I know exactly how they feel."

As all the guests prepared to leave, Achyan looked at his Black Muslim friends and said, "Brothers and Sisters I ask you, please, to spread the word in your community about Ali and David's business. We should help these guys pave the way for a better world."

Everyone applauded.

Hadassah had to leave her dress behind for Ashira to clean. She sat in the back seat of the car next to Aisha. David turned around, looked at her again and said with a smile, "Honey, I'm confused, I don't know if you look like a fine Hassidic or a good Muslim!"

111

CHAPTER 14

The Back-Up Crew

Business was growing steadily. Many of Ali and David's customers were Arab and Jewish merchants extending from Manhattan to Brooklyn and from the Bronx to Queens. They were intrigued by the name of the business, An Arab, a Jew and a Truck, and the statement on their truck -Moving is our specialty, we've been doing it for centuries. Each of their client groups found something to identify with in the name and in the statement. The Jewish Diaspora started in the eighth to sixth century BCE and continued for centuries. The Palestinians were driven from their homeland in 1948 and lived in refugee camps throughout the Middle East. Recently, millions of Iraqis also fled the fighting between the Americans and the insurgents and between the Sunnis and the Shi'as and settled as refugees in neighboring countries. In addition, some of their Arab and Jewish clients appreciated the business partnership between an Arab and a Jew and saw it as a model of a much hoped-for large-scale collaboration between the two peoples. They all wanted to see them succeed.

Their client base expanded to include other residents of the New York area. Dorothy, who was active in her church, spearheaded an effort urging the members of her congregation to use Ali and David's services. Her efforts included the congregations of a few other churches nearby.

Ali and David had to balance several tasks and responsibilities from school and business to social and personal demands. They had limited time to study and they were falling behind in some of their classes. But their immediate challenge was answering and scheduling customers' calls that were becoming more frequent. These calls usually came when they were either attending classes or in the middle of a moving job. They couldn't respond promptly to their potential customers. They needed someone dedicated to answering the phone and making their schedule. But the idea of hiring an additional person and being responsible for someone else's salary, though appealing, scared them. They already had to pay Satish a modest amount of money for taking care of their books, insurance, etc., and had to pay Dorothy and the bank monthly installments for the their loans. They were too timid at that point to make another financial commitment.

Rather than hiring a stranger, they decided to approach Hadassah and Aisha and ask for their help. Ali was comfortable asking Aisha, who was a blood relative and owed him a favor for providing her a place to stay. As a graduate student, she didn't have to be at school every day and could answer the phone while she was at home studying. David, on the other hand, wasn't sure how Hadassah would react to such a request. She was employed by a nonprofit peace organization and worked from home several days a week. He felt she could handle the phone on some of those days. Besides, her involvement in the business would bring them closer together, and would provide him an excuse to see her more often.

To their surprise, Hadassah and Aisha eagerly agreed to help them out and refused to get any financial compensation until the business was well established. They started taking turns on weekdays answering the phone and organizing the schedule. They even had fun dealing with some of the crank phone calls and the wise remarks made by potential clients.

Having someone dedicated to answering the phone and good schedule management resulted in a sharp increase in business. The schedule became tighter and tighter and the customers became more and more demanding. Ali and David had to face a new challenge: how to balance business demands and school requirements. The business was becoming more lucrative, and they realized that they could make a decent income if they could devote more time to it. For the first time since they had started the business they debated whether they should take a year off school and devote more time to the business. They were well aware that their parents would be disappointed if they knew they had dropped out of school. But they knew they could always go back and finish school later. A good business idea came only once in a lifetime. It was an easier decision for David because he had always wanted to have his own business. His choice to study law was primarily driven by his desire to please his father. Ali wasn't particularly interested in engineering either. But, it was a prestigious profession in his country and his uncle, whom he looked up to, made a lot of money as a civil engineer back home.

After a long and exhausting debate, they made the uncomfortable decision to take a year off school and focus entirely on developing and expanding their business.

Hadassah and Aisha were effective in soliciting new customers, and the moving schedule gradually tightened. Ali and David had to work almost every day of the week and that posed another challenge to them. David, as an Orthodox Jew, couldn't work on the Jewish Sabbath, Saturday, which was the day for worship and for him to go to his synagogue. Likewise Ali, a religious Muslim, had to take Friday off. That was the day he went to the mosque to perform the noon prayers and to get together with his Arab friends for a good Middle Eastern meal and listen to the latest gossip from back home. But Fridays and Saturdays were important days for their business. Many of their customers had to be served during those two days. Furthermore, Ali realized that Jewish holidays were numerous and more frequent than he'd known. As a Muslim, Ali had two main holidays, Eid El-Fitr at the end of the holy month of Ramadan, and Eid Al-Adha about two months later. What surprised Ali more than the large number of Jewish holidays was the way some Orthodox Jews celebrated them by refusing to work. That was becoming a serious source of tension between him and David.

Soon after they had started the business in September there was Rosh Hashanah, celebrating the start of the new Jewish year. David had to spend two days at the synagogue and couldn't work. Then, in October, there was Yom Kippur, the Jewish Day of Atonement. David fasted for twenty-five hours and refused to work. Five days later, and fortunately on a Saturday (David's day off), Ali came home and found David sitting in a make-shift tent outside on the landing next to their apartment's front door. He was praying and had some food next to him. Ali learned later that it was Sukkot, a festival commemorating the Biblical period of the Jews' wandering in the desert, and that he was compromising by not working only one day instead of several.

About a month later David again couldn't work. Ali came home and found candles lit everywhere in the apartment, in the Menorah in the living room, in the kitchen, and in his bedroom. Ali accused David of being a pyromaniac and David had to explain to him that it was Hanukkah, the festival of light commemorating the rededication of the Second Temple in Jerusalem in the second century BCE. Heated arguments ensued when Ali found out that there were more holidays to come, including Purim, celebrating the rescue of the Jews from Haman, a Hitler-like figure; Shavu'ot, commemorating the Giving of the Torah at Mt. Sinai; and Passover, celebrating the Exodus of Jews from Egypt, to name just a few.

They brainstormed in search of a way to cover Fridays and Saturdays as well as the Jewish and Muslim holidays. Their first challenge was how to deal with a situation when one of the two Muslim holidays occurred at the same time as a major Jewish holiday. David was willing to compromise on some minor holidays, but not on Yom Kippur, Passover, Sukkot, and Shavu'ot. They both knew that the Jewish and Muslim holidays were based on lunar calendars and that both of those calendars lose eleven days every year relative to the solar calendar. The Jewish calendar, however, makes up the difference by adding a month every two or three years, but the Muslim calendar does not. That meant the Jewish holidays do not fall on the same day every year but within the same month or two. The Muslim calendar does not add a month. Therefore the Muslim Eid El-Fitr and Eid Al-Adha move about eleven days every year, and would occur on the same date about every thirty-three years. Ali and David were glad to conclude that their main holidays would rarely overlap.

Their main task now was how to meet their religious obligations and at the same time maintain their image of an Arab and a Jew with their clients. Many of the customers who planned to use their services looked forward to meeting them and to possibly chat with them. Fortunately for Ali and David the Jewish and Muslim Sabbath fell on different days. They wanted to have someone who could work Saturdays with Ali, looked Jewish, and could speak a few words of Yiddish and Hebrew. In addition, they needed another person who could work Fridays with David, looked like an Arab, and could speak some Arabic. Those were difficult individuals to find. But throughout their long and frustrating search, they never once thought about the two individuals who were the closest to them: Ben and Yasser.

Several members of Ben's family were settlers in the West Bank, and Ben had spent many summers there. Although he never mingled with the Palestinian Arab natives during his visits, he took the opportunity to learn the language. He was dark-skinned and looked like an Arab. Furthermore, he was working only part-time as a telemarketer. If David could convince him to work on the truck with him on Fridays, take his yarmulke off and pose as an Arab, he would solve half the problem.

Yasser grew up in the West Bank and, like many Palestinians, spoke some Hebrew. He also learned some Yiddish in New York. It was Ali's turn to convince him to replace David on Saturdays, wear a yarmulke, and pose as the Jewish partner.

Ali and David knew it was unethical on their part to make such a false representation, and to tell customers that Yasser was a Jew or Ben was an Arab. But they planned not to reveal to the customers the identity of the people on the truck, and who was a Jew and who was an Arab. The looks of the two individuals on the truck on those two days were intended only for appearance and effect. They agreed not to serve Arab and Jewish customers during those two days, since they could easily find out that Ben wasn't a true Arab, and Yasser wasn't a Jew either. Given their unique circumstances, it was the only scheme they could think of that would preserve the identity of the business and allow them to adhere to their religious beliefs concerning the Muslim and Jewish Sabbaths.

The clever plan they'd developed rested on the assumption that they could persuade both the right wing Ben and the militant Yasser to participate in it. David couldn't imagine Ben agreeing to take off his yarmulke in public. Likewise, Ali doubted that Yasser would wear a yarmulke even though he often wore a head cover that looked like one. But his head cover was a couple of inches larger in diameter than a yarmulke and, to him, those two inches made all the difference.

David thought of a ploy to convince Ben to go along with their scheme. In the days that followed the dinner in his apartment, where Ben met Aisha, Ben had been making casual remarks to David about how intelligent and beautiful she was and repeatedly indicated his interest in her. He kept referring to her thick lips that looked like Angelina Jolie's, her femininity, and the way she moved her hips when she walked. It became clear to David that in spite of his interest, Ben was too timid to approach her, and was indirectly seeking David's help. But David never offered to help because he was convinced that Aisha, though a broad-minded person, wouldn't be interested in going out with an Orthodox Jew like Ben.

When David met Ben to discuss his business scheme, he wasn't sure how he'd play the Aisha card. He started by explaining to Ben the sudden increase in the business volume since Aisha and Hadassah began managing their phones and their work schedules. He told him that Fridays and Saturdays had become important days for the business, and that Ali couldn't work on Friday. He asked Ben whether he would be willing to work with him on the truck on Fridays, emphasizing that they would finish working well before sunset when the Jewish Sabbath began. David offered to pay him well for that day of work. Not knowing the full plan, Ben was quick to agree to help David on those days.

"But there is one problem, Ben," David said sheepishly.

"What?" Ben inquired innocently.

"As you know, Ben, we are supposed to be an Arab and a Jew in our business. Not two Jews."

"Well, why don't you find yourself another Arab?" Ben answered impatiently.

"The problem is that most of Ali's close friends will not work on Fridays, and we don't want to bring any strangers into our business. You know, Ben, how hard we've worked to build this business."

"What do you expect me to do? Become an Arab?"

"Yes, but in appearance only."

Ben was slightly irritated, "Do you want me to wear a white robe and ride a camel?"

"No, no," David laughed, "All you have to do is to pretend that you're an Arab." Then he threw his bombshell and hurried to say, "And not wear your yarmulke."

Ben jumped up yelling, "What? Have you lost your mind? I've been wearing this yarmulke since I was seven years old. I think you have been badly influenced by this Arab living in your apartment."

David realized that his plan was about to fail and it was time for him to use the Aisha card, "You know Ben, Ali and I have discussed this plan with Hadassah and Aisha, and Aisha thought that even if you took off your yarmulke you might not look like an Arab. She thought that we need to add another element to make us look convincingly as an Arab and a Jew."

"And what would that be?" Ben asked in a mocking tone, though showing a slight degree of interest after hearing Aisha's involvement in the plan.

"Well, she suggests that every time you and I go on the truck, she'd go with us and pretend that she is with you. This way you would look convincingly like an Arab."

David was lying and hadn't discussed the plan with Aisha. But Ben's negative reaction to his idea was so strong that he had to make such a major change in their plan and bring Aisha into the equation. He thought that if Ben agreed to the idea, Hadassah and Ali could possibly talk Aisha into joining them on the truck. Both Hadassah and Aisha had once asked to accompany them on some of the jobs to help evaluate their performance and the customers' satisfaction.

Ben changed his tone, and with a smile asked, "Did she really say that?"

"Yes," David persisted.

"Does she know that I'll be with you?" Ben asked showing some interest in David's idea.

"Of course, she knows that I'm talking to you right now, and I think she'd be disappointed if she hears that you've refused to help."

Ben interrupted him, "Let me sleep on it and I will let you know tomorrow if I can do it."

David was confident that Ben would ultimately accept his proposal as long as Aisha agreed to join them on the truck.

He ran to Ali, Aisha, and Hadassah and told them about his conversation with Ben. He apologized to Aisha for not discussing his proposal with her beforehand. He explained to her that without mentioning her name Ben would have flatly rejected the idea. Aisha was flattered, "If I can have such an influence on someone like Ben, and make him take off his yarmulke in public, then there is hope for peace in our part of the world."

It was Ali's turn to approach Yasser and convince him to work on Saturdays, and to pretend that he was Jewish. Ali knew how inflexible Yasser was, and his animosity toward

119

Jews in general and particularly those who wore yarmulkes because he considered them the backbone of Israel's support in the U.S. He remembered the day he told Yasser that he was about to move in with David, and Yasser's vehement objections to his plan. Since that time, however, Yasser had a chance to meet David a few times, the first of which was at the dinner in Ali's apartment. That night Yasser also met Ben and chatted with him over dinner; something he'd never done before. Also Yasser had been following with great interest the progress of Ali's business. In spite of his preconceived notions and his mistrust of all Jews, he was impressed by the successful business cooperation between Ali and David, and the rather harmonious living arrangement the two were having in their apartment.

Ali met Yasser at school and started by explaining to him the current dilemma they were having in their business. He added that he wouldn't work on Fridays, and David couldn't work on Saturdays. He further explained that those two days were important for their business, and either Ali or David had to be on the truck during those days.

Without further ado, Ali asked Yasser, "I need you to work with me on Saturdays in place of David, and I will pay you fifteen dollars per hour plus you will be getting good tips from the customers."

Ali knew very well that Yasser was a poor student, and his offer was far better than the hourly rates Yasser was making on a few part-time jobs.

Not knowing the full scope of Ali's offer, Yasser quickly and enthusiastically agreed.

"But there is one favor I will have to ask you to do for me when you're working with me on those days," Ali interrupted his joyous acceptance.

With the smile fading off his face, Yasser asked, "What can I do for you?"

"You will have to present yourself as a Jew."

"And how am I going to do that?"

"You'll have to wear a yarmulke instead of your head cover."

Yasser was visibly annoyed and somewhat insulted by Ali's request.

"Why don't you act as the Jew and wear the yarmulke. After all, you've been living, eating and doing business with them."

Ali expected such a reaction from Yasser as well as Yasser's counter demand, and tried to calm him down.

"I'd have done that, Yasser. But you must remember that many customers know me and know that I'm the Arab. You speak Hebrew and some Yiddish and could fool many people that you're a Jew."

Ali meant every word he said. He'd have played the Jew part and let Yasser be the Arab if it wasn't for the reasons he'd mentioned. The fact that Ali was willing to wear a yarmulke and pretend that he was a Jew demonstrated how business collaboration had managed to sweep away those cultural, religious, and political divisions that separate Arabs and Jews. Ali was ready to pretend he was a Jew for the sake of preserving the integrity of the business he'd struggled with David to build.

Yasser wasn't convinced by Ali's argument, "What happens if our clients are Jews or Arabs? They would know right away that I'm a fake Jew."

"Yasser, we're aware of that, and we'll select our clients carefully on that day. Aisha will be doing the schedule for us. When we meet our clients we'll avoid telling them who is a Jew or who is an Arab among us. The whole thing is merely to preserve our business image of an Arab, a Jew, and a truck. You just let me do all the talking and you don't have to say anything."

Yasser's resistance softened when he heard that Aisha was involved in the process. He, too, was a great fan of hers. But he persisted in quizzing Ali, asking, "Assuming that I work with you on Saturdays, what are you going to do on Fridays?"

"Oh, I forgot to tell you. Ben, David's friend whom you met at the dinner, will replace me on the truck. He will not wear his yarmulke as long as Aisha accompanies them in the truck. Ben felt that Aisha's presence would make him look more credible as an Arab. You know, he also speaks Arabic well."

Yasser was stunned hearing all this information in such a short time. Many thoughts swirled in his head. *Aisha is going with two Orthodox Jews on the truck and one of them is pretending he is an Arab? My dear friend, Ali, is asking me to wear a yarmulke and pretend to be a Jew? What madness!* His world of walls separating Arabs and Jews was crumbling. Soon, he thought to himself, he wouldn't know who was a Jew and who was an Arab!

What Yasser was missing was the fact that Jews had lived in Arab countries for centuries. They lived and worked among the Arabs. They spoke Arabic, and even dressed like Arabs. The only way one could know if a person was a Muslim, Christian, or a Jew in those countries was by his or her family name. Even the first name could sometimes be misleading. For example, if a man's first name was Mousa in Arabic (Moses in English), he could be a Muslim, a Christian or a Jew.

Yasser interrupted his own deep thoughts and, sounding exasperated, told Ali, "I've got to go home and try to digest your shocking proposal. My dear friend, I'll call you, maybe tomorrow. I need to clear my head."

Yasser walked home thinking about Ali's offer. The money was attractive and he'd be working with his friend, and not with David or Ben. Furthermore, he learned that Aisha was involved in Ali's proposal. Two of his closest friends were asking him for a big favor. But what if some of his other Arab friends saw him wearing that yarmulke? What could he possibly tell them; they'd call him a self-hating Arab, or a Jew lover.

By the time he arrived at his apartment he was exhausted and totally confused. He questioned his inner feelings of hostility toward Israelis and Jews in general. How could his friends, Ali and Aisha, who shared his background and suffered the same under the Israeli occupation, learn to befriend and do business with people like David and Ben?

He wondered whether Ali and Aisha's path of friendship and collaboration, rather than hatred and hostility, was the right way for his people to regain their rights in their homeland. He couldn't tell who was right and who was wrong. Most of his Palestinian friends wouldn't agree to do what Ali was asking him to do, and probably wouldn't wish to do business with people like David and Ben. But he thought about the dinner he had in Ali's apartment where he met Ben for the first time. After spending the evening talking to him, Yasser left not feeling the same hostility toward him in spite of the fact that Ben epitomized the Jew he'd always blamed for his people's misery.

Yasser convinced himself that he had no choice but to help his friend Ali and to go along with his proposal. Moreover, the hourly rates Ali was offering him were attractive and would make it easier for him to continue his college education. He would be working fewer hours than his other part-time jobs, but making more money.

Late that evening, Yasser called Ali to tell him that he'd work with him on Saturdays and would wear a yarmulke, "Ali, you know I'm a good Muslim, and I will try to be also a good Jew for you. I sure hope none of my Palestinian friends see me in the truck."

Ali was happy to hear his decision, but couldn't resist teasing him.

"If you see any of them try to push the yarmulke forward on your head and they may not notice the difference."

Ali was relieved that Yasser had accepted the offer, and he and David were waiting for Ben's response. His call didn't come until late in the afternoon on the next day. Ben wanted to be assured one more time that Aisha would always accompany them on the truck. Fortunately, both Aisha and Hadassah were with them in the apartment, and David handed the phone to Aisha, "Hi Ben, I'm looking forward to practice my Arabic with you."

They all could hear Ben's excitement on the other end, "Aisha, I think from now on we should call the business, a Jew, an Arab couple, and a truck."

"No, Ben, we will change the name when I see you coming out of a mosque."

When David hung up the phone, they were all happy that Ben and Yasser were finally on board. Hadassah, though participating in the excitement, was slightly apprehensive. She felt that her role in the business was diminishing in relation to Aisha's. She interrupted the laughter and mumbled, "I also want to be on the truck."

David became concerned and asked her, "Honey, you can't be with us on the truck. The front seat can accommodate only three people."

"I don't mean to be with you and Ben," she interrupted David.

David, his mouth opened, asked in disbelief, "What do you mean?"

"I mean I'd go with Ali and Yasser, and I'd act like I'm Yasser's girlfriend. That would make Yasser look more Jewish, the same way Aisha is doing for Ben."

"But Hadassah, you don't even look like a typical Jewish girl. And you and Yasser would look like an odd couple."

"Relax, David, when I get on that truck I'll look like a true Jew. Remember how I looked coming out of Achyan's house?"

David knew that Hadassah, though religious, didn't observe the Jewish Sabbath. But he was uncomfortable having her spend the whole day with Ali and Yasser rather than with him. He suddenly realized that his scheme had backfired. There was no way Hadassah, who thought of herself as an independent woman, would take no for an answer. To make matters worse, Aisha supported the idea, and the three of them, Ali, Aisha, and Hadassah, started planning the next moves. David had to reluctantly go along.

At that moment, Ali and David's business entered a new phase. Aisha and Hadassah also declared that it was time for the company to begin paying them for their efforts. They felt that they had contributed enough free time for the business.

On the following Friday, Aisha got ready for her first job with David and Ben. She wore dark pants and a long-sleeved blouse and had her usual scarf around her head. She wore bright slippers that showed her pretty feet and freshly painted toenails. She had the same color nail polish on her long fingernails that accentuated her beautiful hands.

Aisha sat between David and Ben in the cramped front seat of the truck. Ben had Yasser's head cover that covered most of his hair. He felt naked without his yarmulke, but sitting close to Aisha and rubbing his leg against hers made him feel at ease. His eyes wandered between her feet and her hands with a discreet and quick pause at her breasts that couldn't be ignored. Aisha felt his eyes piercing through her clothes but kept teasing him about his head cover. She offered him a set of prayer beads that religious Muslim men used and asked him to hold them in his hand to look more convincingly like an Arab. Ben, in turn, clowned around, sometimes shifting his head cover to look like a yarmulke, or holding the prayer beads next to Aisha's ears and asking her to wear them as earrings.

They both were acting silly and obviously having a good time. David concentrated on driving the truck, but was amused by the sudden rapport between Aisha and Ben. He felt relieved that his idea of bringing Aisha along had worked. But he couldn't help thinking about the flip side of his plan that led Hadassah to join Ali and Yasser on Saturdays. The outcome of his scheme was that he'd lost an important day he'd have spent with her alone in the apartment while Ali was working.

One minute Aisha and Ben were teasing and laughing at each other and the next minute they were engaged in a serious conversation about their lives, upbringing, and cultural backgrounds. David noticed that they were gradually feeling more and more comfortable with each other. Some of the remarks that were made by Ben about Arabs, Jews, and Israelis were so moderate in tone that David had to turn his head to make sure that they were coming out of Ben's mouth.

By the end of the day the three of them felt that they had been working together for months, and Aisha and Ben couldn't wait to get back together on the truck. They were disappointed that they had to wait for another week to do that.

The next Friday it was Hadassah's turn to go on the truck with Ali and Yasser. Her role wasn't difficult to play. But she had to tone down her dress and her looks to appear compatible with Yasser who was supposed to be a Sephardic Jew. Hence, she wore pants instead of her usual mini skirts, a scarf around her hair to partially hide her blonde hair, and a necklace that showed a large Star of David for those who'd ever doubt that she was a true Jew.

Yasser didn't expect Hadassah to be with them on the truck. Initially he was embarrassed to wear the yarmulke in front of her. But upon Ali's urging he put it on, and Hadassah helped him positioning it on the top of his head. He tried to cheat and push the yarmulke toward the front of his head to look more Arab than Jewish. But every time he did that, Hadassah pushed it back to the center of his head. Gradually, however, he started playing his scripted role and addressing Hadassah in Hebrew. He kept telling her how beautiful she was. She, in turn, teased him and told him that he'd make a fine Jew.

He looked at her and said with a smirk, "Do you know, Hadassah, that a Muslim male can marry a Jewish or a Christian woman?"

That was the wrong thing to tell a feminist like Hadassah, who replied, "How about Muslim women? Can they marry a non-Muslim?"

"Absolutely not," he responded emphatically.

"Why not? I call that double standard, and if I were a Muslim woman I'd rebel against such hypocrisy."

Yasser sensed that he'd touched a sensitive issue with Hadassah and tried to calm her down by being rational, "The problem, Hadassah, is the children, since they carry the father's name. Just imagine a Muslim woman marries a Jew, say someone like our friend Ben, and they have a son. Would they call him Muhammad Katz? He would be a laugh-ingstock in our part of the world. As a matter of fact he'd have a hard time even here in America."

Ali and Hadassah smiled at Yasser's funny argument but Hadassah wasn't convinced, retorting, "Suppose you marry a Jewish woman. Do the children have a voice in choosing their religion?" she probed him.

"The children must follow the father's religion," he answered without hesitation.

"How about freedom of choice?"

"Not when it comes to my children's religion. I'm no different from a religious Jew or a Christian. I'm surprised that you're even arguing with me about this issue. You know quite well that Jewish families are matrilineal, and a Jew by birth must be born to a Jewish mother. So, we're no different. In our case it's the father instead of the mother."

Hadassah didn't expect such a sound argument coming out of Yasser. Deep inside her, Hadassah agreed with him. Although she was a broad-minded person, she still would want her children to be raised Jewish. Her wish was to marry a Jewish man, but if she fell in love and married a non-Jew, she would insist on raising her children Jewish. So, Yasser and Hadassah, though far apart on the political scale, they were much closer when it came to the religion of their offspring.

In an attempt to change the subject, Ali announced that they were approaching the client's home. Hadassah looked at Yasser and said teasingly, "Now remember, Yasser, who you are. You can't speak to Ali at any time in Arabic."

Ali nodded in agreement, "Please speak only with Hadassah, and in Hebrew. Just act as if she is your wife."

Hadassah objected, "Not unless he promises to raise our children Jewish."

CHAPTER 15

The Prophet

The formation of a back-up crew added momentum to the business, and by December the business had doubled. The client base kept expanding. Aisha continued to accompany David and Ben on Fridays, and Ben kept up his flirtation with her. She enjoyed being the center of attention. On Saturdays, Hadassah played her part with Ali and Yasser who learned how to respond to her teasing remarks. Both Aisha and Hadassah alternated in managing the incoming calls and the scheduling of the moving jobs.

One day when Aisha was assigned to answer the company phone a woman called to schedule a moving job from her house the following Friday. She gave her name as Sarah and her full address on the outskirts of Brooklyn. Aisha forgot to ask about her last name, and assumed that she was neither Jewish nor Arab. Hence she agreed to schedule the job on a Friday consistent with the company's policy of not serving Jewish and Arab customers on Fridays and Saturdays.

On the following Friday, as scheduled, David, Ben, and Aisha pulled in front of an old house in a secluded part of Brooklyn. The house sat on a large piece of land with no other houses around. The three of them walked to the front door and rang the bell. The door opened and a woman greeted them and introduced herself as Sarah and her thirteen-old son, who stood next to her, as Isaac. The woman was dressed in a long-sleeved dress down to her ankles and had a scarf around her head. David turned around and gave Aisha a meaningful look. His first thought was that she was an Orthodox Jew and she and her husband would soon recognize that Ben wasn't a true Arab. Aisha immediately realized her mistake and had an apologetic look on her face. In an attempt to cover up her mistake, she was first to introduce herself to Sarah, "My name is Aisha and I'm the one who talked to you on the phone."

David followed her and introduced himself, and intentionally skipped introducing Ben. The woman was oblivious to all their commotions and called her husband to come out and meet the movers.

A door opened in the back of the house and a man stepped out. David, Ben, and Aisha took one look at him, turned their heads and looked at each other as if they had seen someone from ancient times.

The man was over six feet tall and in his sixties. He was dressed in a long white robe and had a face that looked like it was carved in stone. He had long bushy, salty hair and equally bushy beard that went down to his chest. He held a long wooden staff in his right hand that reached almost to his head. The man looked as if he came out of one of the holy books.

He walked slowly toward them and welcomed them in a soft voice with his eyes focused only on Aisha, "I am Abraham."

David overcame his initial shock and introduced himself. But the man wasn't paying any attention to him and continued looking at Aisha who felt somewhat uncomfortable but intrigued by that unusual man.

Sarah asked David and Ben to follow her, and started showing them the items that needed to be moved. The man, however, stood in the same place completely detached from what his wife was doing. He kept looking at Aisha as if he saw someone he had been searching for. In a tender voice he asked her, "Did you say your name is Hagar?"

Aisha was stunned to hear that, and replied, "Excuse me? No. My name is Aisha, not Hagar."

He ignored her response and asked her to sit down with him in the family room. She started to connect those characters she'd just met. The man referred to himself as Abraham, he was dressed and acted like he were a holy man. His wife's name was Sarah, they had a teenage son named Isaac, and the man was calling her Hagar. A smile swept across her face. She didn't know whether she was with a deranged man or a very special person. But her intellectual curiosity drove her to give him the benefit of the doubt because he struck her as an interesting complex character.

As she sat looking at the man who had called her Hagar, Aisha could see the whole story of the prophet Abraham played in front of her eyes. She revisited the story in her head. *Abraham was married to Sarah and because she couldn't bear any children she asked him to marry her maid Hagar and have a child with her. They named the son Ishmael. Later, Sarah bore a child she named Isaac, and asked her husband to send Hagar and Ishmael away. He took them with him and left them (according to Muslim beliefs) in the wilderness near what is now known as Mecca in Saudi Arabia.*

Judaism, Christianity, and Islam are referred to as the Abrahamic religions because of the prominent role Abraham played in their holy books. Jews, Christians, and Muslims consider him the father of the people of the book. For Jews and Christians this is through his son Isaac by his wife Sarah, and for Muslims, he is a prophet and the ancestor of the prophet Muhammad through his other son Ishmael, born to him by Hagar.

Aisha studied the Qur'an and read the Torah, the Old Testament and the New Testament. She believed, like all Muslims do, that Abraham was the spiritual father of all the prophets and the founder of Monotheism. Her reading of the holy books confirmed her belief that God had blessed all of Abraham's descendents regardless of whether they were the descendents of Isaac or Ishmael. She'd always wondered how the descendents of one prophet could be at such odds with each other, and she was curious to hear what that strange man sitting in front of her had to say about the same subject.

Aisha listened intently as Abraham confided to her that he'd been communicating with God and that was why he'd built a sanctuary in an isolated place in the Bronx. David and Ben were loading the truck with furniture destined to his sanctuary. He asked Aisha to stay behind because he wanted to explain his mission to her. Her intellectual curiosity overcame her apprehension of being alone with a man like him, and she reluctantly agreed. Her fears were somewhat allayed by the fact that his wife and son were with them in the house.

When Aisha told David and Ben that she'd stay behind and wait for them, Ben became concerned and whispered in her ear, "Are you sure you want to be alone with these strange people?"

"Don't worry Ben, I'm a big girl." Then she added with a smile, "Listen, if I can be alone with you and David, I should be able to handle anybody."

Abraham waited until the noise of moving the furniture subsided and David and Ben had left with the truck to make the first delivery. They were scheduled to come back to move the rest of the furniture in a few hours.

Aisha was waiting with great anticipation to hear about his alleged communication with God. Abraham finally spoke in a measured and deep voice and reminded her of what God had told the prophet Abraham, quoting Genesis 12:1.3-- "Now the Lord said to Abraham, 'Go from your country and your kindred and your father's house to the land that I will show you. I will make of you a great nation, and I will bless you, and make your name great, so that you will be a blessing. I will bless those who bless you, and the ones who curse you I will curse; and in you all the families of the earth shall be blessed.'"

Then he surprised her by quoting from the Qur'an (3:25), "You are the descendents of the prophets and of the covenant that God gave to your ancestors, saying to

Abraham, 'And in your descendents all the families of the earth shall be blessed.'"

He continued his sermon-sounding quotation from the Qur'an (2:124), "And remember that Abraham was tried by his Lord with certain command which he fulfilled. He said: 'I will make thee an Imam to the nations.'"

He paused for a minute watching the perplexed look on Aisha's face before continuing.

"You see, God has blessed all Abraham's children, and through his seed, and I mean his sons Ishmael and Isaac, all the people of earth would be saved."

His eyes glimmered as he hit the floor with his staff and raised his voice to say, "My dear, Hagar, what if Ishmael and Isaac were never separated? There would have been one religion and all the Jews, the Christians, and the Muslims would have been one people."

On one hand Aisha totally agreed with his conviction that God had blessed all Abraham's descendents, but on the other hand she had no clue what his goal was. And why every time he mentioned Hagar's name did he pause and look at her. She thought that the family was part of a theater group that was practicing for a play. She wondered whether they were trying to recruit her for a role in such a play. But the more the man spoke, the more she realized that he was for real, and he meant and believed passionately in what he said. Nevertheless, Aisha wasn't the type of a person who would walk away from an intellectual or even an esoteric discussion.

In an attempt to engage him, she asked, "Do you mean that Abraham, the patriarch of the three monolithic religions, made a mistake by casting away Hagar and Ishmael?"

"Exactly," he responded with his arms raised toward the ceiling. "He shouldn't have listened to Sarah and should have raised his sons as true brothers under the same roof. That would have unified all of us who believe in the same God, and would have avoided all the wars and hostilities between the Jews, the Christians, and the Muslims. God didn't intend to have his children kill each other in his name or for his sake."

In a dramatic tone, he continued to lecture her.

"These hostilities continue today. The world has been dragged into the ancient conflict between Isaac and Ishmael in spite of its best efforts to stay out of it. This conflict that has raged between the descendents of these two half brothers for four thousand years is destined to ignite the last war of the world."

Then he paused briefly and said, "I was impressed by the name of your business, an Arab, a Jew and a Truck, because I feel that it is a first step toward bringing together two of God's peoples. But I believe that God wants all his people, Jews, Muslims, and Christians, to be unified."

Looking at him in disbelief, Aisha asked diplomatically, "But how can you reverse thousands of years of history?" and without waiting for an answer she added with a grin, "You don't have a time machine, do you?"

He ignored her sarcasm, raised his eyebrows enigmatically and declared while gazing at her, "God told me that he'd send me a special Muslim woman with whom I'll have a son. We shall name him Ishmael, and we shall raise him with our other son Isaac as blood brothers, and through them and their ancestors we shall spread the unification message."

Since Aisha was the only Muslim woman in the room, she started to feel very uncomfortable, and began to suspect that she was the target of his comments. After all, he'd addressed her as Hagar a couple of times.

She looked at him scornfully, and asked, "How does your wife, Sarah, feel about that?"

Before he could respond to her question, Sarah walked in the room with her son Isaac. She had overheard part of the conversation and hastened to answer Aisha's question, but not in a manner Aisha had hoped for.

"We've been waiting for a long time for that special woman who would bear my husband's son, Ishmael. This is God's will."

Aisha became furious.

"I'm sorry, but you two are living in a dream. You're four thousand years too late."

The wife continued in her calm and composed voice, saying, "We know, Sister, that it's a long journey. But, we must take the first step on this journey together."

"Together?" Aisha exclaimed loudly, looking around as if searching for that missing person they were referring to. She couldn't accept the fact that, in their imagination, she might be that person.

Abraham attempted to calm Aisha down, and asked his wife to bring them some tea. Sarah obediently went into the kitchen and returned a few minutes later with tea and cookies. She poured a cup of tea for Aisha and placed it in front of her. Aisha became suspicious of the tea considering the possibility they slipped something into it. The entire afternoon was becoming quite surreal. She was sitting with a couple who thought that they were communicating with God and they were looking for a special Muslim woman to impregnate, hoping to have a son they'd call Ishmael. The only Muslim woman in the room was she, and they insisted that she drink that tea. But she wasn't about to touch it. She imagined herself falling asleep and waking up pregnant with Rosemary's, or in that case, Abraham's baby!

Aisha sneaked a look at her cell phone and noticed that she had missed a couple of calls from Ben. She excused herself and asked to use the bathroom. She closed the door behind her and put her hands on her face and thought to herself. *How did I get myself into this mess. Does this man really believe what he's saying, or are they part of a cult that forces women to join them; the ones she has often read about.*

She made some desperate attempts to call Ben and David on their cell phones; but they weren't answering. *Where are they? I hope that they arrive soon and save me from these mad people.*

She fiddled around inside the bathroom, taking her time and making a few more attempts to contact David and Ben. Before leaving the bathroom, she looked at herself in the mirror and was shocked to see how pale she was. She tucked her hair completely under her headscarf. She didn't want to show anything that might arouse the so-called prophet.

When she returned to the living room and sat across from Abraham she was visibly breathless and panting. He inched forward and looked at her, "My child, are you alright?"

Sarah got up, approached her and asked with a concerned tone, "Can I bring you anything? Some cold water perhaps?"

"No No thanks." Aisha wasn't about to drink or eat anything they offered.

She was counting the minutes, hoping that David and Ben would soon appear at the door and save her from the awkward situation.

——— ——— ———

On their way to Abraham's sanctuary Ben was concerned about leaving Aisha alone with people whom he thought to be strange. He kept blaming David for allowing that to happen, and David continued to assure him that Aisha was a strong and independent woman who could easily handle those people. Ben tried to call Aisha on her cell phone several times, but that was early on in her conversation with Abraham, and she had inadvertently turned her phone off.

In the past David never took Ben's expressions of admiration for Aisha seriously. He thought that Ben's talk merely reflected an infatuation with an exotic woman. But on that day, Ben talked about his strong feelings for Aisha. David reminded Ben of the vast religious and cultural gulf between them. But Ben was dismissive of those differences. David couldn't believe that Ben, who came from an Orthodox Jewish family of settlers, and who previously had no warm feelings for Arabs in general and Palestinians in particular, was falling in love with a Muslim Palestinian woman.

On his frequent visits to his family's settlement in the West Bank, one of the main subjects he and members of his family talked about was the need to build more settlements and to push the native Palestinians to move to some of the neighboring Arab countries. They often shared their contempt of those liberal Israeli politicians who advocated the dismantling of the settlements in order to achieve peace. He never cared before about the pain and suffering of the Palestinians living in villages surrounding those settlements. Some of the villages had no electricity or running water like the Israeli settlements around them that enjoyed all the modern conveniences. To him all of them were either terrorists or terrorist sympathizers, and they all had deep hatred for Jews in general and especially for the Israelis.

However, his new experience with Ali and David's business allowed him to socialize with some of those Palestinians whom he'd previously detested. He even got along with Yasser, the conservative Muslim and somewhat radical Palestinian. When they met a second time at David's apartment they shared a few laughs and found subjects to talk about other than politics or religion.

His association with Ali and Yasser was causing a gradual moderation in his views toward Arabs and Palestinians, but it was his affection for Aisha that was stirring major shifts in his political outlook. He didn't share his new feelings with any of his Orthodox Jewish friends, or even with David. Only during the short periods of time when he was alone with Aisha in the truck and David was busy talking with clients did he express such a change.

David stopped the truck in front of the address written on a piece of paper he held in his hand. They both sat in the truck for a couple of minutes staring at the unusual building. They looked at each other and shook their heads in disbelief. David was the first to break the silence, "So, this is Mr. Abraham's sanctuary."

The building was a cubical-shaped structure without any windows, surrounded by a large empty piece of land with no neighbors in sight. The whole building was painted black. One of the diagonals of the structure faced east. Each of the four corners of the roof had an iron pole, with one displaying the Star of David, the second a cross and the third a crescent. The fourth pole in the eastern corner had all three symbols bundled together.

David and Ben got out of the truck, walked around the building, and slowly opened the front door. They both understood the meaning of all the symbols. The cubical building resembled the Ka'aba, the cubic shrine in Mecca. According to Islam, the Ka'aba was originally a shrine built around 2000 BC by the prophet Abraham, and dedicated to one God. Muslims all over the world pray five times a day facing the Ka'aba, and if they are able, they will make a Pilgrimage or hajj there, at least once in their lives.

The symbols on the three poles on the roof referred to Judaism, Christianity, and Islam, and the fourth pole in the eastern corner symbolized the unification of the three monotheistic religions.

They walked into a large room with dim ceiling lights. The walls of the room were painted white and carried quotations from the Torah, the Bible and the Qur'an. The writing on the walls was painted in colors like artwork. Spotlights, strategically located, shined on the walls and made the writings easy to read.

On one wall were quotations from Genesis 17.

"And God said, 'Sarah thy wife shall bear thee a son indeed; and thou shalt call his name Isaac, and I will establish my covenant with him for an everlasting covenant and with his seed after him.'"

"And as for Ishmael, I have heard thee: Behold, I have blessed him, and will make him fruitful, and will multiply him exceedingly; twelve princes shall he beget, and I will make him a great nation."

"And Abraham rose up early in the morning, and took bread and a bottle of water, and gave it unto Hagar, putting it on her shoulder, and the child and sent her away-----"

On another wall were quotations from the Bible:

"As for me, this is my covenant with you: You will be the father of many nations."

"I will make you very fruitful. I will make nations of you and kings will come from you."

"I will establish my covenant as an everlasting covenant between me and you and your descendents after you for generations to come, to be your God and the God of your descendents after you."

Ben and David walked around the walls reading these verses loudly, until they reached a wall that carried quotations from the Qur'an:

"when death visited Yagoub (Jacob), when he said to his sons: What will you serve after me? They said: We will serve your God and the God of your father, Ibrahim (Abraham), and Ismael (Ishmael), and Ishaq (Isaac), one God only, and to Him do we submit." (2.133)

"Say: We believe in Allah and what has been revealed to us, and what was revealed to Ibrahim and Ismael and Ishaq and Yagoub and the tribes, and what was given to Musa (Moses) and Isa (Jesus) and to the prophets from their Lord; we do not make any distinction between any of them and to Him do we submit." (3.84)

After reading a number of quotations, Ben mumbled, "Looks like this guy has a message and a mission."

David turned, looked at him, and said with slight sarcasm, "And what is this mission?"

"He may think he is a new prophet, or he may want to start a new movement that unifies all three religions."

David chuckled, "I bet Aisha and Hadassah would be very interested in talking to this man."

"Aisha is talking to him right now. He is probably telling her everything we need to know about his mission," Ben reminded David.

"You're right. I'm curious to hear her opinion. I wonder if she bought any of his ideas."

Ben went back to read more of what was written on the walls in an attempt to understand Abraham's goal. He finally realized what that Brooklyn man was after. He selected quotations to highlight a message, always missed by most adherents of the three religions, that God had established his covenant with Abraham and for all his descendents whether they were the descendents of Isaac or of Ishmael. This man's mission was to make Jews, Christians, and Muslims reexamine why each of them was striving for the sole ownership of the one God they all believe in.

David pulled Ben away from the walls to get him to start unloading the truck. They followed the instructions given to them by Sarah. They finally figured out the use of the wood seating benches they had on the truck. They lined them up in rows facing a small podium. When seated, everyone in the audience would be facing east and facing the building's corner that symbolized the unification of the three religions.

As they moved the benches around, Ben wandered to one of the walls to read some of the quotations again. David, on the other hand, was focused on placing each item according to the floor plan given to them, and ceased to pay attention to the writings. He kept urging Ben to move faster and reminded him that they had one extra load to bring to the sanctuary before sundown. When he mentioned to Ben that they had left Aisha alone in that house he started moving faster and pulled himself away from the scripture on the walls.

As they drove the truck back, Ben whispered, "I don't think he is a strange man. He is trying to make all of us stop and think about the parallelism between the three monotheistic religions."

David looked at him in disbelief. He never expected such a statement from Ben who always talked about Judaism as if it were God's only religion and about Jews being God's chosen people.

When they got closer to the house they received a call from Aisha. Ben quickly picked up the phone.

"Where the hell are you guys?" whispered Aisha in a frantic voice, "I had to go to the bathroom four times to be able to call you. Please come quickly, I feel very uncomfortable here."

"Are you okay?" Ben asked with concern.

"So far, yes," Aisha replied, her mouth touching the speaker of the phone, and placing her other hand around her mouth to muffle the sound.

"Really. Please come quickly."

"We're only a few minutes from you," Ben said in a tender voice trying to comfort her. As soon as he hung up, he turned to David, "Please step on it, I'm worried about her. She sounds frightened."

The truck pulled in front of the door. Aisha heard the noise of the engine. She immediately stood up and rushed toward the front door. She opened the door and walked to the truck. When she felt far enough from the ears of Abraham and Sara, she asked in a reprimanding tone, "Why did it take you so long? Those were the longest three hours of my life. I really don't understand who these people are, but you're not going to believe what they wanted from me!"

David and Ben noticed that she'd been traumatized. Her face was slightly pale and her hands were shaking.

Ben put his arm around her shoulder and squeezed it tenderly, "He isn't a bad man and I'm sure he wouldn't harm you in any way. I think he believes that he has a message. If you'd seen his sanctuary, you'd change your mind about him."

But Aisha wasn't moved by his argument. She told them about him calling her Hagar and that God wanted him to have a second son that he'd name Ishmael and raise him with his son Isaac, and his dream of reversing thousands of years of animosity between Jews, Christians, and Muslims.

With a muffled laugh, David said, "But Aisha, I thought you'd be receptive to his ideas. You should share this story with Hadassah; I bet the two of you could be his first disciples."

Aisha was still freaked out, but mustered a faint smile and said, "I'm all for eliminating animosities between Jews, Christians, and Muslims. But I'm not ready to be impregnated by some aging man to spread his message."

Ben took her hand and went inside the house followed by David. Abraham and Sarah were still sitting in the front room. Sarah offered Ben and David some of the tea and the cookies sitting on the table and they gladly accepted. They sat on the sofa across from Abraham and Sarah and were about to take the first sip of their tea when Aisha tried to attract their attention and give them warning signals not to drink the tea or eat the cookies. She regretted that she'd not mentioned to them her fear of the tea when she was outside the house.

But they were oblivious to her warning looks and drank the tea and ate the cookies while thanking Sarah and complimenting her on her baking skills. When she realized that her signals didn't work, Aisha stood up and walked slowly toward the front door and placed herself in a position to open the door and run in case the two of them became unconscious. But there was no place for her to run to. There were no neighbors in sight, and she wouldn't be able to drive the truck.

She yelled at David and Ben, attempting to distract them from drinking the tea, "Let's move the rest of the stuff, it's getting late."

David turned his head and saw Aisha standing at the door, "Please Aisha, let us relax for a few minutes, we've been working hard for several hours. These cookies are delicious, come and have some."

"Come, my child, and sit down," Abraham addressed her, then leaned toward David and Ben, "And what do you think, my children, of my sanctuary?"

Ben was anxious to engage Abraham in a conversation.

"I was very impressed by the quotations you have on the walls from the three holy books and how they all agree on the role Abraham played in their religions."

"You know, Ben, I'll repeat to you what I told Hagar, I mean Aisha, earlier. The world has been dragged into the ancient conflict between Isaac and Ishmael for four thousand years. Ishmael and Isaac have their father's blood, the blood of Abraham, the father of all prophets. This conflict shouldn't be used as a pretext to destroy the world."

David and Ben turned around and looked at Aisha when they heard him mention Hagar, waiting for her to question Abraham, or respond to him. But she remained silent, and was still standing at the front door. She listened to the conversation and expected that David and Ben would any minute collapse on the sofa. But minutes went by and nothing happened. She thought. *Was I wrong in suspecting this man and not drinking his tea? I bet David and Ben will tease me about this story, and will tell Hadassah how frightened I was.*

She trudged back toward the sofa where Ben and David were sitting looking at their faces and their eyes, searching for any signs of blurriness or dizziness. But they both looked normal, even energized after a short rest and a cup of tea.

David, feeling that Aisha was eager to leave, got up and said, "We better get going; we have another truckload to carry."

David and Ben loaded the truck with the rest of the wooden benches and were about to leave when Abraham stood up and shook hands with all of them, "Please bring your friends and come and visit us at our sanctuary."

Sarah approached Aisha, kissed her on the cheek, "Please come and see us again."

On the way back to the sanctuary Aisha was silent. She kept thinking about the last few hours and her fear of Abraham and Sarah. Ben put his arm around her shoulder and touched her face tenderly, trying to break her thoughts. She pulled her head back. She wasn't used to having men other than her immediate family touch her face. But she realized the irrationality of her reactive move and looked slightly embarrassed. Ben noticed and understood her reaction. He tried to comfort her with his words instead.

"I don't think they're bad people, Aisha. You and I may not agree with them, but they have their own beliefs."

Aisha was surprised by Ben's tone of reconciliation. She always thought of herself and Hadassah as the ones who stood apart from Ben, David, Ali, and Yasser when it came to moderation. She wondered to herself. *What is happening with Ben? Is he trying to join the Hadassah-Aisha camp?* What she didn't realize was that Ben's feelings for her were the main factor behind the apparent change in his views.

When they arrived at the sanctuary, Ben took Aisha around the building pointing out the religious symbols on the roof. Then he took her inside and walked around the various walls reading aloud the quotations from the holy books. He stood in front of the wall that had the verses from the Qur'an and said, "I have to admit that I've not known before that the Qur'an acknowledges Abraham, Isaac, Jacob, Moses, and Jesus as God's prophets. I always thought that Muslims only recognize Muhammad as God's prophet."

"Muslims believe in all the prophets and that Muhammad was God's last one. We even mention their names, particularly those of Abraham and Muhammad, in our prayers."

Then she added, "You can see that our friend's focus was on the story of Abraham and he chose verses from the holy books that are not inconsistent on that subject. But he doesn't include verses that address who the son Abraham was ready to sacrifice. Was it Isaac as the Jews and Christians believe, or was it Ishmael as Muslims believe?"

As they walked around the sanctuary chatting, they felt a certain degree of closeness. David, while busy arranging the wooden benches inside the hall of the sanctuary, observed the ease with which Aisha and Ben talked about their religions and their interpretations of the quotations on the walls.

When they were driving home David was quiet, but Ben and Aisha never stopped talking and teasing each other. It looked like a new phase was about to begin in their relationship.

CHAPTER 16

Growing Affection

When they were not working with each other on the truck on Fridays, Ben called Aisha at least twice a day. In the beginning he felt he had to make an excuse to call her. He'd always start with a question about the meaning of an Arabic word or about a recipe of a Middle Eastern dish. Gradually he didn't have to find an excuse to call her. He just called to chat with her about a variety of subjects. Aisha was flattered by his interest, but couldn't understand what he was really after. They were a world apart in their religious, political, and cultural views and upbringing. But in spite of those differences there was a mysterious pull that attracted them to each other. It was easier to explain in Ben's case. Aisha was an attractive woman who could be noticed in spite of her covered hair and body. In addition, she was an educated woman, had an excellent general knowledge and could intelligently discuss almost any subject.

It wasn't as easy to explain her attraction to Ben. He wasn't particularly handsome. His political views, when it came to Palestinian rights and their aspiration for a homeland were, in Aisha's opinion, deplorable. His family was among the most ardent settlers that opposed any effort by the Israeli government to make concessions to the Palestinians. They were among those people who constantly referred to the Palestinian territory by its biblical name of Judea and Samaria. But Aisha could sense a gentle and sensitive side under his apparent political and religious rigidity.

Furthermore, he had a good sense of humor that appealed to Aisha. She laughed every time he imitated an Israeli or Arabic accent, or when he described a heated argument between an Israeli and a Palestinian.

Gradually Aisha waited with anticipation for Ben's phone calls or for Fridays when they worked on the truck together. David was amazed to hear the two of them picking up a subject and talking about it as if they were continuing a discussion that had started hours before. He had no idea that they were in contact by phone on a daily basis.

Any other man and woman who enjoyed each other's conversation to the degree Ben and Aisha did would have been intimate lovers. But they were held back, not only by their political and cultural differences, but also by their rigid adherence to their own religions.

Aisha often shared with Hadassah her conversations with Ben, and her impression of his apparent interest in her. Hadassah was puzzled and also fascinated by Ben's interest. She thought of him as ultra orthodox and was familiar with his negative views of Arabs and Palestinians. But she encouraged Aisha to pursue the friendship even though she was confident that Aisha would eventually marry a Muslim. She convinced her that such a relationship would be the best way to moderate a man like Ben. She once playfully told Aisha, "Just imagine what a moderating influence I'd have on someone like Yasser if he'd fall in love with me."

Hadassah was the only person with whom Aisha shared her friendship with Ben, and she assured Aisha that she'd keep it a secret. But Aisha always felt that David had an idea of what was going on judging by his expressions when she and Ben were sitting in the truck laughing and teasing each other.

Aisha never shared Ben's friendship with her cousin Ali or their conservative Muslim friend Yasser. She was certain that they'd be shocked and wouldn't accept such a friendship outside the work environment. An ultra Orthodox Jew with a religious Muslim woman would shock anybody, but would drive those two Palestinians insane.

Aisha didn't think of herself as Juliet or West Side Story Maria. She was only having an innocent friendship with someone who happened to be from the so-called "other camp," not any different, in her view, from the friendship between Ali and David.

One day Ben, while talking to her on the phone, collected his courage and asked her, "Would you like to go out to dinner one night this week?"

Aisha was slightly shocked by the question. Several seconds went by before she responded. She knew that Ben, like David, ate only kosher food, which meant that they'd have to go to a kosher restaurant. She didn't mind kosher food, but she remembered her experience in a kosher restaurant with David and Hadassah and the nasty waitress and the stares by the people eating in the restaurant. This time it would be worse. She pictured herself with her hijab and long dress sitting alone in a corner with an Orthodox Jew. She was certain that the stares would be more intense. She also was concerned that one of her Arab friends would see her with Ben and tell Ali or Yasser. They would probably cut all their ties with her and never speak to her again.

But Aisha was a strong-minded and independent girl. She quickly assessed all the undesirable consequences and concluded that it'd be stupid and narrow-minded if she refused to go to dinner with him.

Ben, waiting on the other end of the line, was anxious for her response. The few seconds felt like hours. He thought *maybe I shouldn't have asked her alone. Maybe I should have asked her with David and Hadassah the first time. But, maybe she didn't want them to know.*

Aisha interrupted his thoughts, "Sure, I'd love to go to dinner. Kosher restaurant of course?"

"Yes, if you don't mind."

"I don't mind at all. As a matter of fact I like kosher food. But before we go, you'll have to admit to one thing."

"What?" Ben asked in a tone that reflected his concern.

"You'd have to admit that falafel was originally an Arab dish before it was adopted by the Israelis."

With a sigh of relief, Ben quickly answered, "I do, I do."

Aisha was pleased that Ben had selected a kosher restaurant far from the neighborhood where David and Ali lived. Although she never expressed her concern, he understood her apprehension about being seen having dinner alone with him. Likewise, he didn't want to run into one of his circle of friends from the synagogue.

Ben selected a table in a corner of the restaurant and sat with his back to the rest of the tables in an attempt to partially block other diners' view of Aisha.

It was a night in the middle of the week, and the restaurant wasn't busy. The waitress was friendly, unlike the one who'd served her with David and Hadassah. The stares by the people eating in the restaurant, however, were more intense. One couldn't blame them for staring, because it was an unusual sight, even in New York City. An attractive Arab woman wearing her hijab was eating dinner in a kosher restaurant alone with an Orthodox Jew with a long beard and wearing a yarmulke.

They ordered their food, ignored the stares that were piercing Ben's back, and continued talking as if they were sitting in the truck or they were on the phone. Aisha leaned forward and whispered, "You know, I'd feel a lot more comfortable having dinner with you in a restaurant in Israel or even in the West Bank than here. I can't understand that, after all, this is the United States of America that boasts to be a melting pot of all races and religions."

Ben tried to comfort her, "Remember you're sitting with someone like me in a kosher restaurant frequented by religious Jews."

But Aisha interrupted him, "I bet you we'd get the same stares and more if we walked down Fifth Avenue."

Ben nodded in agreement.

They were both startled by a cheering voice from behind, "My goodness, I never expected to see the two of you here together."

Ben spun around with surprise and Aisha looked startled. It was Dorothy walking toward them. She had met them a few times with Ali and David in her building, but she was the last person on earth they had expected to run into at that restaurant. They didn't know that Dorothy had many Jewish friends, and she was invited to dinner by one of them. They greeted her warmly as she introduced her lady friend.

"Is anyone else from the gang joining you?" Dorothy asked.

"No, this is our evening off from the moving business," muttered Ben.

Aisha's brain raced because she knew how close Dorothy and Ali were. *Would she run and tell him? And if she did, would Ali be outraged? For God's sake, he is my cousin, not my husband. His partner in their successful business is as Jewish as Ben, and Ali is having an affair with a Christian woman. He has no moral or religious grounds to object to or to even frown on my friendship with Ben.*

Aisha felt relaxed and continued to chat with Dorothy and her friend until the waitress escorted them to their own table.

Dorothy couldn't help stretching her neck once in a while to look at them to see how they were talking to each other. She was hoping to see them holding hands or displaying some affection. But they acted properly as though they were having a business dinner.

Dorothy's friend immediately asked as they sat down, "How on earth did those two get together?"

Dorothy boasted, "You know, I feel that I've been an ambassador for peace in the Middle East."

"And how did you accomplish that?" her friend asked. She had no idea what Dorothy was talking about.

"You remember the business called an Arab, a Jew and a Truck I helped establish? That business has done wonders in developing friendships between two groups of antagonists, the Palestinians and the Jews. Ali, a Palestinian Muslim and David, an Orthodox Jew, who are roommates in my building, have become business partners and good friends. And now, look, a Muslim Palestinian woman is on a date and having a kosher dinner with an Ultra Orthodox Jew. I think this is a miracle."

Her friend agreed, "It shows how business can help normalize relations between enemies. I hope those people in the Middle East would learn from that."

"Amen," Dorothy sighed.

Aisha and Ben finished their dinner, said goodbye to Dorothy and her friend and left the restaurant. They chatted as they walked toward Aisha's apartment, not paying attention to some of the people who turned around and looked at them in utter amazement. As they got closer to Aisha's apartment building, the street was dark and empty. Ben reached out and held her hand. She acquiesced until they were in front of her building, then she gently pulled her hand away. She shook hands with Ben.

"Thank you Ben, I enjoyed this evening very much."

Ben looked at her fondly and said, "If I admit that Tabouleh is an Arab and not a Jewish dish, would you have dinner with me again?"

Aisha laughed, "It's a deal."

CHAPTER 17

Bonding in the Face of Bigotry

Ali and David's business was booming after nearly half a year. They were booked seven days a week, and had to turn down few jobs. They were working six days a week while Ben and Yasser were filling in on Fridays and Saturdays, respectively. They were the favorite moving company among the Jewish and Arab communities in New York City and all the surrounding areas. Gradually they were getting more and more customers from other minority groups as well as from white people. They felt that they had reached another milestone in their business and they needed to expand. One obvious way was to add a second truck and another crew. But they were determined to maintain the image of the business as "An Arab, a Jew, and a Truck." Their obvious choice for the second crew was Ben and Yasser.

They were well aware of the shortcomings of a crew composed of Ben and Yasser. Both of them were dogmatic. They weren't sure that the two of them could work together on the same truck without getting into heated arguments, and possible fights.

But they underestimated the positive impact their business had had on Yasser and Ben. The two of them felt that they were an integral part of that business and that they were contributing to its success. They were eager to continue, and possibly expand, their roles in the business. Furthermore, and unbeknownst to Ali and David, there was the Aisha factor. Ben's new friendship with her had softened him and started to moderate his views. As for Yasser, he had the opportunity to be on the truck with Hadassah every Saturday, and was constantly exposed to her charming manner that also had a positive influence on him. He became more sociable and more capable of conducting a conversation without a constant reference to Israel and Palestinian rights, or to Muslims and Jews.

Ali and David discussed their proposal with Ben and Yasser before making a commitment to purchase their second truck. The plan was for them to work the second truck Mondays through Thursdays. On Fridays, Ben would continue working with David as his Arab counterpart, and on Saturdays Yasser would go on posing with Ali as the Jewish partner.

Both of them readily accepted the offer. Ben wasn't happy with his part-time job as a telemarketer and was eager to get more involved in the business as a way to get closer to Aisha. For Yasser, the money was good and even better than any other job he ever had. But he had to drop a couple of his classes to accommodate the new schedule.

The back-up crew consisting of Ben and Yasser provided an opportunity for the business to increase its profit, but posed a problem for Aisha and Hadassah, the scheduling agents. They had to be constantly reminded that Yasser was an Arab Mondays through Thursdays but a Jew on Saturdays, and Ben was a Jew Mondays through Thursdays and an Arab on Fridays. Therefore, the schedules of the main crew and the back-up crew had to be separately maintained and could never be mixed up. The last thing any member of the staff wanted was for Ben and Yasser to appear at a repeat customer who saw either of them working with David or Ali and pretending they were someone else. The business image would suffer greatly, if an old customer of the main crew saw Yasser without his yarmulke and speaking Arabic instead of Hebrew, or Ben without his traditional Muslim head cover and speaking Yiddish instead of Arabic.

A new truck was purchased and a new phase of the business began. This time they didn't need Dorothy to cosign the loan. They had established a good business track record and saved enough money for the down payment. The bank was willing to give them a loan to purchase the truck on favorable terms.

Ben and Yasser were on their way to their first assignment. A woman named Betty Lou called Aisha and scheduled the move. She was crying on the phone and a man was yelling and swearing in the background. They both sensed that that job wasn't going to be an easy one.

They arrived at a house in the outer corners of the Bronx. It was a neighborhood full of poorly maintained houses with yards full of overgrown weeds. There were empty beer cans everywhere, and an old pick-up truck was parked in front of the house. The hood and one door were a different color from the rest of the truck, and the rear tires were twice as wide as the front ones. A rusted old refrigerator with its door opened, leaned against the side of the dilapidated house.

They parked behind the pick-up truck and walked to the locked screen door. They could hear the yelling of a couple inside in spite of the roaring sound of an old window air-conditioning unit. There was no bell to ring. Ben kept knocking on the aluminum side of the screen door and shouting, "Hello, hello." Finally a woman came and unlocked the screen door, "Hello, I'm Betty Lou. I'm the one who called you. I'm the one moving out of this dump."

She was a white woman in her early forties. Her face showed the remnants of an early beauty that had been washed out by years of neglect, like the houses and the lawns around her. She was bursting everywhere out of her clothes, and wore shorts and a halter-top displaying a large tattoo on her flabby stomach.

Right behind her was a man dressed in a sleeveless t-shirt and a pair of blue jeans that hung down low on his hip. His life story was written on his arms that were covered with tattoos. Holding a beer in one hand, he kept yelling at her, "Y'ain't going nowhere. You'll be back by sundown."

"In your dreams," she yelled back.

The man walked behind her through the screen door, took one look at the moving truck and started laughing, "Hey woman, couldn't ya even find a God lovin' Christian moving company?"

He turned to Ben and Yasser, and started singing out of tune, "Your name is A-hab, you're an A-rab, the chief of the desert sand."

Yasser, a newcomer to the United States, looked at Ben for clues. He was seeking his help in understanding what was going on. Ben had figured out the situation and concluded that they were in a redneck neighborhood facing one of those bigoted hillbillies. Ben gave Yasser a look urging him to be quiet.

Ben ignored the man and addressed Betty Lou, "Ma'am what do you want us to move?"

Before she could answer, the man asked in a mocking voice, "Who is the Jew among you? I bet he's the one dealing with the money."

Betty Lou yelled back at him, "Why don't you shut up and mind your own business."

Ben and Yasser were getting impatient. Ben turned to the man, gave him a stern look, and said, "Sir, the lady called us to come here to do a job. We quoted her a price and the longer we stay here talking to you the more expensive it will get."

The man ignored Ben's serious voice, pulled out his pocketknife and started using it as a toothpick. He was obviously trying to intimidate them, "Ya mind if I ask ya what a Jew and an A-rab are doin' in the movin' business? I bet the two of you can't even lift a sofa."

Betty Lou walked inside the house to diffuse the situation and the man, whom she addressed as Bud, followed her. He kept talking to her in a loud voice that Ben and Yasser could hear.

"You're a stupid woman. Couldn't you hire the good Christian people from our church, Smyth Brothers, to move you? What are you doin' with those god damn foreign people?"

"Smyth Brothers were booked for at least one week, and I want to get the hell out of this place and move far away from you," she yelled back.

Ben and Yasser were amused to find themselves lumped together and referred to, either out of ignorance or bigotry or both, as *foreigners*. In an instant Ben and Yasser weren't in opposite camps, but had to unite and pull together to face such a hostile man. It made no difference to Bud that Ben looked American and spoke English without an accent. He didn't differentiate between them. They both weren't white Christian guys like the ones he hung around with.

The confrontation with Bud made Yasser feel closer to Ben. He realized his life would be far better off with someone like Ben than with a man like Bud. The political differences that separated them a few hours before seemed to pale in comparison with the deeply rooted bigotry displayed by Bud.

Likewise, Ben felt the same. He was facing a fellow American who couldn't differentiate between him and Yasser, a foreign student who had been in the country only a short time, and spoke English with a heavy accent.

Ben saw Yasser's irate face and signaled him to ignore Bud and start loading the furniture into the truck. In the meantime, Betty Lou made an attempt to keep Bud busy and away from them.

They worked fast loading the truck. They wanted to leave Bud's place as soon as possible to avoid any trouble. That was their first day on the new truck, and they wanted to make a good impression on their bosses. Betty Lou was equally anxious to leave with them. When they were about to get in the truck, Bud came out of the house, and with a smirk on his face, said, "I bet you two're illegal aliens."

Ben snapped back, "Listen man, I'm as American, and maybe more so, than you are."

Bud wasn't moved, "No, you ain't. First you killed our Lord, and second, you're hangin' around with a terrorist."

Yasser was about to snap. He clenched his fists and turned around. Bud pulled his pocket knife and waived it in the air, "Come on you fuckin A-rab, do you want me to slit your throat like you guys do back home?"

Ben jumped, pulled Yasser's arm and pushed him toward the truck while Betty Lou screamed at Bud, "Why don't you leave these people alone? Please get inside the house and let us all leave in peace!"

She jumped in the truck, pulled Yasser inside and Ben got behind the wheel and drove away hearing Bud ranting in front of the house. She sat in the front seat of the truck between them. They were all quiet for a few minutes trying to get over Bud's hostility when Betty Lou broke the silence.

"I'm sorry, fellows; I didn't mean to put you through all this trouble. I'd have used Smyth Brothers, but they weren't available. I know Bud is mad because he knows the owners who are respectable members of our church."

Yasser and Ben didn't immediately respond. They had already overheard Bud questioning her about why she hadn't called Smyth Brothers instead of them. They knew that moving company was one of their chief competitors. They frequently heard Ali and David mentioning the fact that they had several moving trucks and they were serving the same geographical areas. Ali and David were pleased that they were attracting some of Smyth Brothers' customers and gaining a sizable portion of their market share.

Smyth Brothers Moving Company was a family owned business started by Robert Smyth over fifty years ago, and was inherited by the three Smyth grandsons. All three were Evangelists and active in their Baptist church. They were politically right-wing conservative. Bud and Betty Lou were members of the same church. Ben had heard their advertisements on the radio that were part business and part preaching. They always mixed their business with religion and ended their advertisements with some religious slogans such as, "We're delighted in the love of God the father, Jesus the son, and the gentle Holy Spirit. We want to share with you."

Some other times they'd end their ad with a Bible quotation, "Believe in the Lord Jesus, and you will be saved. You and your household."

They always tried to spread the word that they were followers of Jesus Christ and shared with their audience how, through the acceptance of Jesus, they experienced joy every day, even in the midst of the trials of their difficult business. Their message resonated with some people even in the secular New York Metropolitan area. Their business expanded over the years and they became the dominant moving company in the area. But a small emerging company named "An Arab, A Jew and A Truck" was slowly encroaching on their business territory and they were well aware of it.

After a long pause, Yasser asked Betty Lou, "Is Bud your husband?"

"Unfortunately, yes. I was young and stupid when I met him. I should have walked out a long time ago," she sighed.

"How can a nice lady like you be married to a guy like that?" Yasser asked, shaking his head, baffled.

Betty Lou didn't respond, but a tear ran down her cheek. Ben sat quietly; he didn't want to further embarrass her.

After they finished unloading the furniture at Betty Lou's sister house, Ben asked Yasser whether he wanted to stop for a cup of coffee. Yasser eagerly accepted. He was still fuming over Bud's insults and was anxious to hear Ben's views.

While sipping his coffee, Yasser said, "Let me summarize what I understand about our experience today. This hostile crazy man Bud is a member of the congregation of an Evangelical Baptist church. Our famous competitors, the Smyth Brothers, are members of the same church. Does this mean that they're also bigoted and they hate Jews and all foreigners?"

"Not at all," Ben tried to explain to Yasser.

"Bud is a stupid, ignorant bigot. Yes, he belongs to the same church, but I doubt that he understands what true

157

Evangelism is. Look at Betty Lou; she goes to the same church and she is a very different person. Admittedly, some Evangelists are very conservative politically, and some of them may hate Blacks, Jews, Arabs, Hispanics, and anyone of color. But most of them are rational people who obey the law and are good citizens."

"Hate the Jews?" Yasser exclaimed in disbelief, "I know that Evangelists are the most ardent supporters of Israel, and many of them are against the establishment of a Palestinian state."

"Yes, you're right. But their support of Israel is based on the grounds that the creation and preservation of a Jewish state is a prelude to Armageddon which is the site of a battle during the end of times that will pave the way for the Second Coming of Jesus Christ."

Yasser interrupted him, "Armageddon? That sounds like a Hebrew word. Where is this Armageddon?"

"Yes, it's actually Hebrew for the mount of Megiddo in Israel."

"And what is the role of the Israelis in this Armageddon?" Yasser asked in a mocking tone.

"Some Christians believe that the establishment of a Jewish state is a prerequisite for Armageddon, and they hope for the world to fall apart because Jesus can't come back unless it does. According to them, Christians will escape the worst of it. But, in order for Christians to escape death, most Jews in Israel must perish unless they convert to Christianity. And this may be the main reason behind their support of Israel."

"My goodness, and what will happen to the Muslims during Armageddon?"

"In the bible, Armageddon is the battle between the forces of good and evil that is predicted to mark the end of the world and precede the Day of Judgment. I hate to tell you, Yasser, I have a feeling that the Muslims may be considered by some to be part of the forces of evil."

"Are you telling me that according to the Evangelists the Muslims and many of the Jews will perish to save the Christians?"

"Yes, Yasser, unless they convert to Christianity and accept Jesus Chris! That is my understanding."

"Why in the hell are we fighting each other?" Yasser exclaimed with a loud laughter, "Let us unite against them."

"I'm all for unity, but I don't want to mislead you. Please understand that I'm talking about a small number of Evangelists. The majority of Evangelists and most Christians don't subscribe to the same beliefs, and believe that Muslims, like Jews, are the children of Abraham." Ben clarified.

"Thank you, Ben, that sounds much better. Now I feel I've a chance to go to paradise and be with you and other good Christians," Yasser responded with a chuckle.

They left the coffee shop with Yasser placing his hand on Ben's shoulder; an Arabic gesture of friendship.

Chapter 18

Unfulfilled Dreams

Ali visited his favorite Middle Eastern grocery store, El-Kebir, in Queens on a Friday afternoon to buy some baklava that became Dorothy's favorite dessert. He was with a group of his Palestinian friends who knew the owner, Mahmoud Abd El-Kader, an Egyptian immigrant. Ali had never talked to him before but learned from his friends that he was a follower of the strict Salafist school of Islam that advocates a society rooted in Islamic law and scripture, and aspires to returning Islam to its purest roots. Ali, though a devout Muslim, never subscribed to that rigid form of Islam. Some of Ali's friends knew about Mahmoud's life story and how he ended up owning a grocery store. He grew up in a large family of eight children in a small village in the Nile Delta north of Cairo. His father, a schoolteacher, instilled in him the teachings of Islam and inspired him to study and memorize the Qur'an. From a young age and through his high school years he admired the Muslim Brotherhood, but never joined the organization. However, when he left the village to study at Cairo University, he started to participate in some of the Brotherhood's meetings. They rapidly disillusioned him because of their emphasis on political issues that, in his mind, deviated from the pure Islamic teachings. He became more attracted to a small group of students who called themselves Salafis, and joined their organization. From that point on, Mahmoud became a zealous member of the organization.

Some of the people in the Arab community in Mahmoud's neighborhood felt sorry for him, because running a grocery store in Queens was not his childhood dream. After graduating from Cairo University with a bachelor's degree in science, his dream was to marry the daughter of the mayor of his village and become a science teacher. Her beauty was the talk of the village. Throughout his high school and college years, he dreamt of the day he would graduate and be in a position to approach her father and ask for his approval to marry her. He shared his dream with his mother who always assured him that the mayor would be honored to have him as his son-in-law. But when the day came, Mahmoud was crushed when the mayor told him that he had sworn on the Qur'an not to permit his daughter to marry anyone except a medical doctor. Determined and undeterred as he was, Mahmoud assured the father that he would get a medical degree from the best school in America, and would be back to ask for her hand.

With that in mind, Mahmoud left his family, his village and his Egyptian Salafi friends and came to the U.S. to get his medical degree. He settled in Queens because he had a distant relative living there, and applied to various medical schools. His heart bled every time he received a rejection and felt that the whole world was conspiring against him to prevent him from marrying the girl of his dreams. Several years went by and his determination gave way to despair until he finally gave up completely. The final blow came when he received a letter from his family telling him that his dream girl was about to marry a doctor. He swore never to go back and show his face to the mayor or to his friends in the village.

His medical dreams were replaced by a desire to make a decent and honest living, and that led him to open a Middle Eastern grocery store.

During his time in Queens he joined a small mosque in his neighborhood that was attended by a small group of Salafis. He became immersed in his religion and his store. The daily prayers were the only activity that interrupted his work at the store. Every evening he went to the mosque to pray with a small group of like-minded Salafis. Afterwards they would sit down together to discuss some aspects of their religion or to share their thoughts about some newspaper article that equated Salafism and radicalism. They often shared their disappointment over those journalists' lack of knowledge of true Salafists and their beliefs. Although they were zealous in their views and doctrinally rigid, they were basically peaceful people.

Mahmoud was the only single man among his group of Salafi friends and they often advised him to get married and have a family in order to be a complete person under the Islamic tradition. But the only way for someone like him to find a wife was through an arranged marriage. And he was reluctant to ask his family for help after the humiliation he had received from his own village.

One of his Salafi friends came to him one day with the good news. He knew of a nice Muslim Palestinian girl from the West Bank who could be the ideal wife for him. She grew up in a conservative Muslim family and would not object to resettling in the U.S.

Pushed by his mosque friends, Mahmoud traveled to the West Bank to meet his future wife and her family. Her name was Zena. She was a voluptuous, attractive girl in her early twenties, nearly ten years younger than he. She grew up in a conservative Muslim family as Mahmoud's friends had told him. She covered her hair and wore the usual long dresses, but mainly to please her father who was a devout Muslim. Other than that, and unbeknownst to Mahmoud, she was a Muslim in name only. Zena always dreamt of leaving the West Bank and all its problems and living in America where she would enjoy the luxury and pleasures she often had seen on TV and in the movies. Mahmoud provided her the ticket to fulfill those dreams.

Ali's Palestinian friends told him that when Mahmoud first met Zena, in the presence of her father, mother, brothers and sisters, he was impressed by her looks and the graceful way she walked and sat down in front of him. Mahmoud's looks and demeanor, on the other hand, disappointed Zena. He had a long beard and a thick mustache that overwhelmed his face. The prayer mark on his forehead and the prayer beads moving slowly through his fingers mirrored the religious house she was trying to escape from. Furthermore, he acted awkwardly in the presence of her family, often looking the other way when he addressed any of her sisters. Her parents, however, were impressed by his religious appearance and his business credentials. They felt that such a man could provide a good home and a comfortable life for their daughter and they were eager to approve him as her future husband.

Under pressure from her parents and driven by her desire to leave her village and her dull life in the West Bank and emigrate to the United States, Zena agreed to marry Mahmoud.

During the first few months of her marriage Zena was excited by her new life in the United States. She had a comfortable house in Queens, she enjoyed going to the supermarket around the corner, and spent most of her days watching her favorite TV soaps. But she was mostly alone. Her husband spent all day at his store. Afterwards, he went to the mosque to pray with his Salafi friends and came home late in the evening. Sometimes she was sound asleep when he came home and she had to leave his dinner on the dining table.

Zena was happy to learn from her family about Aisha who came from a nearby town in the West Bank. She was thrilled to find another woman from back home with whom she could talk and share her new experience. They called each other and Aisha visited her a few times. But Zena, unlike Aisha, was not a well-educated girl, and had no interest in political or social issues. Her favorite subject was TV soaps and what transpired in the latest episodes. Aisha was totally uninterested in such a subject. Between her school schedule and her work in Ali and David's business she had little time for Zena's trivial conversations. But, in

163

spite of that, Aisha continued to be cordial and friendly to her.

Zena had no other friends in the US. She hated the wives of Mahmoud's Salafi friends. They were a lot older and too religious for her to bear. They only wanted to talk about religion, cooking, and children, and none of those subjects interested her. After a few months, the initial excitement of a new life in America wore off, and Zena's loneliness affected her relationship with her husband. In addition, Mahmoud started having some heart ailments. He was advised by his doctor to reduce his work schedule, and to consult a heart specialist. But he never listened to his doctor, and Zena was growing impatient with his obstinacy.

One morning she got dressed and as her husband was about to leave the house she said, "Wait Mahmoud, I'm coming with you to the store."

He stood in the doorway shocked to hear that.

"You know you can't come to the store, what would you do there?"

"I'll help you with the customers. I'm sure I can operate the cash register. I can also help you with stocking the shelves. You need help. Remember what the doctor said?"

"Are you crazy? What would the people say? My wife is talking and chatting with strange men in the store. My friends from the mosque wouldn't speak to me if they saw you there."

"I don't care about your Salafi friends. I'm going out of my mind staying home alone. I'm coming and that is final."

Mahmoud was stunned by the determination in her voice, and he finally submitted to her demand. He heard in her voice a desperation he was yet unfamiliar with, but the conviction with which she spoke suggested he abide by her demands or things could go bad between them.

In the first few days he was uncomfortable seeing her at the store, constantly looking around to make sure that she was not speaking to any male customers. But he soon found out that she was helpful to him. Gradually he allowed her to stay alone while he went to the mosque for the noon Friday prayers. When she was alone in the store she enjoyed talking to male customers and was free to exercise the long-hidden flirtatious side of her personality.

Mahmoud was about to hire a moving company to transfer products from a warehouse in New Jersey to his store when Zena suggested An Arab, A Jew and A Truck. She had often heard about that business from her friend Aisha. Her husband ignored her and mumbled, "Who is this Arab fool?"

"He is a Palestinian from a town near us and he is Aisha's cousin."

"I still think he's a fool. Hasn't he yet learned what Jews will do to him? This Jew partner of his will soon take over the business and throw him out."

"This isn't true. My friend, Aisha, tells me that his partner David is a good person, and that they have a popular and successful business."

"Oh come on, Zena, you Palestinians are all naïve. No wonder you lost your homeland."

"Wait a minute Mr. Abd El-Kader, it was you Egyptians and your President Gamal Abd El-Nasser who in 1967 created the mess we're in today."

"Egyptians created the current mess? Thousands of our children died to defend the Palestinians and to help them regain their homeland. The Egyptian economy was ruined in that fight. And you tell me that we're responsible for your tragedy? Go and talk to that Palestinian who is partnering with a Jew. He and those like him who sold their land to the Israelis are the ones behind the current mess!"

Mahmoud suddenly realized that he might have hurt Zena's feelings when he noticed her teary eyes. He abruptly changed the tone of his voice, patted her on the back and smiled, "Ok, Ok. Call your friend Aisha and tell her to schedule those two stooges."

Zena wasted no time in calling Aisha and asking her to schedule a moving job for her husband. She used the opportunity to reconnect with Aisha who had been politely making excuses for not visiting her.

Ali and David were on their way to the New Jersey warehouse to meet Mahmoud when David said sarcastically, "I don't understand those Muslim Salafis who want to take Muslims back to the early days of Islam. They keep their women wrapped up and they deny them their basic rights as human beings."

Ali was surprised to hear him say that, "And when did you become an expert on Salafism?"

"Aisha told me a lot about them when she scheduled this Job, and I also read a little about them."

"What exactly did she tell you?" Ali asked in an exasperated voice.

"I understand that they are zealous in their views about Islam and they want to take Muslims back to the early days of the religion in the ninth century. Aisha tells me that people in the Arab world describe someone as 'Hanbali' when he is very rigid and unbending in his thoughts and behavior. I read that this behavior refers to Ahmed ibn Hanbal who was one of the pivotal figures in the history of Salafism."

Ali shook his head and continued in the same exasperated tone, "Do you ever stop and reflect on your own religion? I'm sure you know of the Haredis among Jews. They follow what they believe to be authentic Judaism that goes back to Moses and the giving of the Torah on Mount Sinai."

"Yes, I know of Haredi Jews, but they are more progressive than the Salafis."

"What? Are you kidding me? Progressive? They cover their women from head to toe like the Afghan women under the Taliban rule. Many Haredi women wear burkas like the most conservative Muslim women, and are restricted to the back of the bus in Haredi neighborhoods. At least Salafi women can sit anywhere they want on the bus."

"And how do you know about Haredis? Have you met any of them?"

"Yes, I've visited Mea Sherim, the Haredi neighborhood in Jerusalem. Have you been there?"

"No, I haven't. But Haredis are a minority among Jews, and the Salafis may also be a minority. But wearing burkas and being covered from head to toe are not limited to Salafi women. Look at women in Saudi Arabia, for example. Not only do they cover themselves but they also can't drive and aren't allowed to leave the country without their husbands' permission."

At that point the truck arrived at the warehouse and Ali looked at David and said in a business-like voice, "Salafis or Haredis; Saudis or Hassidics; Muslims, Jews, or Christians; we treat all our customers the same."

David agreed, "Of course, we're an equal-treatment service company. Let's go and show them how broad-minded we are."

Mahmoud greeted them in a lukewarm way, shaking hands with both of them but mostly looking at Ali. He directed his instructions to Ali pointing out the items that need to be delivered to his store in Queens.

As they drove off, David looked at Ali and said, "Boy, I think our Haredis are more friendly than your Salafis."

Ali smiled, "But your Haredis can't run a business. They want to devote all their time to studying the Torah."

When they arrived at the store they never expected to be greeted by a friendly and vivacious woman. She greeted Ali in Arabic and turned to David and said with a smile, "Shalom." They saw an attractive woman, and the long dress she wore down to her ankle didn't hide the details of her body. The beauty of her face shone in spite of the black scarf around her head.

Ali could deduce immediately from her Arabic dialect that she was Palestinian and that she had to be Mahmoud's wife. David, on the other hand, was at a loss. He had no idea who the woman was. He never expected that a man like Mahmoud would have such an appealing wife. Ali soon clarified the situation by saying, "Your husband told us what to do with the merchandise. If you just show us where the basement is, we'll take it from there."

She turned around to lead them to the basement and Ali followed her. David stood in the same spot for a minute watching her walking gracefully in front of Ali swaying her draped, well-curved body. An expression of disbelief froze on his face. He was startled when Ali turned around and yelled, "David, come on, let's go down and look at the place."

David followed behind while Ali talked to Zena about her family back home, her village and the latest news from the West Bank. Ali was not oblivious to her sex appeal. But while his religious principles were flexible when it came to women and sex, he never flirted with another man's wife, particularly a Muslim wife.

Ali and David carried the boxes from the truck to the basement. Ali noticed that every time David passed by the cash register desk where Zena stood, he stopped and chatted with her for a couple of minutes before he continued down to the basement. He heard Zena giggling every time David stopped at the cash register, and noticed a certain amount of flirtation was going on between the two of them. Ali urged David to speed it up because of their tight schedule. But David ignored him. Finally when they both were outside at the truck Ali yelled at him, "What the hell are you doing? Don't you know she is a married woman? What if her husband shows up and sees you flirting with her?"

Ali wasn't concerned about her husband coming back. He knew that he was busy doing some work in New Jersey. But he was torn between jealousy and being offended. He was jealous watching Zena acting friendly with David, and offended by David's flirtations with a Palestinian woman from his region who was married. The mere thought of a Jew having an affair with a Palestinian Muslim woman angered him. He couldn't see his own hypocrisy and the fact that he, a religious Muslim, was having an affair with a Christian woman. He probably would have had no qualms if Dorothy was Jewish because, in his mind, a Muslim male could have an affair or marry a Christian or a Jew, but a Muslim woman couldn't.

David tried to calm him down, "I'm just being friendly. You know me, I only go out with Jewish women."

"You better stick to that my friend because if her husband sees you flirting with her he'll cut your throat."

"I thought the Salafis are peaceful people."

"They are unless you get too close to their women."

When they got in the truck to leave, David looked at Ali and said sarcastically, "I don't understand you, Ali, you come to this country and you think you can screw any woman regardless of her religion. But God help us, if we touch one of your women."

Ali responded, "How would you feel if you find out that Hadassah is having an affair with someone like Mahmoud?"

"You mean a Salafi? With the same beard?"

Ali felt that he was getting the upper hand in that exchange.

"Yes, exactly like Mahmoud."

David scratched his chin and paused for a few seconds as if he was seriously thinking about the question and answered without cracking a smile, "I really don't understand this analogy. First, Hadassah doesn't like long bushy beards, and second, her skirt is too short for Mahmoud, but if that really happens----I think I'll become a Salafi."

The two laughed as they drove away.

Ali and David's company became the regular movers for Mahmoud's business, transferring goods from the warehouse in New Jersey to his store in Queens, every Tuesday. Zena was always there to greet them and show them where to place the goods. Ali didn't give David a chance to speak to her alone. He always jumped in on the conversation, or made a remark or a joke in Arabic to distract her from what David was talking about. Zena enjoyed the attention and her flirtations were equally divided between the two of them. But naturally she felt more comfortable and more attracted to Ali as they often shared some of their homeland anecdotes.

The business relationship allowed Zena to be closer to Aisha, and forced Aisha to phone her more often. Zena found in Aisha a person she could identify with and could share with her dissatisfaction with her married life. She talked to her about Mahmoud's complete immersion in the religion and in his business, his heart ailments that had affected their sex life, and her lack of any other female friends. Aisha tried to comfort her and encourage her to pursue other occupations besides going to the store a couple of times a week. But in private and in her conversations with her close friend Hadassah, she always brought up Zena's story as a vivid example of unfulfilled dreams and the often sad outcomes of arranged marriages.

Ali and David were at the store one day when Mahmoud was alone. There were no customers and Mahmoud offered to help them to move some of the heavy boxes into the basement. They were upstairs when they heard a thump followed by the sound of items rolling down the steps to the basement. They found Mahmoud lying breathless on the floor of the basement. They tried to revive him, and immediately called 911. By the time the ambulance arrived at the store, Mahmoud was dead.

Ali had the difficult task of calling Zena to tell her the bad news. While wailing on the other end of the phone, she begged him to call Aisha and to help her make the arrangements for her husband's burial. She told him that in respect to her husband and his Salafism's beliefs she couldn't show her face to any men who were not blood-related for at least seven days.

Ali knew that Muslims had to bury their dead within forty-eight hours, and he was in a race with time. He turned to David and asked, "I know this is inappropriate and may even be sacrilegious, but I need your help."

"I'm glad to help, what do you need?"

"You know David, we Muslims have to bury our dead fairly quickly and we're not allowed to embalm the body to preserve it."

"We do the same in Judaism, and we've to bury our dead within forty-eight hours."

"Oh my goodness, no wonder they call us cousins."

Ali told David that they had to have the body transferred to Mahmoud's house to prepare it for burial. He frantically called Aisha to tell her about Mahmoud's sudden death and asked her to help with the preparations.

David asked Ali, "What will happen after you move the body to the house?"

"I asked Aisha to find the people who would come to the house and prepare the body for burial. They thoroughly clean the body and wrap it in clean white cotton or linen cloth."

"This is exactly what the Jews do. How about cremation or open caskets? We don't allow either."

"Cremation is forbidden in Islam, and the body is never displayed at funerals."

Ali and David rushed to receive the body at Mahmoud's house. Zena left the basement door opened for them while she stayed on the second floor hidden. She didn't want to be seen by unrelated males. Ali left David in the basement with the body waiting for the people who were supposed to arrive to prepare it for burial while he went to pick up Aisha.

By the time Ali left the house, David was totally drained. He sat alone in a basement with the body of a Salafi lying in a room next to him. He couldn't comprehend how he ended up in that situation. He went into the bathroom, took off his yarmulke and washed his face, hair, and arms to cool off. He was startled when he heard a loud voice with a heavy Pakistani accent coming through the door of the basement. With water dripping from his hair, face, and arms he quickly tried to put his yarmulke on, but it fell on the floor and he couldn't find it. The Pakistani man hurried in looking for the body.

"I'm here to prepare the body for burial. I'm sorry my assistant got sick and I'm alone today. Would you please give me a hand?"

"Wait a minute, I----"

The man interrupted him thinking that David had washed himself to perform the Muslim prayers.

"Sir, you can pray later. I'm in a hurry."

"But---"

"Sir, I've three other bodies to wash after this one and I'm alone. I need your help."

He walked toward the body and David felt obliged to follow him. They carried the body to the bathroom, laid him on the floor and undressed him. The Pakistani looked for something to hide the dead body's genitals as dictated by Islamic traditions. He looked around and found a black round piece of cloth on the floor. He picked it up and placed it on the genitals.

At that instant Ali and Aisha arrived at the house. Aisha went upstairs to be with Zena. Ali walked into the basement and saw David and the Pakistani man kneeling on the floor washing the body and David holding the body's feet. His jaw dropped as he looked at David in disbelief. He had to control himself from screaming. He couldn't bear that scene and started to turn around to leave when his eyes caught David's uncovered hair, which he'd never seen before. His jaw dropped further down as his eyes focused on a black round piece of cloth covering the dead body's genitals.

——— ——— ———

Zena mourned her husband for forty days, as is custo-mary in some Muslim societies. At the end of the mourning period, she called Aisha to tell her that she was going to reopen the store and run it by herself. She decided not to adhere to conservative Muslim widows' ways of mourning for a period of four months during which they couldn't marry or interact with men whom they could marry.

A few weeks later, Ali stopped at the store to say hello to Zena. He was stunned when he saw her. The long dress was not solid black any more, but had pink and yellow flowers, and the headscarf matched her dress. The scarf wasn't wrapped around her face but only covered her hair except for a few strands that were left hanging on her forehead. Her face that had never seen make-up during her husband's life was fully made-up with lipstick, eye shadow, and tweezed eyebrows. Ali kept telling her how beautiful she looked and she was happy to hear that from him.

When he left the store he whispered to himself, "I think Zena has come out of the box."

CHAPTER 19

Aisha at Passover

When the phone rang in Aisha's apartment she trudged toward it with a smile on her face. She knew who was on the other end because she was expecting his regular daily call around the same time. She picked up the phone and said hello as if she didn't know who was calling. A cheerful voice answered, "Do you miss me yet?"

Aisha gave her delicate laugh, "It hasn't been twenty-four hours yet."

Ben was always the one who made the phone calls to Aisha. Although she liked Ben and felt at ease with him, she couldn't rid herself of some of the old Arabic traditions that a woman shouldn't take the initiative and call a man.

Ben was eager to tell her about his experience with Yasser the day before when they went to the home of Bud and Betty Lou. He described to her how hostile and bigoted Bud was and how he had to restrain Yasser from getting into a fight with a man wielding a knife.

"I think it was Yasser's first exposure to real hostile bigotry," Ben said. "But what surprised me most was Yasser's unawareness of the role right-wing Evangelical Christians play in the Arab-Israeli problem. He always claims to know all the facts, and he never misses a beat stressing the blind support the Jewish Americans give to Israel. But at the same time, he underestimated the support of the Evangelicals." Ben laughed, and added, "He didn't understand what Armageddon is and what it means."

Aisha was well aware of the role of right-wing American Evangelists, not only in supporting Israel, but also in defending and financing illegal settlements in the West Bank. She'd recently heard a well-known American preacher, whose charities had donated millions of dollars to projects in Israel and the occupied territories, "Israel exists because of a covenant God made with Abraham, Isaac, and Jacob thirty-five hundred years ago and that covenant still stands."

Aisha had nothing against the preacher's support of Israel, but she was critical of his continued advocacy of building and expanding Jewish settlements in the West Bank that was destined, together with Gaza, to constitute a future Palestinian state. She shared with Ben the content of a recent article in the *New York Times* about U.S. tax-exempt funds aiding settlements in the West Bank. The article explained the inconsistencies in U.S. policies. On one hand the U.S. government was committed to end the four-decade Jewish settlement enterprise and foster a Palestinian state in the West Bank; on the other hand the US Treasury Department helped sustain the settlements through tax breaks on donations to support them.

Ben reluctantly pointed out that the American tax law was more lenient than Israel's and the outposts receiving tax-deductible donations were illegal under Israeli law.

A few months earlier, and before Ben had met Aisha, this conversation would have taken a completely different course. He would have vehemently supported the US favorable tax laws and the expansion of settlements. But his growing love for Aisha made him adopt the new position that many of those settlements were obstacles to peace. He was hopeful, though, that the large settlements adjacent to Jerusalem and Tel Aviv would be integrated with Israel in any future peace agreement, and didn't care if the other settlements were dismantled. He felt at ease with such a compromise because his family's settlement was like a suburb of Jerusalem.

In the past, Ben welcomed the American Evangelicals' support of Israel and the settlements, but never believed in the motivation behind that support. He often ridiculed them in private among his religious friends. He didn't believe in Armageddon, or in Jesus coming back, or in the Evangelicals' belief that most Jews in Israel would perish unless they converted to Christianity. He remembered his Israeli friends jokingly telling him that as long as those Evangelicals kept sending their millions, they'd go along with their prophesies.

"How about dinner tonight?" Ben switched the subject. "I've discovered an excellent kosher restaurant."

"A new one? I thought I'd been to every kosher restaurant in New York already."

"No, I guarantee you'll like this one. They have typical Middle Eastern dishes prepared in a kosher way. You've got to try their lamb, it's delicious."

"You know lamb is my weak spot. Sure I'll go."

At the restaurant they sat, as usual, in a corner to avoid the curious looks of other diners. Aisha was about to dig into the delicious looking lamb shank when Ben got up to greet a couple approaching their table. He introduced them as Dr. Bob Hoffman and his wife Judith. In his introduction he emphasized that Bob was the best orthopedic surgeon in the New York area. They were a good looking couple in their mid thirties. Bob was tall with an athletic built. Judith was an attractive blonde dressed in expensive clothes. Aisha could tell that every piece she had on carried the name of a famous designer. She didn't look like the typical person one would meet in a kosher restaurant in the Bronx but rather in one of Manhattan's more expensive fine dining establishments.

Aisha noticed right away that they were both intrigued by seeing Ben with someone like her. She inferred that they knew Ben from their synagogue. Judith took immediate interest in Aisha. She asked about where she was from and what she was doing in New York. Aisha's answers further fueled her curiosity and drove her to ask more questions. Finally, her husband had to interrupt her and point out that they were keeping them from their food that was getting cold. He grabbed her arm to lead her away from their table. But before she turned around to leave, she looked at Ben and said in an enthusiastic voice, "Ben, please bring Aisha and join us at Passover this Sunday." Then she turned to Aisha, "Would you mind joining us? I hope you can come. We'd love to have you in our house."

Aisha was surprised by the sudden invitation. A confused look came across her face. She wasn't a stranger to Jewish holidays. She had a close Israeli girl friend back home and she used to spend a lot of time with her before it became difficult to cross from the West Bank into Israel. But her friend's family rarely celebrated religious holidays. Although Aisha was quite familiar with the meaning of Passover, she'd never been to a Passover dinner.

Bob and Ben were equally startled by Judith's invitation, and noticed the confused look on Aisha's face and her hesitation in responding to her. Ben jumped in to save Aisha from making a commitment she wasn't ready for.

"Thanks. We'll talk it over and I'll let you know."

"Great. But you know me, Ben. I don't easily take no for an answer."

With her husband passively looking, Judith sounded like a wife who usually got her way.

They walked to their table at the end of the restaurant. As soon as they sat down, she whispered, "I'm flabbergasted. Our friend, Ben, the Orthodox Jew who weaves Hebrew words and religious quotations every time he talks, is dating a Palestinian Muslim woman wearing hijab! I feel I'm dreaming and I want to pinch myself. I personally like her, and I find her very attractive and intelligent. But not sure I see her with Ben!"

"Maybe the differences between them are the source of attraction," Bob tried to help her get over her shock. Then he told her in a measured and softly reprimanding voice, "But honey, your invitation may have been inappropriate. We should have discussed it first. You know our usual guest list. The girl may feel very uncomfortable."

Judith shrugged her shoulders scornfully, and retorted, "I'm tired of our usual guest list. We need to liven things up a bit and make it more exciting."

"You mean exciting or controversial?"

"Both. If it weren't for me, we'd be spending our free time with either your parents or your friends from the synagogue. You know I like eclectic friends."

Knowing that it was feeble to argue with her, he took refuge in silence.

Ben and Aisha continued their meal and neither of them spoke much. It was unusual for them not to get into long discussions. Ben was thinking about the awkward situation Judith had put him in. He wasn't sure that Aisha would be comfortable at their Passover dinner. He'd been to it once before. Although Judith wasn't the religious type, her husband and his parents were. Her parents came from Prague. She wasn't brought up in a religious home like Ben and Bob. She went to the synagogue and celebrated all the Jewish religious holidays in order to please her husband and his parents.

Aisha, though not the type who walked away from challenges, predicted that she'd be the odd one out at such a religious celebration. Ben could read her mixed emotions. He finally broke the silence, reassuring her, "You don't have to go to that dinner if you feel the least bit uncomfortable. I could go alone and make an excuse for you. I can see that Judith likes you and wants to make friends with you. But you can always see her for lunch or coffee. It's no big deal."

"Let me think about it, please," Aisha said softly without lifting her eyes from the food in front of her.

Ben and Aisha finished their dinner and walked over to Bob's table to say goodbye. Judith seized the opportunity once again to say, "I hope to see you both on Sunday." Then she turned directly to Aisha and reached out for her hand, and said, "Aisha, it was a pleasure meeting you. I would love the chance to get to know you better. Please come on Sunday."

"Thank you very much," Aisha said without committing herself to accepting the invitation.

The restaurant was not far from Aisha's apartment. Beneath the harsh street lighting Ben and Aisha could see the signs of spring. The head of purple crocuses were breaking thru a patch of dirt. Out of the reach of man-made lighting, hundred-year old oak trees glistened under the bright light of a near perfect full moon. Slipping off his parka, the night air had lost its mean icy bite and now felt cool and refreshing against Ben's skin. For the shivering Aisha, this was not the spring of the West Bank. Ben gently placed the dark blue parka over her shoulders and for a brief moment they both felt the warmth of spring in the Bronx.

"Tell me more about your friends," Aisha asked.

Ben stressed what was apparent to Aisha.

"You can see they are very different. She always expresses her feelings and views regardless of whom she is with. She has a strong personality and is unconventional in her behavior. Those were the traits that attracted him to her and finally drove him to marry her. She is the exact opposite of him, almost in everything. He is religious, she isn't; he is a man of few words, she is talkative; he is gloomy and she is always cheerful and excited; he is calculating and methodical, and she is spontaneous and uninhibited. But I know that Bob loves her very much. I also know that his parents were against the marriage, but he didn't care. They found her to be Jewish in name only, and that she didn't care about Jewish traditions. They'd never traveled much and they probably felt she was too unconventional for them."

"And how did they meet?"

"They met at a friend's party and he fell in love with her at first sight. By that time he had established a successful practice and had made a lot of money. I think that helped her to fall in love with him too."

"Do you think she married him for his money?"

"No, no. But considering how different she is from him, I think his distinguished career and wealth may have been a factor."

As soon as he finished his sentence, he realized that he'd committed a grave mistake. He turned his head and looked at Aisha and saw the puzzled look on her face. He almost could read what was going on inside her head. *How could he be going on and on about the differences between Bob and Judith that paled in comparison to those between us. There is a mountain separating us, but nonetheless we still are good friends.* He tried to correct himself.

"Those were his parents' feelings. He often shared their comments with me. I personally find her to be the best thing that ever happened to him."

Aisha smiled to help him get over his embarrassment, thanked him for the dinner, said goodbye, and walked into her apartment building.

Aisha rushed to call Hadassah to tell her about Ben's friends. She shared with Hadassah her apprehension about going to the Passover dinner, particularly after hearing of Bob Hoffman's conservative parents. After a long talk, however, Hadassah was able to persuade her to go to the dinner and to make friends with Judith. When Hadassah heard Aisha's description of Judith, she became interested in meeting her. She felt they had so much in common and that she could become a friend of hers as well.

On Sunday Ben picked up Aisha in a car he had borrowed from a friend. Aisha looked beautiful that day. She had great skill in fine-tuning her dress in response to the occasion. Her hijab was wrapped in such a way so as to look like a headscarf. She wore black silk pants with a long green blouse and a pearl necklace hung down between her well-formed breasts.

Judith greeted them at the door with a cheerful hello. She was visibly excited that Aisha had come. Aisha was impressed by the size and location of the house. The backside of the house opened to a large patio and a lap-size swimming pool facing the Long Island Sound. The patio extended the whole length of the house. Large windows and French doors brought light and the water views into every room of the house.

Judith introduced Aisha to the other guests. It became apparent to Aisha that Judith had alerted her guests as to who was coming to dinner. None of them showed any visible sign of surprise when they met her.

There were about twenty-five adults and children. All the males, including children, wore skullcaps. The guests included a couple that looked like Ultra Orthodox Jews. The man and his young son had side locks and the wife had a head covering not much different from Aisha's. The only non-Jew among the guests, besides her, was the girlfriend of Judith's young teenage son. She was a beautiful Italian-American girl.

Aisha saw two maids busy at work in the kitchen, but Judith bragged that she'd prepared the whole meal, and that she'd refused to let her in-laws or her husband help in the preparation. She took Aisha's hand and walked with her outside on the patio.

"I want you to know that I'm not very religious. I do this only for my husband and my son. As a matter of fact, I've very little in common with most of these people," she whispered to Aisha.

Then she confided in Aisha some intimate details about her family and how she didn't get along with her in-laws who disapproved of her son's Italian girlfriend because she wasn't Jewish. She talked to her as if they had been friends for years. Aisha was impressed by her warmth and openness, but it was obvious that Judith needed someone new in this gathering; someone she could talk freely to, and Aisha provided that opportunity.

Their intimate conversation was interrupted when a distinguished looking man approached them on the patio. Judith introduced him to Aisha.

"I want you to meet our dear friend, Dr. Joseph Friedman. Joe works at the Middle East Institute in Washington, D.C." Then she boasted, "Aisha is getting her Ph.D. at Columbia University in international relations."

"Columbia! I'm impressed," he said while shaking Aisha's hand.

At that moment one of the maids came to the patio seeking Judith's attention. They needed her in the kitchen for last minute preparations. She laughed and announced, "Would you please excuse me? I better rush to the kitchen to save our Seder family meal." She held Aisha's hand and said, "I leave you, my dear, in good hands. I'm sure the two of you will enjoy an intellectual discussion. But please, make it short because we'll be eating soon."

Dr. Friedman and Aisha spoke briefly about Columbia University and about his job at the Middle East Institute. He mentioned an article he'd just finished writing about energy and the US dependence on foreign oil. He highlighted the well-known fact that the US imported over 60-percent of its oil, and added, "We can't be dependent on those insecure oil sources in the Middle East. Also, why should we be sending money to Saudi Arabia, a country that exports terrorists and supports terrorism?"

Dr. Friedman was apparently unaware that he had touched on a subject that was quite familiar to Aisha.

"But Dr. Friedman, the United States imports only a small percentage of its oil from Saudi Arabia. As a matter of fact, the US total imports from the Gulf, including Saudi Arabia, Kuwait, Qatar, and the United Arab Emirates, amount to only eight-percent of the total US oil consumption."

Dr. Friedman realized that he was talking to someone who was well informed, but held his ground.

"Yes, but this is a volatile region and we shouldn't be dependent on it at all."

Aisha, like the rest of the Palestinian intellectuals, didn't usually defend Saudi Arabia or the Arab Gulf countries. She felt contempt for the Saudi Monarchs and the rich Arab Gulf sheiks she saw in London and Paris driving their fancy cars and shopping at expensive stores such as Giorgio Armani and Louis Vuitton on Bond Street and the Champs Elysees. But she was tired of reading and hearing about the American money going to Saudi Arabia. She'd always wanted to respond to this issue and Dr. Friedman provided her a forum to do that.

"You know Dr. Friedman, the United States should worry a lot more about imports from China than those from Saudi Arabia. In 1960, manufacturing accounted for a quarter of the US Gross Domestic Product and employed twenty-percent of the labor force. Today manufacturing has gone down to eleven-percent of the Gross Domestic Product, and employs a small percentage of the work force. Most of these jobs have moved to China, and the US has become dependent on China almost in everything Americans consume."

Dr. Friedman interrupted her, "We're losing manufacturing because we can't compete against cheap Chinese labor."

Aisha fired back, now fully engulfed in the debate, "This isn't totally true. Germany has remained a manufacturing powerhouse even though it has a workforce that is more unionized and better paid than the American one."

"Are you telling me that it's ok to keep importing oil and sending money to Saudi Arabia?" he tried to test her.

But Aisha was unrelenting.

"What I'm saying is that you and others should put everything in the right perspective. You're dependent on Saudi Arabia for less than five-percent of your oil while you're shipping jobs and your manufacturing base to China. You have become dependent on China in almost everything you consume. You've got to keep in mind that the US exports more to the Gulf Arab countries than it imports, while its balance of trade deficit with China runs into the hundreds of billions of dollars."

"But China doesn't export terrorists and isn't a breeding ground for religious zealots," Dr. Friedman interjected.

"I do agree that some of the eleven fanatics who participated in 9-11 came from Saudi Arabia. But you can find fanatics everywhere. The truth is Saudi Arabia isn't an enemy. In fact, Saudi Arabia has been an ally of the United

States for decades, and it's China that, until recently, was the enemy and is the one you should fear the most."

Dr. Hoffman, though impressed by Aisha's knowledge, didn't show any sign of agreement with her. Judith showed up on the patio to ask them to come to the table since dinner was about to be served.

Everyone looked for his or her place card around the table that was beautifully decorated. It was still light outside and the large windows provided a stunning view of the Sound.

As the host, Bob, started by distributing a twenty-five page pamphlet entitled, our family's modern Passover, but with a traditional feel. After welcoming all the guests, he started reading the story of Passover.

"The Torah tells us of our forefather Jacob. A long time ago, Jacob led his people from Canaan to Egypt, due to a severe drought in Canaan. The Pharaoh, leader of the Egyptians, welcomed the small group of Jewish people into Egypt. They worked hard and earned the respect of the Egyptians. In fact, Jacob's son Joseph worked for the Pharaoh and helped the Egyptians become a great community.

One day the old Pharaoh died, and a new one took the throne. He was scared of the Jewish people because there were so many of them in Egypt. He thought that they might hurt him one day, and so he made them slaves. He wanted to know where the Jewish people were at all times, so he made them work day and night, building huge pyramids and statues to the Egyptian gods.

The pharaoh was mean to the Jewish people. He didn't give them enough food to eat, had them beaten, and took away their homes, animals and, sometimes, their family. They were very unhappy and cried out to God to save them.

God heard their prayers and sent a message to Moses, leader of the Jewish people. A plague was to befall the Egyptians if they didn't release the Jewish people from their bonds of slavery. The Pharaoh didn't believe Moses and the first plague struck the Egyptians. This was followed by nine more plagues, each worse than the last.

As each of the ten plagues struck the Egyptians, the king became more and more stubborn. Finally, after the last plague in which the first-born male of each Egyptian family died, the Pharaoh demanded that the Jewish people leave immediately. They had such little time to get ready that the bread they were baking didn't have time to rise.

Under God's guidance, Moses parted the Red Sea to allow the Jewish people to cross and reach the desert through which they wandered for forty years. During that time, God gave them the Ten Commandments, and sustained them with manna. Finally, Moses led the Jewish people to Canaan, where they live today in the land we now call Israel."

Bob continued his reading, "We celebrate Passover each year with the Seder, telling the story of how God came to our aid in a time of need and delivered us from bondage."

He began by lighting the candles and saying, "By lighting the candles in our home we hope to illuminate our eyes, our minds, and our hearts to the potential of the future and the holiness these observances bring into our homes."

He then poured the first cup of wine to celebrate the passage from slavery to freedom, and to emphasize that this story should be told and handed down from generation to generation.

Aisha sat at one end of the table facing the host. Judith sat on one side of her husband at the other end, and his parents on the other side. Judith, knowing that Aisha didn't drink alcohol, had placed a bottle of diet Coke next to her. Aisha could see some of the guests sneaking a look at her during the ceremony trying to study her reactions. But she was listening intently as Bob spoke. A lot of what she was hearing wasn't new to her because she was familiar with all three holy books.

The host broke the middle of unleavened matzos placed in the folds of a napkin as a reminder of the haste with which the Jews left Egypt. Karpas (vegetables) were passed around

185

with a bowl of salted water representing the tears shed by the Jews.

Bob asked his dad to explain each of the items on the Seder plate, including a shank bone symbolizing the lamb offered as the Passover sacrifice in biblical times; a roasted egg, symbol of life; bitter herbs, symbol of the bitterness of Egyptian slavery; and a mixture of chopped nuts and apples symbolizing the mortar used by Jewish slaves to build Egyptian structures.

Finally the host asked everybody to recite the ten plagues that God wrought upon the Egyptians. All the guests named the plagues one-by-one starting with the Blood Plague until they reached the Death of the First Born plague, then Bob read again, "One morning when the Pharaoh awoke in his bed there were dead firstborn on his pillow, dead firstborn on his head, dead firstborn on his nose, dead firstborn on his toes. Dead firstborn here, dead firstborn there, firstborn were dying everywhere."

Aisha didn't participate in the songs. She was touched but also saddened by the service. She was touched by how the Jewish elders impressed on their children to recite, every year on Passover, a story that had happened over four thousand years ago. But she was saddened to hear children singing and celebrating the death of the firstborn Egyptian children. She thought about her own story and her people's suffering. She was sitting among intelligent, prosperous people reflecting on the suffering that had happened thousands of years ago. But her people's misery was happening as the guests sang the "Death of the First Born Plague." Millions of Palestinians were currently homeless or aspired to establish their own homeland. They were not slaves to the Israelis and they were not building pyramids, but many of them were living in an occupied territory and had been deprived of their human dignity.

She suddenly found herself overcome with emotion, and a tear ran down her cheek.

CHAPTER 20

Declaration of Love

Ben and Aisha said goodbye to Judith, Bob, and the other guests, and got into the car to drive home. Ben noticed the tear on Aisha's cheek during the Passover ceremony. He didn't understand the reason behind the tears. He sat close to her and was anxious to see her reactions, and how she would handle herself in the midst of a religious Jewish gathering. Part of his anxiety stemmed from being worried that any of the guests would make a comment that in any way would offend her. On the contrary, no one made an offensive remark and all the guests were polite and welcoming. He wondered whether she'd found any of the words or the stories in the Haggadah pamphlet distributed at the dinner offensive. He was reluctant to ask such a question, or probe the issue.

They sat quietly as he drove home. After a while he summoned his courage and broke the silence by asking, "How did you like Judith's cooking?"

He knew deep in his heart that food was the last thing on her mind. He was afraid to stir a divisive argument, and that was the only question he could think of at the moment.

During their short friendship and their daily phone conversations, Ben and Aisha always avoided certain sensitive issues that separated them politically and ideologically. They frequently talked and laughed about the similarities between their religions and why their people were fighting. They shared pleasant stories from Israel and the Arab world. But they rarely discussed Israel's occupation of the West Bank, Palestinian terrorism, Israel's inhumane blockade of Gaza, or the thorny and divisive issue of the Jewish settlements in the West Bank. They learned to enjoy each other's company and found refuge in other politically and intellectually charged issues. They both, independently, made a concerted effort to avoid any argument that would adversely affect the time they spent together.

Aisha gazed at his face for few seconds searching for any clue of whether he understood her feelings. In the absence of any, she answered, "The food was good, but for some reason the songs at the dinner table, particularly the ones about the Egyptian plagues, made me sad."

Realizing the reason behind her tears, he explained, "You've got to understand Aisha that the elder Jews feel it's their duty to remind their children over and over again of the persecution and suffering the Jews have borne throughout history."

Aisha wasn't convinced. She sighed audibly and challenged Ben, "But all these people sitting around the table, including you, keep talking about suffering and you have no firsthand knowledge of what suffering really is. If you really want to know about suffering, I can tell you a thousand stories about people's suffering in my country at the hands of the same people celebrating the death of the firstborn Egyptian child. And much of that suffering continues today."

As soon as she finished her sentence, Aisha burst into tears. She realized that she'd hurt Ben's feelings and she was ashamed of it.

Ben pulled the car onto the side of the road and stopped, put his arm around her shoulder, and whispered in an injured tone, "I wish you could understand how sad your words make me."

"I'm very sorry. Please forgive me for being so mean," Aisha said in a choked voice and continued to cry.

Ben held her tighter and tried to comfort her.

"I understand and respect your feelings about these issues. Knowing you has opened my eyes to many things

I've chosen to ignore in the past. Through you I've learned to sympathize with all the Palestinians and to appreciate their plight. You don't have to tell me about their suffering, I have firsthand knowledge of it."

Then he turned his head to face her, took out his handkerchief and wiped her tears. With a delicate smile on his face, he continued, "All I know now Aisha is that I love you, and I wish I could freeze this moment with you in my arms."

His mentioning of embracing her suddenly awakened her traditional Arab impulse to push him away from her, but she didn't. She sighed again, turned her head and looked off in the distance and muttered, "But Ben, there are mountains that separate us."

"Aisha, mountains were made to be crossed," he replied defiantly. "I know I want you to be mine, and for me to be yours. What is wrong with that?"

She was stunned to hear Ben confessing his love for her. She always knew that he liked her a lot, and she also liked him. But the way he expressed his love to her was a turning point in their relationship. She gazed at his face for a long time reflecting on what he'd just said, lowered her eyes, and spoke softly.

"You're an Orthodox Jew, brought up to marry a Jewish girl and to raise your kids in the Jewish faith. Likewise, I'm a religious Muslim woman who has been taught that someday I'd marry a Muslim and raise my kids to be Muslims. Friendship is one thing, but love and marriage are another matter. How can we cross these steep and tortuous religious and cultural mountains?"

Ben looked at her tenderly and watched the tears pouring out of her beautiful dark eyes down on her cheeks. His eyes also filled with tears. A feeling of despair overwhelmed him. He fully understood every word she'd said, and was under no illusion of the difficult obstacles that lay ahead in his relationship with her. But he also knew that he was in love with her and was determined, at any cost, to overcome those obstacles.

Ben took his handkerchief out and dried Aisha's tears as well as his own. When he saw a tear coming down on her lips he had a strong urge to kiss her, but restrained himself out of respect for her beliefs and traditions. His urge was not motivated by lust, but rather by a desire to have his skin touch hers, thus allowing him to be closer to her.

The two of them sat quietly in the car for a few minutes. They were reflecting on the new development in their relationship. Their deep thoughts were occasionally interrupted by the sound and bright lights of a passing car. Ben, still holding her in his arms, tried to console her, "Let us not allow our relationship to be a source of pain to either of us. Let us not think or talk about the cultural and religious gulf that separates us. I know that I love you and I want to be with you always. I also feel that you, at least, enjoy being with me. The stronger our friendship grows, the less we'll think about this gulf."

He gazed at her face, searching and hoping for a positive response. She turned her head towards him and, in the lights of an incoming car, he saw a faint smile on her face.

CHAPTER 21

Crisis in the Ranks

The phone calls between Ben and Aisha increased substantially from once a day to several times a day, and their meetings became more frequent. They felt comfortable holding hands whenever and wherever they walked. Although they always tried to avoid busy streets, and chose to go out at night, they couldn't escape an occasional sneer, or a look of hostility and contempt by a passerby. His love for her grew stronger and she became more overtly affectionate toward him. He loved to hear her calling him "ya habibi" which meant *my darling* in Arabic, because he was aware that an Arab woman wouldn't use that expression casually. He knew the difference between someone calling him honey or darling in the United States and an Arab woman addressing him as habibi. In the US cashiers and waitresses constantly called him honey and they didn't even know his name. He remembered his female cousin scolding a man on the phone who was harassing her and addressing him as honey. But habibi from Aisha was something special. Even the way she said it sounded endearing and was like music to his ears.

Their relationship, though, remained platonic except for the handholding, a kiss on the cheek, or an occasional hug. Although he loved her and had a burning desire for her, he was reluctant to try anything that would offend her or risk losing her. The more he abstained from expressing his physical desires, the more she admired and liked him. On many occasions he was tempted to have his lips touch hers, to let his hands wander around her body, or to hold her tightly in his arms and whisper his love for her. But he resisted this innate temptation and was content with holding her hand, and listening to her calling him habibi.

They kept their friendship a secret from Ali, Yasser, and all her other Arab friends. Initially Hadassah was the only one who knew about their relationship. But gradually David, being on the truck with them every Friday, took notice of it. In the beginning, David and Hadassah thought that the relationship was a case of mere infatuation. But they slowly realized that it was a lot stronger than that, and finally Ben confessed to David that he was in love with her, and that he couldn't get her off his mind day or night. That was quite a shock to David because he vividly recalled the hysterical phone call he'd received from Ben when he was visiting his parents in Miami. Ben was disturbed when he went to David's apartment and saw Aisha, Ali, and the others there. He told David then that his apartment had been taken over by a bunch of Arab terrorists and wanted David to call the police. David and Hadassah often laughed how ironic that story was in view of Ben's new transformation.

Any time the four of them went out to dinner, Ben never stopped talking about Palestinian rights. He even argued for the need to dismantle Jewish settlements in the West Bank, but he always ignored mentioning the one his uncle had founded. In addition to all of that, and following their experience with the bigoted Bud, Ben and Yasser became comfortable with each other. Whenever they worked together on the truck, they went for coffee and shared a few laughs.

Ali and Yasser were completely unaware of the evolving friendship and growing affection between Ben and Aisha. They had noticed a recent moderation in Ben's views and in his relationship with them, and they attributed that to his exposure to Aisha's rational arguments and effective persuasion. They had never imagined that the emerging moderate side of Ben was driven by his love for Aisha.

Ali and Yasser maintained certain traditional views that stemmed from their upbringing as well as their religion. They believed that a Muslim woman wasn't allowed to marry a non-Muslim, unless he adopted Islam. According to the tenets of Islam, children follow their father's faith, and hence the father must be a Muslim. In Ali's and Yasser's minds there was a big difference between friendships and relationships that could lead to marriage. Aisha was quite familiar with their thinking and their beliefs, and that they'd be up in arms if they found out what was going on between her and Ben. Therefore, she was determined to keep her relationship with Ben a secret.

Aisha was successful in keeping Ali and Yasser in the dark. But there was one weak link in her careful plan – Dorothy. She saw her once in the restaurant alone with Ben and another time in the street holding hands with him. Dorothy was fascinated by their relationship, and naively thought that it was an interesting romance that should be brought up in the open and publicized. Somehow she imagined herself as an instrument of friendship and peace between Arabs and Jews. After all, it was her money that helped Ali and David start their business and cemented their friendship, and through that business she saw other friendships and romances blossom. She was proud of herself and started to share those stories with her friends and the congregation of her church.

Not once did Dorothy, however, mention the ongoing romance between Aisha and Ben in front of Ali in their regular evenings together. She innocently assumed that he was aware of it. Whenever Ali arrived at her apartment, he was exhausted after a full workday. They either had dinner together or headed directly to the bedroom. Their conversations focused mainly on the business and Ali's ambitions to expand the company's territory beyond the New York area.

One evening as she lay next to him stroking his arm she blurted out, "I'm very happy for Aisha and Ben. I think their romance can be a subject of a great novel, like Romeo and Juliet or Maria and Tony in West Side story."

Ali spun around, and with a searching, inquisitive look, he asked in a disapproving tone, "What romance? Between whom? You don't mean Aisha my cousin?"

Still unaware of the blunder she'd committed, she continued with an involuntary laugh, "You must have seen them. They look so cute together holding hands."

He got out of the bed and shouted at her in a voice full of resentment and anger, "Stop that stupid talk. You saw my cousin Aisha holding hands with that fuckin Jew?"

Dorothy was astonished by his reaction. She didn't grasp the reason behind the sudden change in his behavior. She thought *How can a man like him make passionate love to me, but doesn't accept his female cousin being in love with another man or holding hands with him? Is his reaction due to the fact that Ben is a Jew? Would he react the same way if the man were an Arab?*

She thought that Ali had moderated his views about Arabs and Jews since the first dinner she had in her apartment for him, David and Satish, and the subsequent establishment and success of his business with David. *Would an Orthodox Jew, like Ben, react the same way if he saw his sister holding hands or in love with an Arab?* She had no answers to the questions running through her head. But she suddenly realized that she'd made a gross error in sharing this information with him. His fury was a reality check for her. She became unsure of herself and wondered whether she was naïve in believing that she'd helped or even made a dent in establishing peace and harmony between Arabs and Jews.

Ali was fuming, and put his clothes on and left her apartment without saying goodbye. It was late at night and David was asleep. But Ali didn't hesitate to knock on his door to wake him up. David was startled when Ali turned on the light in his bedroom. He reached for his eyeglasses and put them on speculating what had caused Ali to behave that way. There was an unwritten rule between them to never enter each other's room when the door was closed. But Ali, in his anger, ignored that rule. When his eyes adjusted to the light in the room, David saw Ali glaring at him.

"Ben is out of our business. He must be fired," Ali shouted with a look full of contempt.

David shook his head, completely baffled and shocked by Ali's combative tone. He exclaimed in disbelief, "Why? What has he done?"

"He has dishonored me and my family. There are a million Jewish girls in New York, why should he fool around with my cousin, Aisha? She is a religious Muslim woman."

David attempted to calm him down, "Aisha is a grown-up and you aren't her father. Who are you to tell her whom she can see or go out with? Besides, let me assure you that she and Ben are only friends."

Ali wasn't moved by David's rational argument, because Dorothy told him that she'd seen them holding hands in the street. He thought about what they could possibly be doing in private, if they were holding hands in public. The mere thought of his cousin Aisha in the arms of an Orthodox Jewish settler made him snap.

"I'm warning you. We either fire Ben or we close this business." He left the room and slammed the door behind him. He continued shouting in Arabic as he walked to his room cursing Ben, his religion, and his family, "I'll kill this dirty Jew if I ever see him touching my cousin. I won't allow that son of a bitch to dishonor our family. I will pull every hair of his beard with my own hands and I'll take his yarmulke and wipe my ass with it."

Ali couldn't sleep that night. He tossed and turned waiting for the morning to call Aisha and express his anger to her. He kept repeating to himself every word he would tell her and the tone of each word. He was determined to pressure her into ending her relationship with Ben.

At eight o'clock he jumped out of bed and before he even thought about his morning prayers, he called her. Without any introductions he started screaming at her in the phone, "How could you do this, Aisha? How could a good Muslim woman like you have an affair with a man who stole the land of your people and continue to inflict pain and suffering on your family, friends, and neighbors? How can you stand before God and pray knowing the sins you've committed? Aren't you ashamed of yourself?"

Aisha was shocked by his remarks and the tone of his voice. It took her a few seconds to absorb what he'd said before she yelled back at him, "Who told you those lies? Ben and I are just friends. He is a gentleman and he respects my religion and my traditions."

Ali continued his rampage as though he didn't hear a word of what she'd said.

"I told David that if we don't fire that guy, I'm shutting down the business. I'll not sit idly by watching my Muslim cousin copulating with a Jewish settler. I want you to know that I'll forever hold you responsible for ruining my business and my life."

Aisha, who was normally a composed and rational person, screamed hysterically at him, "What the hell are you talking about? Who has fed you all these lies? I've just told you, Ben and I are friends, same like you and David. And who are you to tell me what to do and whom to befriend! I'm older and a lot more educated than you. You're the last person who should lecture me. You having a flaming affair with a Christian woman who's as old as your mother!"

Her way of referring to his affair with Dorothy intensified his anger like she'd poured gasoline on the fire burning inside him and made him yell louder until he finally slammed the phone down.

Ali's reaction was the outcome of his upbringing and years of indoctrination in a society that placed a high value on male dominance and female virginity. Growing up, he was conditioned to believe that it was normal for men to be non-virgins, but not females. Women's bodies belonged to their husbands and should be used to give pleasure to their husbands and not to other men. His jumping to the conclusion that Aisha had lost her virginity to a Jewish man compounded his rage.

Aisha was a virgin, and her will to maintain her virginity until marriage didn't impede her or other Palestinian women from winning political, economic, or social equality. Placing a high value on women's virginity in her society wasn't limited to Muslim women. Christian Palestinian females were also expected to be virgins at marriage. As a matter of fact, many religious women in the Middle East, whether Muslims, Christians, or Jews, believe that western women should follow the tenets of their religions as they appear in the holy books and should abstain from premarital sex.

Ali sat on his bed trying to control his anger and felt like talking to someone else who would sympathize with his feelings and support his position. His immediate choice was Yasser. He called him and woke him up, and recounted his conversation with Aisha. He described her as a person out of control. He spoke like someone who had been betrayed by a close friend.

"Can you imagine my innocent, devout Muslim cousin has lost her virginity to this fuckin' Jewish settler? She is a traitor. If she was in Saudi Arabia, they would have stoned her to death."

Yasser, who was to the right of Ali when it came to religion and Middle East politics, was overtaken by rage. He mumbled, "We shouldn't allow that traitor to dishonor our family and our religion."

He was referring to Aisha, but he forgot that he wasn't even related to her. He kept repeating how he'd trusted Ben, and talked as though Ben had double-crossed him personally and had violated a loyalty oath.

Ali recalled how Yasser was vehemently against him moving in with David. If he'd listened to him, he thought, Aisha would never have met Ben and he would have protected the family from a looming disgrace when the neighbors back home found out that Aisha was having an affair with a Jewish settler.

However, Ali failed to remember that ignoring Yasser's unreasonable pleas led to his fruitful friendship with David and the founding of a successful business with such promising potential. All of a sudden he was becoming as entrenched in his beliefs as Yasser and threatening to destroy his friendship with David and to ruin the business they'd worked so hard to build.

After a long pause Ali asked in a voice devoid of any emotion, "What do you suggest we do? We can't allow this affair to go on. If our family or any of our neighbors find out, there'll be a scandal. I don't think Aisha's parents would be able to show their faces in our town, and they'd probably blame us for that."

When Ali asked for Yasser's advice, he had forgotten the Arab saying he'd often repeated to his friends, "It is always better to have a wise enemy than a stupid friend."

Yasser didn't hesitate for a second to answer Ali's question. He raised his voice as if he were giving a speech to some students back home, and answered passionately, "We'll not show up for work, and we'll bring this business down unless this son of a bitch Ben is fired and is prohibited from seeing Aisha."

"But how can we prevent him from seeing Aisha even if he was fired?" Ali asked.

"I'll take the responsibility of watching her, and I'll not hesitate to beat his ass if I ever see him come near her."

Yasser was demonstrating his typical self-destructive personality by advising Ali to bankrupt his own business to punish Ben and Aisha. By listening to Yasser, Ali was about to replay the story he once read about Saint Ebba and her nuns. In 867 AD, Saint Ebba urged her nuns to protect their chastity by disfiguring themselves, so they might be unappealing to the Vikings who'd landed in Scotland. She demonstrated this by cutting off her nose and upper lip, and the nuns did the same. She succeeded in protecting their chastity, but the ultimate result was catastrophic, because the Viking raiders were so disgusted that they burned the entire monastery of Coldingham to the ground.

Yasser's demagoguery was infectious. Ali lost his sensible judgment and went along with him. They agreed that they wouldn't show up for work, thus making the business unable to operate.

Ali sat in his room with the door closed until he heard David leave the apartment. He, David, Ben, and Yasser were supposed to meet at nine where the trucks were parked. They had a full schedule that day. When they didn't show up, David called them but got no response. The clock approached ten, and they were already late for their first job on the schedule. Ben sat in one of the trucks yawning and watched David panicking. But he had no idea what was going on or what had transpired the night before. He was unaware of Ali's accusations and his ultimatum. Finally Ben realized that something serious had happened. He got out of the truck and approached David. He overheard him talking to Hadassah on the phone and telling her about Ali's story and his ultimatum.

"What is going on?" Ben demanded with a puzzled look on his face.

David turned to Ben and said, "Ali is beside himself. He learned about your relationship with Aisha and he thinks that the two of you are having an affair. I tried to explain to him that you're only friends, but he doesn't believe it. I didn't take him seriously last night when he told me that either I fire you or he'd close the business. I now understand why he and Yasser haven't shown up. I think he is serious and he is going out of his mind."

David's explanation didn't alleviate Ben's confusion.

"But how will firing me change my friendship with Aisha? I'll continue to see her and be friends with her whether I work with you or not. I'm also confident that Aisha isn't the type who can be ordered around by Ali or any other man."

"I agree with you. I'm waiting to hear from Hadassah. She is trying to get hold of Aisha and find out what she knows."

After waiting for a couple of hours, and not hearing from anybody, David and Ben decided to work together on that day and let Ben play the Arab partner that he became so accustomed to perform. They selected, as usual, a few clients that wouldn't suspect Ben's Arabic role. They asked Hadassah to cancel the rest of the jobs that day.

While David and Ben were on the truck trying to serve a few customers and maintain the business, phones were ringing everywhere. David was calling Hadassah who was talking to Aisha who had called Ben. David felt obligated to call Dorothy and share with her the crisis they were going through. After all, she was the one that had financed the start-up and had a vested interest in its success. Dorothy, in turn, contacted Satish, her financial consultant, seeking his advice and guidance. Beside his knowledge of the finances of the business, she felt that his friendship with both David and Ali could help in negotiating some form of a compromise that would save the partnership between them.

Dorothy called several of her friends asking for their recommendations and help in resolving the crisis. She was sad because she felt responsible for the apparent collapse of the business. If she hadn't inadvertently mentioned to Ali that she'd seen Aisha and Ben holding hands, all the problems would have been averted, or at least delayed. She was always bragging to all her friends that she'd helped establish a successful business owned by a Palestinian Arab and a Jew that was the talk of the Arab and Jewish communities in the New York area. Any time she met one or more of her lady friends or when she went to church on Sundays she talked about the business named An Arab, A Jew and A Truck that she was associated with. All of a sudden she found herself contributing to the destruction of a beautiful arrangement that was incubated in her apartment building and financed by her own funds.

What worried Dorothy most was her relationship with Ali. She was concerned that he would move out of the apartment and would stop seeing her. She was afraid that he might suspect her of being a party to this imaginary affair between Aisha and Ben, or had helped cultivate it. She never realized until that time that she was truly in love with him. She enjoyed every minute with him and loved hearing his thick accent and his impassioned arguments, particularly whenever he discussed politics. She was always aware of the difference in age between them, and that someday he'd go off and marry a young Arab girl. But her aim was to push that eventuality as far into the future as possible, and the new business, that she was part of, provided a natural way to accomplish that. His heavy work schedule allowed him no time to look for or date other girls. He often came to her apartment in the evening exhausted after a long hard day of work. She'd have a nice meal prepared for him and he'd share with her some funny experience he'd encountered with a customer that day before they retired to the pleasures of her bedroom.

She reminisced about the first day she saw Ali coming down the steps of her building. She vividly remembered his dark, beautiful eyes that were full of lust piercing through her tight blouse, and his head turning around as he came down the stairs to glance at her hips. She thought about the first dinner she had in her apartment for him and the other guys, and how Ali couldn't stop giving her those meaningful looks even when he got into a heated political argument with David. Her mind also turned to the day she asked Ali and David to help her move the furniture into an apartment in her building and how that experience became the nucleus of their partnership. *How irrational and foolish can Ali be? A successful and promising venture is about to be squandered on the basis of misconceptions and stubbornness.*

She wondered whether the sudden disintegration of the business was symbolic of what was happening between the Arabs and the Israelis. Any success or forward steps toward peace were usually lost to irrational and senseless acts by both sides. She felt like a US peace envoy working hard to bring the two sides closer together to see all the efforts going into smoke as a result of a foolish step taken by one or a few individuals.

Ali and Yasser were nowhere to be found. Ali wasn't in his apartment and wasn't answering his cell phone. Dorothy finally got hold of Aisha who was depressed and crying because she believed that she was the cause behind all the drama. Dorothy found in Aisha a partner in her own guilt. But while Dorothy wished that she had never discussed Aisha's relationship with Ali, Aisha wasn't about to be influenced by Ali or anybody. She had no regret about any of her actions. She was determined not to succumb to Ali's reactionary views, and wouldn't surrender an inch of her freedom even if it meant the destruction of his business. Her friendship with Ben or anyone else was only governed by her own judgment and not by what her family and neighbors thought.

Ali and Yasser didn't show up for business the following day, or the next day, or the days that followed. One of the two moving trucks stood idle in the parking lot and David and Ben teamed up to do a few of the jobs that had been already scheduled. But they were pushing back their bookings, which meant lost revenues.

Meanwhile Aisha and Hadassah called customers and made excuses such as the crew was sick, the truck's brakes were being repaired, or the truck driver's grandmother was killed in a horrible car accident. Their objective was to gain some time and provide an opportunity for Ali and David to reach a compromise. David, however, announced that he was determined not to let Ben go just to please Ali who'd declared that he'd rather break up the business than see Ben working there. Dorothy and Satish couldn't figure out a way to overcome that impasse.

CHAPTER 22

New External Crisis

The congregation of the Baptist Evangelical church in Brooklyn was diverse and representative of the local community. Its members included individuals such as Bud the unemployed bigot, who had an altercation with Ben and Yasser when they were hired to help his wife Betty Lou move out of his house, as well as wealthy and respected people like Robert Smyth, Jr., the oldest brother and President of Smyth Brothers Moving Company. Robert Smyth was a stalwart member of the church congregation and a large contributor.

Smyth didn't know Bud, but had seen him often at Sunday services. He was startled one Sunday when Bud intercepted him on his way out of the church. He was in a rush because he had a prior engagement. Bud was still fuming about the Arab and the Jew movers who had been at his house and, for some illogical reason, he held them responsible for his wife abandoning him. After saying hello and introducing himself, Bud recounted his experience with the moving company called An Arab, A Jew and A Truck. He immediately got his attention because Smyth had been talking about that business a few days before with his brothers. They were alarmed by the amount of jobs they'd lost to Ali and David's company, which was now a major competitor in their territory. Before Ali and David established their business, most of the Jewish community in the area had been regular customers of Smyth moving services. But that was changing fast and a large percentage of their prior customers were switching to Ali and David because they were intrigued by the name and what it stood for. The Smyth brothers were actively seeking ways to reverse that trend and started to be concerned about the viability of their business.

Robert Smyth, Jr. listened intently to Bud as he falsely described the competition's performance to be substandard and unprofessional. His interest peaked when he heard Bud say, "And they employ illegal aliens. You should have seen that Arab Muslim on the truck. He looked like a real terrorist. We shouldn't let that go on in our backyard."

Smyth nodded in agreement. He was one of those right wing Evangelists who regularly listened to and supported the evangelical preachers who were dedicated to spread hatred toward Muslims. He responded in a calm and deliberate voice as though he had thought long and hard on the subject.

"I agree with you, Bud. We've got to defend America from the satanic horde of hateful Muslims. Thank you very much for this useful information and I assure you I'll be looking into this matter right away."

"Thank you, Mr. Smyth and good luck. I hope you break these bastards and put their asses out of business," Bud cried with a broad smile on his face.

Robert Smyth bowed his head slightly and gave him a questioning look. He realized that, in spite of the useful information he'd just received, he was talking to an ignorant man who didn't differentiate between Muslims and Jews and grouped them together. Smyth and few members of his congregation looked at them quiet differently. They were strong supporters of Jews and advocated that all Jews should flock to Israel because it would trigger the second coming of Christ and the end of the world. They believed that the Jewish nation would ultimately be reconverted to Christianity. But Mr. Smyth believed what his favorite preachers had been saying that Islam is a wicked and evil religion, and that the Christian God and the Muslim God are two different deities. Either way, the information Bud gave him could be useful for his means.

Smyth got in his car and drove away. He started to develop a strategy to break up the new business that was threatening his company. He thought that since he and his church were strong supporters of Jews and Israel, he might be able to persuade the Jewish owner of the business to dump his Arab partner and join forces with Smyth. He became comfortable with his idea and decided to contact the Jewish partner and make him an offer he couldn't refuse.

Smyth's phone call came during the same period when Ali and David were going through their internal crisis. Aisha was in charge of the phones on that day and dreaded every incoming phone call because she had to make excuses for the delays in the pre-scheduled jobs, and listen to customers' complaints and threats. In spite of that, she answered the phone in her usual cheerful voice. Smyth asked her about the names of the business owners. At first, she thought he was a customer who wanted to register a complaint. She tried to evade his question by telling him that she was the manager and that she'd help resolve his problem. But he was persistent and told her that he wanted to discuss an important business matter with them. She finally yielded and gave him the names of the owners. He immediately asked to speak to David, who happened to be in her apartment at the time. She signaled to David to pick up the phone, but stayed on to listen in case he was an irate customer.

He started by introducing himself as the president of Smyth Brothers Moving Company. David was quite familiar with the name and aware of the adverse impact his company was having on the Smyth business. Smyth first spent a long time talking about his church and the contributions they had made to Israel, and how the members of his congregation were solid supporters of Israel's security, and against the dismantling of any Jewish settlements in the West Bank or the establishment of a Palestinian state. David was perplexed by the man's political introduction and couldn't understand what he was after. He kept smiling and winking at Aisha who was listening and shaking her head. Suddenly Smyth said without a change in the tone of his voice, "I know you're Jewish and I've a lot of respect for your religion. But I also know that your partner is Muslim. I need not tell you, David, that the God of Islam is not the same God of the Judeo-Christian faith. It's a different God, and I believe Islam is a very evil religion."

David noticed that Aisha was about to scream at the man on the phone, but he pushed his fingers against his lips as a signal for her to remain quiet, "But Mr. Smyth, the overwhelming majority of Muslims are good, decent people and their faith provides them the structure through which they live good, decent, and moral lives."

Smyth was unmoved by David's defense and continued in a controlled and deliberate voice, "I agree with you, David, that some of them are decent individuals. But people like you and me who belong to the Judeo-Christian faith should unite together."

"What are you exactly after, Mr. Smyth?" David asked impatiently.

"I'd like to propose that you bring your share of the business and join our company, and I'm ready to make you a very attractive offer if you agree to do that."

"You're asking me to break up my business and join you? Why would I do such a thing? I have a fifty-percent partner; we started this business together," David exclaimed in exasperation, giving Aisha a look indicating how disgusted he was with the man on the other end of the phone.

"David, I know you're a religious man," Smyth continued in his brazen persuasion. "Jews and Muslims couldn't unite. This is the will of God, yours and mine, not theirs. Your future is with us in the Judeo-Christian faith. Let me quote one of our great preachers and one of the strongest supporters of Israel, 'Our long term goals are the sacking of Mecca, the defiling and final destruction of the Kaaba and the creation of a Judeo-Christian state with Mecca as its capital.' For it is written, 'But thus ye deal with them; ye shall destroy their altars, and break down their images, and cut down their graves, and burn their graven images with fire.'"

David and Aisha continued listening to what now began to sound like a full-blown sermon. He talked as though he represented the Judeo-Christian faith. They were both stunned and amused at the same time. David interrupted him and continued to speak to him politely.

"Mr. Smyth, as far as I know the crusades ended hundreds of years ago and we're now in a period of peaceful coexistence between the three monotheistic religions: Judaism, Christianity and Islam. I really don't think you should mix business with religion. We, as well as you, are in business to make a profit and to serve the public regardless of their race or religion."

"Don't be naïve, David," Smyth protested. "You should know who your partner in business is. Let me quote a passage from the Qur'an, the book he believes in, 'Slay the unbelievers wherever you find them.' Do you know who the unbeliever in this context is? It's you David. You're the one to be killed. Do you want to be a partner with a person who believes in murdering you?"

At that point Aisha lost her patience and composure, and she interrupted him, "Stop right there, Mr. Smyth, and lift that veil of ignorance from your eyes. When you quote a passage from my Holy Book, you ought to quote the end of the passage that says, 'and when the unbelievers cease to threaten you, when they cease, then remember that God is compassionate and you have to stop fighting.' Mr. Smyth, there're no two Gods. Your God is the same as ours and we believe in all the prophets from Abraham, Isaac, and Jacob to Jesus and Muhammad. Please stop your malicious and divisive talk and preach peace, love, and cooperation among all mankind."

Smyth was startled to hear someone else on the phone and yelled at her, "Who are you? And why are you listening in on our conversation?"

"My name is Aisha, and I work for this company. Moreover, I'm one of those Muslims you've been downgrading and accusing of murder. I wish to assure you sir that no one I know has any plans to hurt you. As much as I abhor what I've been hearing from you, my religion has taught me forgiveness and not to interfere with your religious beliefs. Let me quote a passage from the Qur'an that you and others like you wish to ignore-- 'You have your religion and I have mine.'"

Smyth overcame his initial shock, and quickly regained his composure. He wasn't expecting a debate, much less with an unknown party, or someone of intelligence. But he ignored Aisha and continued to address David.

"It seems to me that you've chosen to partner with the devil. You've befriended the Antichrist. But I warn you, my friend, that Lord Jesus shall return in power and glory and regain the earth, and shall build a temple in Jerusalem. You'll someday regret your decision."

David and Aisha remained silent as they listened to him blurting some biblical quotations that he erroneously presumed were directed at all Muslims. Their expressions of shock and amusement gave way to serious concern when they heard him saying before he hung up the phone, "I tried to work with you as a man who belongs to the Judeo-Christian faith, but it seems that I've failed. May the Lord be the witness I've tried! Rest assured, David, I'll not let you build an empire with the devil. I'll bring you and the devil down. I know that you're employing illegal aliens in your business, and I'll make sure that you lose your business license."

His last comment had a far worse impact on David and Aisha than his entire talk that was merely full of hatred and inaccurate interpretations of scripture. He was suddenly not talking about prophecies or the unknown, but about tangible actions that could destroy their business. Their expressions of amusement gave way to panic and despair. Their internal crisis caused by the alleged affair of Ben and Aisha was compounded by a far more serious external crisis that would be spearheaded by their competition and directed by the Xenophobic Mr. Smyth.

Aisha had an agonizing look on her face as she muttered, "Do you think he meant what he said? Do you believe that he can have our license suspended?"

David didn't respond to her questions right away. Many thoughts swirled around in his head. The only one who had no work permit was Yasser. Thus a new dilemma evolved. He would have to let Yasser go to save the business while Ali insisted on firing Ben as a punishment for his relationship with Aisha. Firing either of them or both would considerably hurt the business. They wouldn't be able to operate both trucks and they'd be stuck with the expenses of one truck that remained unused in the parking lot. Furthermore, because of their religious obligations, Ali and David could only work together five days of the week. As a result, their business would regress and they wouldn't be able to meet all their financial obligations. Replacing employees like Ben and Yasser, so trustworthy and reliable, would be hard. Finding these qualities in workers with cultural backgrounds that suited their business model would be even harder.

Finally he looked at Aisha with a haggard look and answered her, "First, we need to get hold of Ali and brief him on this serious issue and make him snap out of his irrational behavior. I think Dorothy is the best person to explain to him the serious situation we're facing."

By the time David answered her, she'd forgotten her own question and was immersed in her own thoughts about what Smyth was telling David. She looked at him inquisitively, "Do you believe what that guy was saying? He thinks you're naïve enough to believe that you're an equal partner in the Judeo-Christian faith. The truth is that your people are a bridge to the second coming-- a second coming in 'our land.' It's not about you and me, it's about real estate."

Our land? David savored those words. *Our land, our house, our children. Is it possible?* Instead he snapped back.

"It's always about real estate."

She refused to let go, "A bridge to the second coming, the great orgasmic rapture. You and your people will then have to accept Jesus and be converted to win the right of passage and be rescued from Satan. That is why Mr. Smyth and his buddies strongly support Israel because they believe it's the gate through which they'll pass to eternal peace. They might take you along. You'll be a tolerated visitor. You'll get the external guest pass. If you don't convert, you'll be banished from club rapture. You see, David, it's a selfish motive. And Mr. Smyth is denying passage to all Muslims because he is too ignorant to know that Muslims accept Jesus and refer to him as a great prophet. They even name their sons after Jesus."

David was no different from many Jews in general and Israelis in particular who understood the motives behind the support of people like Smyth and some of their charitable giving to Jewish organizations. But it'd be foolish to turn down such support. They were content to let them believe what they wanted to believe as long as they continued giving and supporting Israel.

Aisha's talk was getting wearisome. David wanted to retreat to his thoughts about the incoming financial tsunami that was about to wipe out his business.

David thought she, like most women, wouldn't stop. And he was right.

"Why can't the big three use a spirited space like the Buddhists or the Hindus?"

"Now there's an idea," mocked David. "Even the Dalai Lama wants his real estate back, or have you forgotten Tibet or Kashmir? Does that ring the bell? The Political Science 101 bell?"

David said goodbye and left her apartment heading to Dorothy to share with her the new threatening developments.

John Smyth, Jr. knew exactly whose help to seek to defeat Ali and David's business. He immediately went to see his friend and member of his church who was in charge of business licenses in Bronx County. Mr. Christian Abialbon, whose last name meant *father of understanding*, was the consummate bureaucrat. He was sixty years old and had spent close to two-thirds of his life working for Bronx County. He was well versed in the ins and outs of the bureaucracy and often used his extensive knowledge to help friends and bring down enemies.

Smyth met Abialbon on a Sunday after the church services. They both shared the same philosophy of the extreme religious right, and often met on Sundays to exchange new information they had learned from their favorite right-wing evangelical preachers. Smyth knew that Abialbon admired one religious scholar in particular. After warmly greeting his friend, Smyth said, "You know, Christian, I love the article I read the other day by our favorite professor."

The mere mention of the professor attracted Abialbon's attention, and he asked, "What is he writing about this time?"

"He is warning us about the modern horsemen of the apocalypse that are riding forth to wreak havoc in our society. He describes them as representing the denial of the sanctity of human life, the rise of hardcore Internet pornography, the radical homosexual agenda and its attempt to undermine marriage, and the radical Islamic Jihadism."

"I tell you, Bob, it's that fourth horse that worries me the most."

"Absolutely," Smyth said in support of his friend. "And the liberals in this country keep telling us that those Muslim radicals only constitute a small percentage of the billion Muslims in the world. But we may have a bunch of those Jihadists right here in New York."

Abialbon became visibly alarmed.

"I fully agree with you. What bothers me is that our government is spending hundreds of billions of dollars and sacrificing the lives of thousands of our men and women to help and defend Muslims everywhere from Bosnia and Iraq to Afghanistan and Pakistan. And they still hate us and want to kill us."

"I tell you, my friend, you and I have discussed this before. This religion is a wicked and evil one. Again, those liberals keep telling us how America can expect Muslims to believe in the sincerity of our efforts and the nobility of our sacrifices when some of our preachers keep referring to their religion as evil?"

"To hell with those liberals; they will destroy our country."

After that discussion, Smyth had an easy task convincing Abialbon of his case against Ali and David's business, and provided him with the bureaucratic justification to suspend their business license because they were employing illegal aliens. He presented the business as a haven for Muslim terrorists who had tricked David Goldstein, a well-meaning Jew, to join them. In the blink of an eye, Abialbon could see Ali, the part-owner of the business -An Arab, A Jew, and A Truck- with a keffiyeh on his head and a belt of explosives riding the fourth pale horse, symbolizing death, and heading to Manhattan over the RFK bridge to wreak the havoc and destruction some of his preachers had talked about.

At that moment, Mr. Abialbon lost the right for what his name meant-- *father of understanding.*

CHAPTER 23

Change of Heart

The Astoria neighborhood of Queens, which is one of the five boroughs of New York City, is home to large communities of Arabs, Greeks, and other minorities. Immigrants from across the globe have made this neighborhood look like a colorful ethnic tapestry, famous for its varied cuisines. From many street corners you can see foods from five continents represented by nearby restaurants and cafés. People who love to eat flock to Astoria where the ethnic food is more traditional and cheaper than other places in the New York Metropolitan area.

Steinway Street below 28th Avenue is a center of Arabic restaurants, cafés, and shops. The smell of falafel, shawarma, and Middle Eastern spices lead pedestrians to delicious eating-places such as the Lebanese Taverna, the Egyptian Café, or the Restaurant of Morocco. The scenes you encounter walking down the streets of this neighborhood are almost carbon copies of what you'd see in Cairo, Beirut, Istanbul, or Ramallah.

Before he became totally preoccupied by his business, Ali often came to this neighborhood to eat or to meet some of his Palestinian friends. They would meet at Café Palestine, which was their favorite spot, to drink mint tea, smoke the nergila, and spend hours on political, religious, and social debates. He savored those meetings and took pleasure in participating in the discussions that usually ended up in laughter when they started making fun of one of the

213

debaters, or when his friend Imil Habbash interrupted the discussion to tell them the latest joke he'd received from home.

After his outburst with David and his screaming match with Aisha, Ali stayed in seclusion for a few days at his friend Ahmed's apartment, and didn't show up for work. He didn't respond to the numerous phone calls from David, Hadassah, and Dorothy. Nobody knew where he was or what he was doing. They left messages pleading with him to return their calls. His mind was taken over by obstinacy and irrationality. He could see his business going down in flames and he acted as if he didn't care.

His friend, Ahmed, was worried about him and he was finally able to convince him to get out of the apartment and meet with his old buddies at Café Palestine. When they arrived at the Café, the group had already assembled on the patio around two large tables. Several water pipes were being passed around among the group. When they saw Ali approaching the patio, they stood up cheering and welcoming him. Many of them had not seen him for months. Ali's face beamed and he wore a broad smile. It was the first time he'd smiled in days. After shaking hands and giving the traditional hug and kiss on both cheeks with each one of them, they asked him to sit at the head of one of the tables. They all, almost simultaneously, called on the waiter to bring him his favorite cup of Turkish coffee and the water pipe was immediately placed in front of him.

Imil Habbash was the first to congratulate him on the success of the business and to tell him how much they'd missed him. Each one of the group started flattering him by recounting an incidence when they'd heard people talking and praising his moving company. Ali thanked them warmly and was happy that none of them was aware of the internal crisis he'd started and that was about to wipe out the business they admired.

The topics of discussion among the group usually ranged from the serious to the irrelevant. But the Palestinian-Israeli problem was always the leading topic. From there the discussion would branch off to subjects that were in the headlines on that day or that week. The group was a microcosm of the Palestinian population. The majority of them were Muslims, but a few, such as Imil Habbash, were Christians. When it came to peace negotiations with Israel, there were the moderate rational ones and the others who refused to compromise on some of the thorny issues such as the future of all the settlements in the West Bank, or the right of return of the Palestinians who left Israel in 1948. Among the group Ali was considered to be mildly moderate and Yasser was one of the stubbornly uncompromising ones. For that reason, none of them was surprised when Ali decided to share an apartment with an Orthodox Jew, or when he started a business with David. They would have been shocked if someone like Yasser had done the same.

Ali sat quietly as the group started their traditional discussion about the new events in the Middle East, and the on-off peace negotiations between the Palestinians and the Israelis. Imil loudly protested, "How can we trust this man, Netanyahu, when he talks about peace and compromise while building or expanding Jewish settlements on our land? He'll never agree with dismantling the settlements or on sharing Jerusalem."

In the past Ali would have joined his friend Ahmed Mansoor, who was arguing to continue the negotiations with whoever was the Prime Minister of Israel because further delays in reaching a compromise on a Palestinian state only hurt the Palestinian cause. In spite of Imil's interruptions, Ahmed tried to explain his point.

"Look, Imil, at where we're today in terms of Palestinian land compared to where we were following the 1947 United Nations partition of Palestine. A Palestinian state today would be much smaller than the one proposed by the UN at that time, and every year we wait the Israelis will expand their settlements and the negotiations and the compromises will get even harder."

Another member of the irrational faction of the group jumped in to defend Imil, "Listen, Ahmed, history isn't made in fifty or one hundred years. It may take several hundred years before we restore Palestine again as a secular country where Jews, Muslims, and Christians live together in peace."

Ahmed shook his head in disbelief and countered, "But why do we have to wait a few hundred years? Just imagine if a smaller Palestinian state were established today I mean smaller than what we'd hoped for, and peace were restored in our region. Cooperation and trade would thrive between the two states and thousands of businesses like Ali's would be formed. These businesses would, in turn, hire thousands of Israelis and Arabs who would work together, exactly like what Ali and his partner are doing today. Look at what Ali has accomplished. Even our friend, Yasser, is now working on the same truck with an Orthodox Jew whose family we all know is one of the major proponents of building more Jewish settlements on our land. I believe that social contacts and friendships would flourish through those businesses."

Ahmed then looked at Ali and asked for his opinion. But Ali remained quiet for a minute as the whole group stared at him, wanting to hear him speak. Ahmed had just described his business as the prototype of partnerships that would flourish between Israelis and Palestinians once a final peace solution was reached, and how cooperation and friendships through such businesses would ultimately make the contentious and difficult issues being negotiated at that moment, irrelevant. He felt he was in agreement with Ahmed's moderate and logical views, but in his personal life he was acting like the most irrational of the group. He was about to destroy what Ahmed was describing as a model of collaboration between Palestinians and Jews because he was suspecting that his Muslim cousin Aisha was having an affair with an Orthodox Jew. *And what if Aisha were to marry Ben? Wouldn't that be one of the possible consequences of establishing a free and democratic secular region?* he wondered.

Ali was relieved that none of the people sitting around the table, except Ahmed, was aware of the ongoing crisis inside his business and his own personal dilemma. But he felt that he was pushed in the discussion's arena with the spotlight shining on him, and he had to take a position in the debate. His recent personal behavior placed him squarely in Imil's corner, but his reputation among his friends, particularly after he'd launched a successful partnership with David, put him rightfully in Ahmed's. If he sided with Imil, he'd be abandoning the principle he'd often championed in the past, that collaboration and trade would enhance and cement peace between his people and the Israelis. On the other hand, siding with Ahmed would require him to reexamine his own behavior, ignore his pride and ego, and retreat on the threats he'd made to David and Aisha. He'd often admonished his friends when they repeatedly talked in terms of defending Arabs' pride, and warned them that pride was the right hand of Satan at work. He remembered a statement by Plato he'd once read. *The cause of all sins in every case lies in the person's excessive love of self.*

With all the eyes focused on him, Ali finally opened his mouth, "As much as I mistrust Mr. Netanyahu, I believe we should continue talking to him and everyone else until we achieve a mutually agreeable, win-win solution."

Ali then stood up and said, "Sorry, I've got to go to work."

His brief meeting with his friends, and his listening to their repetitive arguments, made him return to his senses and realize how irrational he'd been in dealing with the issue of Aisha and Ben. As he rushed down Steinway Street heading to his apartment, he heard someone calling his name. He turned around and saw Abdul Raheem, his wife Zeinab, and their son Elijah sitting outside one of the Middle Eastern cafés. He hadn't seen them since their meeting at Achyan's house for dinner, but he called Abdul Raheem a few times to thank him for referring members of his community to his business. Zeinab insisted that he join them for a few minutes, and Ali felt obligated to do so.

Ali was surprised to find out that Zeinab had been regularly chatting with Aisha over the phone and had gone to lunch with her at least a couple of times. She laughed when she repeated Aisha's story about her meeting with Abraham, his wife Sarah, and their son Isaac, and when he kept calling her Hagar and how uncomfortable and frightened she had been to be alone with them. Ali knew the story well because he, David, Ben, and Hadassah continued to tease Aisha about her multiple visits to the bathroom to make phone calls, and her refusal to touch the cookies for fear of being drugged.

Zeinab interrupted her laughter and said in a serious tone, "I believe this man Abraham is sincere in his mission to bring Jews, Christians, and Muslims together and have them realize that they are praying for the same God and that there're more similarities among their religions than differences."

Ali concurred, "I agree with you. We've visited his sanctuary twice and had tea with him and his wife Sarah. Aisha didn't refuse to drink their tea during those visits."

Zeinab smiled again and said in a tone bordering on reverence, "I love this girl, Aisha. She is intelligent, compassionate, and has a great deal of inner strength. I find the name Hagar is appropriate for her. I don't know, Ali, how much you know about the role the Hagar story plays among African American women?"

"To be frank, Zeinab, not much," he answered, sneaking a look at his watch. He was anxious to leave and head to his apartment.

"You know, Ali, we consider Hagar's story to be comparable to that of the slaves in American history. We admire her strength and her ability to support her son on her own, like many Black women do. I remember by heart what Professor Delores S. Williams once wrote about her that, 'Hagar has spoken to generation after generation of Black women because her story has been validated as true by suffering Black people. She and Ishmael together, as family, model many Black American families in which a lone mother struggles to hold the family together in spite of the poverty to which ruling class economics consign it. Hagar, like many Black women, goes into the wide world to make a living for herself and her child, with only God at her side.'

That is why I find Aisha's experience with Abraham and his wife Sarah fascinating."

At that instant, Ali's cell phone rang. He immediately answered when he saw Satish's name on the screen. Satish briefed him on Robert Smyth's threats and his remarks about employing illegal aliens. Satish warned him that Yasser's employment could cause a serious problem to their business. Ali told him that he was on his way home and to quickly arrange a meeting with David and Dorothy in her apartment. He apologized to Abdul Raheem and his wife and rushed home.

In the span of a few hours, Ali had a complete change of heart. First, listening to his friends it became clear to him how foolish and irrational he was to abandon his business that offered a success story of cooperation between Arabs and Jews that could resonate back in his home country. Second, he recognized once again the admirable qualities of his cousin Aisha and the harshness of his unsubstantiated accusations of her.

When Ali arrived at Dorothy's apartment he found her, David, and Satish sitting around her dining table. Although they were happy to see him back, there was a gloomy look on their faces. They were staring at a piece of pink paper that had an official look. David handed him the paper. It was a notice of suspension of their business license from Bronx County signed by Mr. Abialbon. David repeated once more his conversation with Robert Smyth and his attempt to sabotage the business by offering David to take his share of the business and join his firm. David was confident that Smyth was behind the notice. Ali was embarrassed because as he was hiding and threatening to bring the business down, David was carrying the entire load on his shoulders. Moreover, David had refused to betray him and join the Smyth Brothers Moving Company. He took that stand even though he wasn't sure whether Ali would come back.

The discussion around the table focused on how to best deal with the current crisis. Finally Satish proposed that the first step in facing the suspension was for Ali and David to go and meet Mr. Abialbon and attempt to diplomatically convince him to reinstate their business license and allow them to operate pending an investigation of the validity of the charges filed against their business. He recommended that they explain to him that Yasser was waiting for his work permit, and that they would immediately stop employing him until his work permit was approved. They all supported Satish's strategy, and Ali and David decided to go and meet Mr. Abialbon the following day.

When Ali and David left Dorothy's apartment and walked up the stairs, they looked at each other with genuine affection. They felt closer to each other than ever before. They recognized that the imminent threat to their business and to their livelihood had created an unshakable bond between them. Ali felt guilty for his behavior, and was about to apologize. But David looked at him as if to say, I know. It's ok. We'll be ok.

CHAPTER 24

Challenging the Bureaucracy

Christian Abialbon was in charge of all business licenses in Bronx County. The small size of his office was inversely proportional to his authority over small businesses in the area that needed to maintain their licenses in good order. He had no formal education and was hired in the county as a clerical assistant when he was a young man straight out of high school. He had no special talent except obeying his bosses and catering to their whims. He was the typical yes-man bureaucrat. For that reason, and nothing else, he was routinely promoted until he became the head of the office that was in charge of business licenses. He was an excellent example of the Peter Principle and he rose in the county ranks until he reached his level of incompetence. Nowhere is the Peter Principle more evident than in government agencies. As long as they do what they're told and don't make waves, individuals in a bureaucracy are promoted. Sooner or later they reach a position at which they are no longer competent and there they remain being ineffective and unable to earn further promotions.

Mr. Abialbon, the consummate bureaucrat, was the man Ali and David had to face to appeal the suspension of their business license. He was nobody in the realm of government bureaucracies, but he was the one who held the future of their business in his hands.

Ali was quiet familiar with bureaucracy and bureaucrats. They work in the same way whether they are in Russia,

221

Turkey, Egypt or the United States. Bureaucrats may dress differently or speak in different languages, but they behave almost identically. He knew how large bureaucracies in the Middle East tend to evolve into complex economic machines that have their own agendas serving their own benefits, independent of what is good for the public they are supposed to serve. He'd read about similar bureaucracies in the United States such as the military-industrial complex or the more recent homeland security bloated apparatus that generated crises, both domestically and internationally, as means to profit and to justify its existence.

When they entered Abialbon's office they saw an older man with grey hair, thick gray eyebrows, and glasses that hung down on his large nose. He sat in a small office in Bronx County building where he'd worked for over thirty-five years. The few walls of the office were adorned with family and religious captions. High stacks of files were piled on both ends of his small, old, wooden desk. A large poster was hung on the wall behind his desk that listed all the steps needed to obtain and maintain a business license in Bronx County. He was looking at a pile of papers on his desk and didn't immediately acknowledge them. They stood in front of his desk for a couple of minutes holding the pink piece of paper they had received from his office before he finally raised his head and gave them a look implying that they were interrupting something important he was working on. He knew who they were as soon as he laid his eyes on them. They looked exactly as he'd pictured them after talking to his friend Robert Smyth, Jr, David with his skullcap had to be the Jewish partner, and the person standing next to him, a brown-skinned male with a thick mustache, had to be the Arab partner. In his mind, Ali's looks fit the image he had of an Arab terrorist or a Muslim Jihadist. All that was missing was the biblical fourth pale horse. He pictured hundreds of young men like Ali on their horses galloping down the bridges toward Manhattan to cause havoc and to hold a victory rally at the sacred Ground Zero site.

Abialbon saw a great danger to his faith in Ali and David's partnership. *What if thousands or millions of such partnerships were formed in the Holy Land? Wouldn't that delay the arrival of Armageddon?* He belonged to one of those right-wing religious groups that wanted to hasten it rather than delay it. His determined intent to break up their partnership was driven more by his beliefs than by his friendship with Smyth.

Evangelists are not alone in their belief in the promised arrival of a messiah. Some Muslims believe in the return of a Muslim Messiah known as the Mahdi, and Iranians assume that he'd come to Tehran. Likewise, Jewish groups in Jerusalem hope to clear the path for their own messiah by rebuilding a temple on a site now occupied by the Al-Aqsa mosque, one of Islam's holiest places. Unfortunately, all these groups, in spite of their declared good intentions, help to cultivate the seeds of division and hatred among the three Abrahamic faiths.

David spoke first, explaining that it was unfair to suspend their business certificate on the basis of allegations and unfounded charges that they were employing a number of illegal aliens. Abialbon nodded his head while listening to David as though he was sympathetic to his pleas. When David finished his prepared remarks that he'd memorized before coming in, Abialbon pointed out to the poster above him listing the terms and conditions of a business certificate and spoke in a level tone.

"You see, Mr. David, I only follow rules and regula-tions. There are witnesses who submitted written affidavits claiming that your business is employing undocumented workers. Therefore, until an investigation is launched and it proves otherwise, your license has to remain suspended based on such complaints."

Every time David attempted to interrupt him to explain his position, he pointed up to the rules and regulations on the wall behind him.

Ali was restraining his fury as he listened to Abialbon's bureaucratic monologue and David's pleas. The scene in front of him stirred flashbacks to when he was trying to get an exit visa from his home country to come to the United States. He stood then in front of a low-level government employee who looked like Abialbon and had a large poster hanging on the wall behind him outlining all the documents he needed to obtain an exit visa. The only difference was that the Palestinian bureaucrat had a sign on his desk that instructed the applicants not to ask too many questions. Abialbon had no such sign, but might as well have. It was implied in how he treated them. Ali had a vivid memory of his traumatic visa experience.

He desperately needed the exit visa to leave the country, because college classes were about to start in New York. He couldn't understand some of the requirements listed on the wall, and every time he asked a question, the government official pointed his finger to the poster behind him. When Ali requested clarifications of the items listed on the poster, he pointed to the sign saying not to ask too many questions. One empowered bureaucrat caused him to miss a few weeks of college classes and a lot of agony until he discovered that one of his relatives was a friend of that man's supervisor. Then, and only then, was he able to leave the country. The anger and frustration he'd experienced in that visa office made him detest bureaucracies everywhere.

Faced with Abialbon's inflexibility and unreasonableness, Ali and David left his office feeling defeated. They understood that the investigation Abialbon had demanded would take weeks or months to conclude. Meanwhile, their business would collapse under the burden of mounting expenses such as truck payments, insurance, telephones, etc. Furthermore, a long absence from the marketplace would drive most of their potential customers to other moving companies. Smyth Brothers Moving Company would be the natural choice for those customers and Robert Smyth, Jr. would achieve his declared goal of driving them out of business.

When Dorothy found out the disastrous result of their meeting with Abialbon, she organized a meeting in her apartment that included Hadassah, Aisha, Ben, Yasser, Satish, Ali, David, and herself to plan the next steps they ought to take to fight Abialbon's arbitrary decision. As they sat across from each other around her dining table their faces reflected the sadness of the situation. But one positive outcome of the crisis was clearly evident. All the hostilities toward Ben and Aisha by Ali and Yasser had given way to unity and determination to fight the external threat that was about to wipe out every thing they had worked so hard for. Ali never mentioned a word about Aisha's relationship with Ben, and was genuinely friendly toward both of them. Likewise, Aisha teased Ali, in Arabic, about his mustache and the fact that he'd neglected to trim it.

Aisha and Hadassah were the first to speak. They had thought of several steps to take on their way to the meeting. They suggested that each person call several customers and share with them the unreasonable position of Bronx County, and ask for their support in fighting the suspension of their business license.

Dorothy stated that she would announce the county's decision at her church where many members of the congregation had used Ali and David's services and were supportive of the business. She also volunteered to contact all her friends who attended other churches in the area and were enthusiastic about the business and the positive message of cooperation it stood for. Hadassah and Ben declared that they'd call a number of the Jewish customers and David promised to seek the help of Achyan and several of his Hassidic Jewish friends. In turn Ali committed to contact his customers in the Arab community as well as his Black Muslim friend Abdul Raheem who had referred many members of his community to them.

Aisha hesitated for a minute when her turn came before she thoughtfully declared that she'd contact Abraham, the self-declared prophet, and his wife Sarah. They all had heard of Abraham and they immediately expressed reluctance on using his services in their fight. They were worried that his Messianic appearance and unrealistic message might turn off some of their customers. But Ben was quick to back Aisha's idea and to propose that Abraham's sanctuary could be used as a meeting ground for all their supporters. He argued that Abraham should be taken seriously and his message could provide a unifying platform for all those diverse potential supporters they were seeking.

Soon after they'd left Dorothy's apartment, each one of the group started making phone calls. They presented their situation as a typical case of big business using their connections to squeeze out an up-and-coming small business from its market. They avoided discussing other reasons behind the suspension of the business certificate and the fact that it was collusion between two religious zealots. They were encouraged by the positive response they received from their customers who declared their readiness to voice their support to the highest government officials in the county. All the people contacted were invited to a meeting at Abraham's sanctuary to get to know each other and to coordinate their future efforts in the fight to restore Ali and David's business license.

Abraham and Sarah were excited about being part of this effort and about receiving such a large ethnically and religiously diverse group at their sanctuary. They felt that such a gathering would provide Abraham an opportunity to spread his message of interfaith healing, and to attract more and more people to join his sanctuary.

On the scheduled day of the meeting Abraham stood at the door of the sanctuary greeting a stream of people who came in support of Ali and David. He was dressed in his usual long white robe and held his long wooden staff in his hand. In a solemn voice he welcomed the influx of supporters that included Hassidic Jews in their large black hats and long beards, Orthodox Jews with their skullcaps, Muslims holding their prayer beads in their hands, and Black Muslims wearing their traditional black suits and black hats. Intermingled with this diverse and colorful group, there were ordinary men and women who came from many other churches in the area, including Dorothy's church.

Ali and David stood next to Abraham, greeting the people and chatting with those customers whom they had served. In the midst of this crowd, David squinted as if he had to avoid the piercing glare of a hot afternoon sun. His eyes focused on a rainbow of color protectively clinging to a sensuous sculpted figure moving in his direction. Unrestrained long black hair framed what David recognized as a hauntingly beautiful face. Between an artful balance and a sway she walked toward them in high heels that matched her rainbow-colored dress. She was alone and oblivious of David's stare. She was obviously looking for someone she was supposed to meet at the sanctuary.

David grabbed Ali's arm and whispered, "Look straight ahead. This lady looks very familiar. She may be from your part of the world."

Ali's eyes settled on the swath of moving colors and thought. *Sure, our part of the world is famous for its immodest flesh-flaunting females.*

David, growing impatient waiting for Ali to solve this puzzle, pleaded again for help, "Who is she? Do I have early dementia?"

Coming to David's rescue, Ali put the features of the face together. Almost too stunned to speak, he murmured, "My God, it's Zena!"

"Shut up. No way!"

"Yes, it's her. Her Salafi husband Mahmoud may be turning in his grave."

Ali couldn't share David's excitement. He was ashamed of his conflicted feelings that oscillated between an admiration of Zena's liberation and condemnation because of his respect to her late husband's beliefs and traditions. Like Ali, Zena was shedding hundreds of years of customs. And like him, she belonged to this new world and Mahmoud lived in the old one.

David mistook Ali's silence for anger, "Look at the positive side, Ali. The color of her dress is a symbol. At the end of every storm there is a rainbow. She is telling us that our business will endure this storm. I believe this is a good omen."

Ali looked at him and smiled, "Let us pray for that, David."

At that moment, Zena saw them and approached them, "Ahleen Ali, keif halak, I haven't seen you for a long time," then turned to David, "Shalom David, how is the business?"

Before waiting for an answer, she saw Aisha and rushed toward her. The two hugged and kissed each other.

Watching them, Ali could see the clash of cultures being played out in front of his very eyes. Two Arab Muslim women were trying to assimilate in a new western environment. One was clinging to her beliefs and traditions and continued to wear long dresses and wrap a scarf around her head, while the other submitted to the temptations of her new society, got rid of her hijab and uncovered her arms and legs.

Ali realized that those who found head scarves and other Islamic religious expressions repellent would welcome someone like Zena in their midst more eagerly than Aisha who was far more superior in education and intellect. That realization depressed him for a moment until he looked around and saw the sea of people who transcended race, religion and everything else, and came to help him and David save their business.

Ali's thoughts were interrupted by Dorothy's voice saying hello. She introduced Ali and David to an elderly couple she was with. The couple told them how much they loved their company and how impressed they were with the service they received from their crew. Before the couple followed Dorothy into the sanctuary, they whispered to Ali and David, "You should consider adding a Christian to your crew. How about calling your business: An Arab, A Jew, A Christian, and A Truck? I bet, Mr. Abraham, would support this addition." They shared a laugh at such a notion, and David thanked the couple.

"This is a great idea, we'll certainly look into it." When the couple was far enough from them, he turned to Ali, "Ben would hate this idea because there would be no room for Aisha on the truck."

With a Cheshire smile Ali was quick to approve, "Good, that will keep him away from my cousin. But let's pray that the third crewmember isn't an ultra religious Christian, otherwise we'll have one more Sabbath to worry about. Two are bad enough."

"This whole thing is putting me on edge," David's voice suddenly sounded strained and anxious. "I think we need a back up plan. What if Abialbon refuses to reinstate our license?"

Oh my God, don't tell me we are going to change roles and I have to play the optimist now.

"David, have you forgotten your dream? You wanted to start a business called Kosher Food on Wheels. We can always start another business."

"So what are we gonna do, convert you to Judaism and convert the trucks into Kosher food mobiles?"

"Not quite my friend. This time the kitchen will be fifty percent kosher and fifty percent halal; Ali and David's Kosher and Halal Food on Wheels."

"You mean David and Ali's Kosher and Halal Food on Wheels."

"Hey, no problem. We'll just put Halal before Kosher."

"Let's end this war over bagels and pita before it begins. We're going to fight to keep our first business before we start a new one."

Ali was relieved to see David's spirit back, and said playfully, "You worried me for a second. I thought I lost you,"

"Are you kidding? You can't lose me now. We've got the same bank account."

Grabbing Ali's Arm he led him into the sanctuary.

Abraham encouraged everyone to mingle with the rest of the people and to wander around the sanctuary and read the messages on the walls that were taken from the Torah, the Bible, and the Qur'an.

The benches in the main hall of the sanctuary were totally full and the corridors and the space in the back of the hall were filled with people standing and waiting to hear Abraham. Many of them had mixed feelings of admiration and apprehension about this man who'd dedicated his life to interfaith healing and to promote dialogue, understanding, and unity among the three Abrahamic faiths.

Abraham walked slowly toward the podium. The light rhythmic pounding of his staff on the floor, as he inched toward the front, was the only sound that broke the silence prevailing in the room. When he reached the podium, he invited his wife Sarah and Aisha to join him. They stood on either side of him as he welcomed the guests one more time before he addressed the subject of their gathering. He introduced his wife and his son Isaac who was sitting in the front row. Then he turned his head toward Aisha and referred to her as Sarah's close Muslim friend. He didn't call her "Hagar" as he had done repeatedly at their first meeting, much to Aisha's relief.

He started by reminding the audience that the injustice that was facing Ali and David was motivated by the same prejudice, intolerance, and lack of understanding that had prevailed for centuries among the Abrahamic religions. He explained that lack of interfaith understanding was behind many of the devastating wars throughout history. Abraham pointed to one of the walls and read the Abrahamic Covenant from Genesis of the Old Testament written more than 3800 years ago-- "Now the Lord said to Abraham. And I will make you a great nation (Genesis 12:2). And the Lord appeared unto Abraham, and said, 'Unto thy seed will I give this land.'" (Genesis 12:7)

He looked at the crowd in front of him and said with clear conviction, "You see, my brothers and sisters, God was talking about Abraham's seed. Isaac and Ishmael were his seeds that multiplied into Jews, Christians, and Muslims."

He then pointed to another wall that contained quotations from the Qur'an, and read "You are the descendents of the prophets and of the covenant that God gave to your ancestors, saying to Abraham, 'And in your descendents all the families of the earth shall be blessed,' (3:25) 'And remember that Abraham was tried by his Lord with certain command; which he fulfilled; He said: I will make thee an Imam to the nations. (2:124)'"

Abraham raised the pitch of his voice and warned loudly, "Let us not allow the bigots, the demagogues and the uninformed to hijack our beautiful religions, and let us focus on the similarities between our beliefs and not the differences. If we fail to do that, we'd be allowing an ignorant minority with the wrong dogma or belief to divide us and cause havoc in our nations. I'd like to repeat what Dr. Hans Kung, Professor of Ecumenical Theology, once said, 'There will be no peace among the nations without peace among the religions. There will be no peace among the religions without dialogue among the religions.'"

The audience listened intently to Abraham. Some nodded their heads in approval and others murmured words from one of the holy books. His deep voice, his imposing figure, his long salty-color beard down to his chest, and the long mast in his hand, which he raised once in a while to emphasize a point in his sermon, had a magnetizing effect on the crowd.

Abraham finally announced that a rally would be held in front of the Bronx County building at noon on the following Tuesday, and urged each person to invite his or her friends to that rally.

"We all have a vested interest in seeing this beautiful cooperation among the children of Abraham, Ali and David, expand and flourish. We're not seeking revenge for the loss that Ali and David have suffered, but rather justice and the reinstatement of their business license. And let us not forget my friends the famous words the great African leader Nelson Mandela once said, 'There is no future in South Africa without forgiveness.' If the Black South Africans were able to forgive the Whites for all their injustice and atrocities, we can forgive those individuals who were behind the suffering of our brothers Ali and David."

While everyone clapped and voiced their support, Abraham leaned his mast against the podium and invited his son Isaac to join them. Deeply touched by Abraham's words, Abdul Raheem pushed his son Elijah to run to the front and stand next to Aisha. They all held their hands and raised them upwards and the audience's clapping and cheers got louder and louder.

CHAPTER 25

The Beginning of a Long Journey

News of the planned rally spread rapidly in the New York area and gained the support of different groups. Each group had its own motives for their support. Arab, Jewish, African-American, and Hispanic minorities admired Ali and David's business not only because it was successfully competing with big businesses such as Smyth Brothers, but also for its message of cooperation between Arabs and Jews. Some conservative groups' support was inspired by their desire to demonstrate the danger and foolishness of bureaucracies and big government. The intellectual liberals wanted to publicize the evil acts of some extreme elements of the Christian Right who spread the seeds of hatred and dissension between Arabs and Jews as means to fulfill their rigid biblical prophesies. The support of those dissimilar groups helped to spread the story of Ali and David. Rumors and innuendos started to build up around the main story of the successful new business of a Palestinian Arab and an Orthodox Jew, a model for peaceful collaboration in the Holy Land, that was about to be unfairly terminated by a local government bureaucracy.

The news media got wind of the planned rally and the reasons behind it. Each newspaper and TV station raced to find the facts or to secure an interview with one or more of the main characters of the story. Various headlines, some exaggerated, appeared in a number of publications charging Bronx County with damaging the chances of peace in the

Middle East, or claiming collusion among some members of the Christian Right to help the business of one of their own.

The other issue that attracted the attention of the news media was the spiritual leader who was behind the rally. His goal of reenacting the four-thousand year story of Abraham the prophet filled the talk shows and radio waves. Rumors spread that a woman whose name was Hagar was moving in with him, his wife Sarah, and their thirteen-year old son Isaac. And Hagar was pregnant and was about to have a son whom she'd name Ishmael. Sarah and Hagar were going to live together like friends and equals and not as a wife and servant as in the biblical story. They planned to raise Isaac and Ishmael as true brothers, living in the same home and learning to spread a unified message of God and faith. They wanted the followers of the Abrahamic faiths to ponder the consequences had Abraham kept Hagar in his home four thousand years ago, treated her as a true second wife, and raised Isaac and Ishmael like brothers.

The news media kept repeating that the goal of Abraham was to dispel the notion that Ishmael was kicked out of Abraham's home because he was a troubled child since, throughout history, many families had to cope with raising children who had different personalities. Both Abraham and his wife Sarah as well as Ali and David never denied or confirmed any of those rumors. They decided to let the rumors go on because they played in their favor. *No press is negative press* they thought. They knew that Aisha was the mystery Hagar and that she wasn't pregnant or about to move in with Abraham, but they didn't feel the need to address that issue.

National and international news outlets picked up the headlines of the stories. Radio and TV talk shows from Cairo to Tel Aviv and from Paris and Rome to Berlin discussed every aspect of the stories. Internet chat rooms buzzed with opinions, recommendations and insults. Christian, Jewish, and Muslim religious leaders, while supporting Ali and David's business, vigorously attacked Abraham and his intentions, referred to him as a mad, ignorant man, and described his acts as blasphemous. Many other people admired and supported his goal of making adherents of the Abrahamic faiths reexamine their roots and focus on their similarities rather than their differences.

All of a sudden the New York Bronx, and not Jerusalem, Mecca, or Cairo, became the focus of world attention and the launch pad for peace in the Middle East, and for reconciliation between Judaism, Christianity, and Islam.

On the day of the rally, the streets were cordoned off around the county building. A green, blue, and white truck, carrying the name, An Arab, A Jew and A Truck and displaying a logo that included the Crescent and the Star of David, parked in front of the County office steps. Scores of television crews representing news outlets from all over the world scattered around the site looking for new stories or new twists on the main story behind the rally. Hundreds of people arrived at the site in support of Ali and David's business. They looked like a collage of Jewish, Christian and Muslim pilgrims converging on Mecca or Jerusalem. But in that case it was the Bronx County building. The signs carried by some of the participants were as dissimilar as the people carrying them. One sign read: An Arab, A Jew and A Truck is Our Road to Peace in the Middle East. Another one read: Bronx Bureaucrats-- Keep Your Hands Off Ali and David's Business!

People stood shoulder to shoulder, holding hands and facing the County building. Muslims were holding hands with Orthodox Jews who held hands with Catholic priests. The large black hats of the Hassidic Jews mingled with the smaller black hats of the Black Muslims. Some of the young news reporters couldn't tell the difference between Jewish males wearing their yarmulkes and some Muslim men who had their own head covers. A few Muslim women wearing their hijabs stood side by side holding hands with Orthodox Jewish women who covered their hair in an almost identical way. These were historical images that flashed on TV screens around the globe.

In the middle of the crowd, Abraham stood next to Aisha and Sarah who held her son's hand. Abraham's tall imposing figure and distinct clothes attracted the attention of the news hunters. Several of them surrounded him, asking questions about his philosophy and how he planned to spread his message. Several other reporters approached Aisha. One of them asked, "Is your name Hagar?"

"No, my name is Aisha."

"Are you pregnant?"

She laughed in response, "No, I'm not even married."

The news' hunters looked at each other in disbelief. They were too immersed in the rumors they'd helped to spread to believe her denials.

The attention of the crowd and the news media suddenly shifted when the Bronx Borough President appeared on the steps of the county building to address the crowd. He was brief and to the point. In a few words he declared that the county was reinstating Ali and David's business license. In a typical bureaucratic response he defended the initial suspension as a legitimate step, but announced that the unusual amount of support and enthusiasm for that business had persuaded him to veto the initial decision of suspension. The crowd roared with applause and broke into cheers in various languages from English and Arabic to Hebrew and Yiddish, and congratulated each other. Arab women expressed their pleasure by ululation as if they were celebrating a wedding in their home countries. Ali hugged David, David kissed Hadassah, Ben congratulated Aisha, and Sarah hugged and kissed Aisha. Ali noticed Ben looking at Aisha with great affection, and thought. *I know I'm a close friend and a business partner with an Orthodox Jew, but marriage---this is another story. Maybe our friend Abraham can solve that one.*

In a matter of days, the business was back in full swing. The phones in Aisha's and Hadassah's apartments were ringing continuously and prospective customers were eager to schedule their moving jobs.

When Ali and David drove their truck again for the first time through Steinway Street, people sitting at the restaurants and cafes lining the streets of the Astoria neighborhood jumped to their feet cheering and clapping. Ali and David waved and honked their horn repeatedly. The media frenzy died down as the weeks passed, but rumors continued to build. Rumors transformed into undisputed facts. Some tried to convince the skeptics that God was working through Abraham to unify his people, and this time it wasn't in a far away land but in the Bronx. None of these rumors were confined to New York. People swore they saw arch old enemies working side by side. The media didn't take much notice of this until CNN news interrupted its nightly broadcast with this bulletin:

"These photographs are from a security camera posted on a street corner in the Old City of Jerusalem, and they give some credibility to the hundreds of phone calls made to our network claiming that a man who has uncanny resemblance to the Israeli Prime Minister was seen sitting next to a shorter older man who looked almost identical to the President of the Palestinian National Authority. Both men appeared to be laughing as they slowly turned a major corner. The grainy photos showed a large green, blue, and white moving truck that carried the emblem: **An Arab, A Jew, and A Truck.**"

FINAL NOTE

TO ALL PEACE LOVERS:

I hope you've enjoyed reading this book as I've taken the pleasure writing it. Ali and David's story is a symbol of hope for the Middle East. An Orthodox Jew and a devout Palestinian Muslim were able to recognize the similarities between them rather than their differences, and started a business that became a model for collaboration between two historically adverse groups.

Ali and David's success story has convinced my wife, Lynn Skynear, and me that there is light at the end of this dark tunnel of hostility between Arabs and Jews. We decided to transform that business from fiction to reality and form a non-profit foundation named **"Arab-Jewish Truck to Peace"** that spreads the message of hope Ali and David started.

Arab-Jewish Truck to Peace aims at expanding friendship and understanding between Arabs and Jews as well as between Israelis and Palestinians, through collaboration among Jewish and Arab artists, writers, actors, and entrepreneurs. Ali and David's truck managed to bring the militant Palestinian, Yasser, and the ultra Orthodox settler, Ben, closer together and planted the seeds of love between Ben and the devout Muslim, Aisha. The propagation of such stories through creative collaboration will ultimately bring peace and understanding to a region that was the source of our civilization.

www.anarabajewandatruck.com